The Jane Austen Quilt Club

a novel by
Ann Hazelwood

 American Quilter's Society

PO Box 3290
Paducah, KY 42002-3290
americanquilter.com

Ann has pieced together her extensive knowledge of business and quilting to create the exciting Colebridge Community. You quickly become engaged in the life of Anne Brown and her family. Mystery, romance, and quilting—what more could you want, other than the next book in the series.

Jan Copeland
Patchwork Plus Quilt Shop
Wood River, Illinois

Ann Hazelwood's quilt fiction series is a delight. We grow attached to her characters and eagerly await the next book. They are a best seller in our gift shop. What a treat to have a quilt fiction from an extraordinary quilt expert.

Carla Jordan
Owner of CL Jordan Preservation Firm and director of the Lutheran Heritage Center and Museum
Altenburg, Missouri

Located in Paducah, Kentucky, the American Quilter's Society (AQS) is dedicated to promoting the accomplishments of today's quilters. Through its publications and events, AQS strives to honor today's quiltmakers and their work and to inspire future creativity and innovation in quiltmaking.

EXECUTIVE BOOK EDITOR: ELAINE H. BRELSFORD
COPY EDITOR: CHRYSTAL ABHALTER
PROOFREADER: JOANN TREECE
GRAPHIC DESIGN: LYNDA SMITH
COVER DESIGN: MICHAEL BUCKINGHAM

This book is a work of fiction. The people, places, and events described in it are either imaginary or fictitiously presented. Any resemblance they bear to reality is entirely coincidental.

 American Quilter's Society

PO Box 3290
Paducah, KY 42002-3290
americanquilter.com

Additional copies of this book may be ordered from the American Quilter's Society, PO Box 3290, Paducah, KY 42002-3290, or online at www.AmericanQuilter.com.

Text © 2014, Author, Ann Hazelwood
Artwork © 2014, American Quilter's Society

Library of Congress Cataloging-in-Publication Data

Hazelwood, Ann Watkins.
  The Jane Austen Quilt Club : a novel / by Ann Hazelwood.
     pages cm
  ISBN 978-1-60460-130-5
  1. Quilting--Fiction. I. Title.
  PS3608.A98846J36 2014
  813'.6--dc23
                              2013047772

The pattern for this block is available at:

**http://www.americanquilter.com/
friendship_daisy_hazelwood**

With Appreciation

One does not fulfill one's success without the help of
family and friends. I would like to acknowledge and
thank the following;

First and utmost, my heartfelt thanks to my husband,
Keith Hazelwood, and my sons, Joel and Jason Watkins,
who continue to give me love and support. I love you!

My writer's group, The Wee Writers, Jan, Mary, Janet,
Hallye, Ann and Lilah. Their talent and friendship are
such an inspiration to me.

My friends and former employees of my former
business, Patches etc. who continue to cheer me
on and occasionally share my travels.

Last, but certainly not least is the AQS staff, especially
Meredith Schroeder, who believed in this fiction series,
and my patient editor, Elaine Brelsford, whose wisdom
makes me a better writer. I feel they are on this journey
with me and I hope to make them proud.

CHAPTER 1

I sat shivering in our snow-covered gazebo, staring across the yard at the former Taylor mansion that now belonged to me and my husband, Sam. The loneliness I had experienced in these past few days at 333 Lincoln was enormous. I felt so empty without Sam. Sam's emergency aortic valve surgery on Christmas morning was frightening for both of us and an early wake-up call as to what my life would be without him.

I needed to go into the house to get warm, but I felt so close to Sam in our gazebo. I had surprised Sam with this marvelous addition to our yard on his last birthday. It was such a risk, but with the skillful help of Kevin from my flower shop, it was constructed from a kit in no time. Sam loved it and we have enjoyed it immensely. I was trying to reflect on good times as I fought the depression of Sam's illness.

Peering across the yard, I marveled at the historic home we had discovered together right before we got married.

Sam fell in love with this top-of-the-hill architectural masterpiece when we began to house hunt. With his love of history and skill at carpentry, he found it irresistible. I was quite skeptical until I miraculously found my dream in a run-down potting shed in the backyard. We both saw the home as a great challenge to our busy lives. My Brown's Botanical Flower Shop on Main Street was growing day by day. Sam had just received the title of vice president with the hope that he would someday be president of Martingale. We both worked hard for our achievements. Why we would want to add more headaches to our hectic life was like asking, "Do you want whipped cream with that hot fudge sundae?" Yes, we wanted it all. Did we now have to pay the price for the stress it seemed to bring?

I was so cold. My warm tears were quickly freezing down my cheeks. I needed to go into the house where I knew a fire was burning in the study. Nora, our housecleaner, was busy preparing a temporary bed downstairs and off the study where Sam could rest for a few days when he came home from the hospital. It would work nicely until he would be ready to climb the long staircase to our bedroom.

Our heavenly master bedroom was as beautiful and white as our wedding cake. The beautiful linens and new furniture were hardly used before Sam was rushed to the hospital with a heart attack. My favorite spot in the room was the charming bay window that looked out onto our yard and side driveway leading to the house. The other window provided a small view to the street below. We loved sitting high on the private hill, which provided a mystery to the folks of Colebridge. The only information most folks wanted to share with us about the former owners was the Taylors were rich folks who had a ghost in their house.

Nora was trying to get my attention without coming out into the cold. She called my name aloud. "Anne, Anne," she yelled into the cold air, "your mother has been trying to reach you. She is on the phone in the kitchen. Please come in from the cold, girl, or you're going to catch your death of cold!"

That sounded too much like my mother! I lived with Mother until I married Sam. I regained my senses and stood to walk slowly into the house like a good girl.

Keeping my coat on, I picked up the phone. Nora was pouring me a cup of hot coffee. "Yes, Mother," I answered in my chilly, somber mood.

"How is Sam?" she asked in an anxious tone.

"Amazingly well, so they say!" I said, not believing my own words. "I'll be bringing him home tomorrow morning. Can you believe it? He seems quite chipper and glad to be alive! I wish I were doing that well." I regretted those words as soon as they were out of my mouth and tried to make light of them. I stopped to catch my sniffle that was going to lead to a big cry. I had to get a grip, for her sake. This was my first real test of being a mature married woman with real-life problems.

"That's great news, Anne. He is a lucky man," she said sincerely. "It sure was a scare for all of us. I'll be by this morning to see how I can be helpful. If you need me to go with you tomorrow, I will. How about I pick up some lunch from Donna's Tea Room? I'll bet she'll have some of that corn chowder you love and that will hit the spot on this cold day." Mother always had a way of making everything better with food.

"Sure. See you then, but I will bring Sam home myself, like a good wife should," I said firmly. "Sam would not like the fuss, and you never know what time they'll release him, so it will be best if I just go. I appreciate all you do, Mother, but as you warned me, once I got married, it was no longer about me. I am just so grateful he has gotten through this. This whole experience has been overwhelming!"

"Yes, honey, I know," she said sympathetically. "It was for all of us. I hope he'll continue to do well and will listen to what the doctor tells him. Men do not always make the best patients."

Well, I guess I'll find out!

Nora stayed busy doing domestic things around the house. My mind was not fully aware of all she was busy accomplishing. She seemed to know what might be needed, as if she had been through this herself. It felt good to have her here, even though her conditional request was only to work here when someone was home. That was not always convenient with my busy schedule. She knew I was upset about Sam and she thought of all the details that my mind was perhaps overlooking.

"I'm happy to help you when you want this tremendous Christmas tree taken down, Miss Anne," Nora offered. "New Year's Eve is tomorrow, so I don't suppose you want it down before then. It's a beauty, Miss Anne. You sure had some great insight when you said you pictured a tree to the ceiling in this grand foyer. I think it was a treat for many folks who came to that nice trimming party you hosted."

Oh yes, there was a tremendous party. It was another happy occasion to remember fondly. We had no ornaments, so Sam suggested we have a tree-trimming party where everyone would bring an ornament for the big tree. It was also a perfect time for many of our friends and family to see 333 Lincoln for the first time.

"After the new year begins, there will be plenty of time to take it down, Nora," I said, not wanting it to go away. "Yes, it was fun bringing everyone together for the first time as a married couple and it was also sort of a housewarming, I guess." I beamed as I looked up to see the sparsely decorated tree. "I wonder if it all was too much for Sam," I posed a thought to Nora. "He, Al, and Kevin worked so hard to set this tree up. It's hard to imagine a muscular, handsome, young man having any health restrictions, isn't it?"

Before she could answer, Mother was knocking at the door. I went to answer and Nora got back to her chores.

"You're in luck, my child," she said, handing me the take-out lunch. "Corn chowder was on the menu. Of course, Donna is concerned about Sam and said to tell you so. She sent several pieces of her coconut cream pie! You know Donna. She thinks a good dessert can cure the soul."

"She's a dear," I said, walking into the kitchen. "Calls, e-mails, and cards have now started coming. Boy! You can't keep any secrets in this town, can you—especially when it's bad news!"

"Not with the presence you and Sam have in the community, Anne," she noted. "I think it's a good thing. I think most folks are very sincere. How are things at the shop?"

Oh yes, my shop. "Business is pretty good, actually. Making Sally the manager happened just at the right time," I said, setting bowls on the kitchen table. "She is so reliable and the new girl, Abbey, is working out really well. I'm going to stop by there today to check on things."

We asked Nora to join us when we sat down to eat, but she declined, as she had to do some errands on the way home. She reminded me that Sam's room was ready and she would be on call for any extra assistance. We both thanked her and sent a piece of pie home with her.

"I don't suppose you are up to going to the Jane Austen Literary Club meeting tonight, are you?" Mother hesitantly asked. "It might help get your mind off of things, and they're all concerned about you!"

"Oh no, no," I immediately responded. "The Janeites will have to do without me. I need to be with Sam. I need to reassure him all is well and that everything will be fine." I began tearing up again and put down my iced tea.

"Of course, Anne. I just wanted to make sure," she said, now tearing up herself as she touched my hand. "Sam is so strong. He will be fine—just you wait and see. I'm sure this incident will alert him to be more careful with his health. By the way, Sue was nice enough to offer to pick me up. She had a feeling you would not be going." She held back any further emotion and picked back up on the literary club discussion.

"We are going to discuss Jane's book *Northanger Abbey*, which I have to admit is not my favorite of all of Jane Austen's novels. They say it is the most humorous of all her books, but I suppose I just don't get it most of the time. It will be good to hear if anyone else liked it."

"If I remember, Catherine Morland, the main character, does have an interesting romantic life. I never quite finished it, but Jean said it has a good ending. She also said that this was the book originally written as *Susan*. It was actually published after Jane's death and her brother Henry changed the title to *Northanger Abbey*. This is a good book discussion to miss if I have to miss any of them. I love seeing everyone, though, and Jean does such a good job with our literary club. Her English accent adds the perfect touch as our hostess and our customers in the shop love her accent, too. Please tell everyone the good news of Sam coming home and that I promise to be there next time."

"This soup really hit the spot, didn't it?" Mother commented as she took the last spoonful of chowder. "I must get going. Oh, I just remembered—I came across the crazy quilt still in the garage. Didn't you say you wanted it to keep with the Taylor house treasures?"

"Oh yes, I do," I remembered. "I guess my first response was to save and clean up the beautiful vase that was inside that quilt, remember? That quilt turned out to be more important, however, so I want to keep it here in the house. The vase looks great on that mantle, don't you think? Nora tells me it's in a different place each time she comes to clean, but I sure haven't noticed that. She's always looking for the Taylor ghost she hears about. I'll have to let that quilt air out some more, like Jean recommended."

"It's filthy, remember?" Mother reminded me as we went out to the car.

"Yes, but without that quilt, we would not have discovered Mr. Taylor's mistress, who just happened to be my grandmother." I was trying to be cute, recalling our discovery. "I will treasure those cut-up letters we found behind the pieces. Jean said I should shake out any bits and pieces of paper still in the seams. Since we can't wash it, it will have to be used, as Jean called it, as a parlor throw."

The wind was fierce, blowing in from the open door, so I ran quickly to grab the bag and kissed Mother good-bye. "Give Sam my love," she yelled from the car window.

I took the bagged quilt inside and took it directly to the sunporch where I could later shake out more paper pieces from the backside. Thinking back to Albert's letters, I was still puzzled as to why Marion chose to cut them up for the quilt. Why not newspapers or even plain paper? Was she angry or was she trying to pressure them by keeping their history in a quilt? Was she hoping no one would discover his infidelity? Little did she know that the very people that cared about it would take the pieces apart, one by one, and put them together again.

CHAPTER 2

S am was walking down the hall with a pretty young blonde nurse when I got off the elevator. I'm sure they didn't get a young, good-looking patient like him every day. He was laughing and looking like his old self.

"Look at you! You're already out and about with the prettiest young chick here at the hospital," I teased. He quickly grabbed me around the waist and planted a nice kiss on my lips in response. The nurse was blushing.

"I feel fine. Sore, of course, but fine," he bragged. "Am I lucky or what? This is Samantha, Anne. She's been taking good care of me."

Samantha gave me a big smile. "He's doing really well, Mrs. Dickson, but he should rest a week or two before he starts that rat race I'm told he practices," she warned, trying to be professional. "I hope he's learned a good lesson about how to handle work and stress."

"That will be the challenge of his lifetime, I'm afraid!" I said, shaking my head.

"I'll let you take him from here, Mrs. Dickson," she instructed as she left us alone.

Sam clung closer to me as we continued walking slowly down the hall to a sitting area overlooking Main Street and the river. We took a seat where no one else could hear us talk. "Tomorrow we'll be together again," Sam said, smiling. "It will be good to be home. I've certainly had no complaints, but I don't belong here."

I nodded, smiling. "I'll be here bright and early to pick you up," I confirmed, now trying to show more confidence. "I hope no one changes their mind, because I'm taking you home, regardless. Don't they know we are practically newlyweds?"

We both grinned at one another recalling those thoughts.

"By the way, Nora has done a nice job taking the sitting room off the study and turning it into a temporary bedroom for you," I bragged. "She just knew what to do and it looks fine. I guess it's good to know, as we get older with progressing aches and pains."

He shook his head as he smiled into my eyes. "I take it you'll be sleeping there as well, Annie?" he ventured, grinning with suggestive thoughts on his mind, judging from the look on his face.

"No chance!" I responded, now showing a more serious look on my face. "You need rest, and I don't seem to have that effect on you! I'll be at your beck and call, but you need rest until you can do the stairs."

"I can do the stairs now, if they let me," Sam interjected, looking frustrated.

"You will not be doing stairs for awhile, Sam, or anything else, if I can help it!" I spoke to him in a stern voice. "You scared me half to death, so it's going to take the doctor's advice to convince me that you are ready for me...or the stairs!"

We both giggled and then were interrupted by Samantha bringing Sam some pills to take. We were sharing a couple of soft drinks when Sam's cell rang. It was his mother.

"I'll use the restroom while you talk, Sam. Tell her hello for me," I requested, kissing him on the cheek.

I knew his mother and sisters were frantic with worry, but Sam was insistent they not come in from out of town during his unfortunate health situation. Helen, his widowed mother, had been here for Thanksgiving. Frankly, I was grateful I did not have to deal with her mothering Sam and her sometimes insensitive remarks. I was worried about Sam and wanted to concentrate on him without interruptions. Sam, her only son, was perfect in her eyes. Therefore, sometimes my feelings became a secondary concern of hers.

When I returned, Sam was off the phone and sent his regards from his mother. He said I looked tired and should go home. I wanted to stay until at least visiting hours were over, but I wasn't very good company. I think Sam seemed more rested than I felt at the moment. After I gave him a recap of my visit to the shop and the messages they all had sent for him, I agreed to go home. No matter how he wanted to pretend, he was still not his normal self.

I walked into the dark, quiet house and turned off the alarm that Sam insisted we have installed on this secluded hill. I was feeling safer with the alarm, and in a short while, 333 Lincoln really had become home. We shared the house with the spirit of my grandmother who, for the most part, left us alone. She especially liked me, and that was a good thing since her lover, Albert Taylor, had lived here previously with his wife and not my grandmother, who was his mistress. She meant no harm, but undoubtedly she was the ghost that everyone in town seemed to know about. She made it clear she wasn't moving on until she was good and ready.

Besides my occasional journaling, I started what I hoped would be a book about the Taylor house. I wasn't sure where it would lead me or when I would find time to continue to write. Marion and Albert had been fascinating and prominent citizens in the community, but the house itself held a mystery all its own. I loved to write, and living in this house gave me more than enough to write about!

I went to the kitchen to pour myself a drink and saw the bag on the porch containing the quilt that had revealed so much to us. Quilts could often divulge much information about their makers. Jean and Nancy, the most avid quilters in our literary club, said no two quilts were alike for that very reason. When Aunt Marie had taught some of us to quilt in the basement of my mother's home, it opened up a whole new world to us, not only about the world of quilting, but about our family as well. We discovered secrets we never would have known otherwise. My dominant but now deceased Grandmother Davis began to insert herself into our activities. Why her presence did not scare the daylights out of us, I don't know.

I pulled the filthy quilt top out of the bag, bringing back memories of when I had found it under the potting shed bench. It had been wrapped around a beautiful vase, as if someone meant to hide it there and then forgot about it. I took it to the back door to shake it out in the darkness, and I could see little flakes of paper falling out onto the grass. While we carefully removed the old letters from the paper-pieced quilt, it had been impossible to remove them completely from the seams. I left it inside on the sun porch. I laid it across the drying rack I used for my hand washing. I planned to hang it outdoors to air when the weather was nicer. I hoped Marion Taylor, who was no doubt the maker, was watching me care for the quilt that had nearly been ruined. I washed my hands and then decided to take my drink upstairs to our bedroom.

Going up the grand staircase, I thought of everyone enjoying the Jane Austen Literary Club tonight. I could hear my ears ringing from their discussions, which I know included Sam and me. I smiled, thinking how we all loved and admired Jane. It was such a romantic era for all of us. Mother, who was once a librarian, had read all of her books. My favorite was *Pride and Prejudice*, like most members in our group. Sam's Christmas gift of a trip to England to visit the Jane Austen museum would now have to be postponed indefinitely. I always wanted to go to England. Having Jean, my British employee, reminded me of that desire nearly every day. I decided it would stay on my "bucket list."

There was part of me that could really relate to Elizabeth Bennet in *Pride and Prejudice*. She had higher and different priorities than just getting married. She would rather be alone than let anyone arrange a husband for her. However, when she found the right man, everything changed.

Jane Austen had that independence also, which was so rare in those days. My business venture on Main Street was like writing was to Jane: a passion that alone could fill my life.

When I think of Jane trying to escape for a private

moment to write in her room, I could certainly relate. It was difficult for me to do the same, and I, unlike her, was not a professional writer.

My phone on the bedside table began to ring. It startled me into the reality of being at 333 Lincoln alone. "Hello, sweet Annie. Are you ready for bed or shuffling papers?" Sam's voice whispered.

"Oh, honey, why are you still awake?" I gently scolded, sounding more like a mother than a wife. "I brought my drink to my room to help me sleep; however, I may fall asleep before I drink it."

"That sounds good," he agreed. "I'm too excited about coming home to sleep. Harry stopped by from work and began filling me in on various things. Of course, he got me thinking and now I'm wide awake. At least at home, I'll be able to take care of some business more easily."

"Hey, wasn't this call supposed to be about you missing me?" I teased. "Maybe some of that work could just wait for a while."

"You got that right, baby," he said, laughing. "I do miss you and love you very much. I am so sorry this spoiled our first Christmas together."

"We had a great Christmas together," I countered, cheering him up. "The big tree, the party, Mother's dinner, and all our gifts—we had it all!"

"All good stuff, my lady," he agreed, "I just couldn't quite make it to the finish. I had no idea my discomfort could lead to this."

"Well, we'll have a nice, quiet, romantic dinner on New Year's Eve," I said with a cheerful voice. "It will be just the two of us. I hope you can have a little bubbly champagne and a few of your favorite things. The doctor may have other plans for you, however."

"You are the favorite thing I really want, but we do have a lot to celebrate and be thankful for, don't we?" he bragged. "What would my life be like without you, sweet Annie?"

"I think it would be a little less stressful with no 333 Lincoln, no wife, and no flower shop, don't you?" I knew I might have said too much.

"Stop this nonsense talk," he snapped, sounding agitated. "If I were there, I'd prove to you how you are the best thing that ever happened to me."

"Good night, Sam. I love you!" Touched by his warmth, these were my last words to him for the evening.

CHAPTER 3

Getting Sam home around noontime put his arrival much later than I expected. It was nice to see his mood so good after what he had been through. Flowers from the shop were waiting for us on the doorstep. I told him I had nothing to do with their arrival and considered how lucky I was to have my little flower shop family.

We were barely settled when Uncle Jim called to see if he could do anything for Sam. I was so grateful, that in spite of it falling to Sam to have to fire Uncle Jim from Martingale, it did not seem to impact their relationship. I was forever grateful that it was Uncle Jim who had introduced Sam to me. When he hung up, Sam rested his head back, trying to grasp that he was now home again.

"Has Uncle Jim had any luck finding a job?" I asked, unpacking Sam's overnight bag.

"No, and I figure he'll tell me if there is any news," Sam

replied, sounding a bit down. "Has Julia said anything to you?"

"No, she hasn't," I confirmed, shaking my head. "How about I fix you some lunch, handsome?"

"Not right now. Come here and sit with me a minute," he said in a serious tone. "Are you okay?"

"Sure. It's just been scary for me," I confessed as I sat down next to him. "I have some nice filets to fix tonight. How does that sound?" His look was serious.

"Don't change the subject on me," Sam pointed out as he put his arm around me. "I hope to never put you through this again. I don't want you to be afraid of each and every move I make, or it will be an additional stress for me. I also don't want you to ignore your business. Feel free to go there today, if you like."

I interrupted and stood. "I hear you. Just don't be so bossy," I said, putting my hands on my hips. "I guess I would feel the same way if this had happened to me. Today is the last day of the year, and I am going to fuss over my husband, whether you like it or not. I'm going to do some things in the kitchen and it would be nice if you took a nap so you'll be able to stay up until midnight with me!"

"So, who's bossy here?" he questioned, pulling me close to give me a kiss. A knock at the door was not what I wanted to hear. I looked through the peephole to see it was Mother holding what looked like food.

"I hope I am not overstepping my place, but I thought some homemade soup might be just the thing for both of you," she said kindly, handing me the package.

"Great, but come in for heaven's sake," I greeted her, giving her a kiss on the cheek. "Sam doesn't want lunch now, but I'm famished," I told her. "Please join me. Besides, I am anxious to hear about last night's club meeting." She reluctantly came in and removed her coat.

"Hey, Mother-in-Law!" Sam announced as he came to greet her. They hugged.

"I knew there might be some perks to being out of commission. What's in the container?"

"Well, of course, my own chicken soup. There's nothing like it for what ails you, if I have to say so myself," she bragged with a grin.

We all walked into the kitchen, making small talk about Sam's condition. Sam excused himself to take a rest, which was a good idea, considering the morning's activities.

"Will you join me in something to eat, Mother?" I offered, opening her pot of soup. "I am going to help myself to this right now, if you don't mind. You are spoiling me."

"I always have and always will," Mother confirmed, sitting down at the kitchen table. "I'll have a cup of tea and stay for just a bit." She paused as she watched me. "Are you handling things okay, Anne?" Why were questions going to be about me now, I wondered.

"I am. It's just all new, as you can imagine," I admitted, but determined I did not really want to discuss my feelings any longer with anyone. "I want to hear about last night."

"Well, first of all, they all sent their best to both of you and wanted to know as much as I knew about Sam's condition. All and all, we missed you very much." She went on to explain. "It was a pretty fun night, actually. Isabella, from the quilt shop, was curious about our group, so Nancy brought her as a guest last night. I think we may have convinced her to join. No one was too keen on *Northanger Abbey*, I must say, so there wasn't much discussion. Isabella said there is much interest now in English fabric designs and patterns in her quilt shop. She took note, of course, of how many in our group were quilters. Because of Isabella's presence, Jean showed us a quilt she was working on and then Jean asked when and if the basement quilters would be meeting again."

"Yes, I sort of miss those afternoons myself," I lamented, recalling fond memories. "It seemed like a nice ritual with the delicious treats, not to mention the gossip. I guess when we finished my floral appliqué quilt was the last time we quilted, right?"

"You're right. I miss it too, Anne," she said sadly. "We never know what twists and turns may come around the corner, do we? I have been thinking. I think we should offer to help Jean quilt her quilt when it's ready. However, since Isabella does machine quilting now for people, she may want it machine done."

"Jean's quilt? You've got to be kidding," I said with sarcasm in my voice. "Jean is a purist to the bone. She would want it hand done. I think she is piecing that quilt by hand, if I'm not mistaken. We owe Jean a lot for helping us with the potting shed quilt, so I think we should offer to do that for her."

"Then we shall. It'll be fun to get back together," Mother noted. "Mother and Aunt Marie would be so pleased to know our quilting continues in that basement."

"Trust me, Grandmother knows, but I'm not sure about Aunt Marie," I teased. We continued the chatter just like we did most every morning when I was still living at home. It was good to have her with me for encouragement. The soup hit the spot. From the silence coming from the rest of the house, I knew Sam was resting.

CHAPTER 4

S am was impressed with the candlelight dinner I arranged
for us in the dining room with the flowers from the girls
placed in the center of the table. It was nice having just the
two of us enjoy this beautiful room together. My steaks
were not cooked to perfection, but the baked potatoes and
salad were a hit. Sam loved my own salad recipe of lettuce,
mandarin oranges, toasted almonds, and blue cheese with
red wine vinegar dressing.

He seemed well rested and we had nice conversation
about our past year and what the future might hold for us at
333 Lincoln. It was getting close to midnight so I told Sam I
wanted to be on the south porch to toast in the New Year, but
only if he didn't mind bundling up for five minutes. I knew
there would be fireworks in the distance from downtown
Colebridge to bring in the New Year. He thought it was a
grand idea, so we grabbed our heavy coats and glasses of

champagne as we opened the door to the cold night air. There was still a light covering of white snow that remained with the constant cold temperatures of the season. The dark sky displayed a full moon that was just waiting for the sparkle of fireworks. Looking out to the gazebo, 333 Lincoln looked like a Christmas card. My touch of garland and red bows added a festive touch that I hoped I could keep for some time.

Sam checked his watch and proceeded to count down the minutes. I looked into his magical eyes and knew how darn lucky I was to have him standing next to me. As the New Year struck, he drew me close and gave me that powerful kiss that he kept for special occasions, just like this. The fireworks in the distance erupted into multicolors and suddenly the lights in the house flashed on and off. When we looked into the window, the colorful Christmas tree in the foyer joined in the rhythm of flashes, which left us speechless.

"How's that for a private show, Mr. Dickson?" I teased. Sam did not see the humor, because it had happened before. He knew it wouldn't last. We knew it was Grandmother Davis's way of reminding us how she had taken residence here, whether anyone liked it or not. Sam did not appreciate the humor as much as I. I knew there was part of him that would never quite acknowledge her presence. I took it upon myself to raise my glass for the second toast and said, "Happy New Year, Grandmother!" Sam smiled and shook his head in dismay as he reluctantly joined me in the second sip of champagne.

I told him to chill. As always, it wasn't but a few minutes and then all the power was restored back to normal. Sam shivered and grumbled as we went back into the house. This interruption in the home he loved was not always going to be amusing, I gathered.

We took our champagne into the den by the fire. We sat there in each other's arms in silence as we continued to hear fireworks going off in the distance. "Happy New Year," we once again whispered in each other's ears as we fell asleep.

We were closed on New Year's Day, so I thought it would be a good time to check things out at the shop without folks seeing my car and wanting to visit about Sam.

After Sam awoke, which was later than his normal routine, I brought in the paper and had his favorite orange rolls and juice ready for him. I can do all this, I told myself. Sam was going to be a good patient, so I needed to be the good wife. He was preoccupied reading the paper, and there was plenty of coffee in the pot, so I left in my walking clothes for the shop.

It was a good feeling going to the cold empty street on the holiday. I wanted one-on-one time again without the others around. I wondered if the shop had missed me as much as I had missed being here. Was it going to turn into someone else's business if I wasn't careful? Everything seemed in order when I walked into the warm, colorful shop that smelled heavily of roses. I glanced at the orders on the computer and it appeared we were doing quite well. The next day would be a busy one with two funerals and a Kiwanis Club banquet. I made a note to be there to help. I then checked my neglected e-mails. I knew there would be lots of questions about Sam's health, and it strangely irritated me instead of giving me comfort. How could word about Sam have spread so fast, I asked myself. They say bad news always spreads fastest, right? Ted Collins, oh no, not Ted! The e-mail read, "Sorry to hear about Sam's heart condition. I hope he's doing better. I wish you much success and good health for the two of you in the coming year. If you want to talk, I am still a good listener, despite your decision to move on. Happy New Year, Ted."

"What the heck!" I said to myself out loud. Ted Collins, my former boyfriend, would be the last person I would want to talk to right now. I figured that when he heard the news about Sam, he was probably delighted. He could once again rub it in that I had chosen a man too old for me and that my troubles had just begun. I never regretted for a moment that I left him for Sam. Besides, Wendy Lorenz, his former girlfriend, was eagerly waiting at his fingertips. I was sure they were likely still together, and would not be surprised if there was a holiday engagement announcement. I wish he would truly move on. I shut down the computer. I was no longer in a mood to hear anyone else's concerns or good wishes.

CHAPTER 5

My cell phone rang and it was Nancy, my only real personal friend. "Hey, I called the house thinking you were there and Sam said you were itching to get to the shop," she began explaining, in what sounded like a happy frame of mind. "Sam sounded really good. Are you doing okay? Am I interrupting some work?"

I couldn't answer for what seemed like a whole minute. "I'm fine," I stated strongly as I took a deep breath. "I wish everyone would quit asking how I'm doing. I am not the one who nearly died here!" I started to cry and abruptly hung up on her. I evidently wasn't okay. Oh, what have I just done? Hanging up on my very best friend made me sob even harder. I rested my head on the desk. What was happening to me? I slowly raised my head trying to get a grip of myself. I sat and stared at my blank computer screen. Somehow, just staring, simply just staring at nothing in particular was what

I needed to console me right now.

When anyone would ask how I was doing, it hit a nerve. It was a nerve that cried out how I wasn't doing well. It wasn't my nature to whine or ask for help. I was a strong only child and now an employer. It was others that always needed help from me. Did they think I couldn't handle a husband that now needed me? Ten minutes later, hard banging on the front door startled me. It was Nancy. I got up to let her in as I wiped my eyes. Not good timing, I thought.

"Girl, I am so sorry. I didn't mean to upset you," Nancy said, grabbing me for a hug. I backed off, not really wanting her sympathy.

"I am the one to apologize, Nancy, for heaven's sake," I spilled out, sounding sad, angry, and out of tears. "I am ashamed of myself, Nancy. Please sit. I guess I could use a good friend right now."

"I purposely tried not to visit or call because I know how much commotion this had to create for the two of you," she explained as she took off her coat. "I wanted to call last night and wish the two of you Happy New Year, but we decided it may not be a good idea, especially if Sam went to bed early."

Sure, like two elderly folks, I thought to myself. "No, we had a nice quiet dinner, which I prepared myself, I'll have you know, and then we went out to the south porch to hear the fireworks and toast in the New Year," I said, gaining my composure. "We are fine. Sam is, anyway." I managed a smile and then a giggle. "Oh, and Grandmother Davis blinked her lights right on cue for the New Year." I laughed again, getting a bit silly.

Nancy wanted to laugh too, but wasn't sure how to take me. She didn't ask what that all meant, of course.

"You'll get through this, Anne. Give yourself some credit here," Nancy said, looking me straight in the eyes. "This was a serious incident for the two of you. You've had so many changes in your life in a very short period of time. You amaze me, you know that?"

I wanted to change the subject from this pity party of mine. "I hear you brought Isabella to the literary club last night!" I interjected, deliberately changing the subject.

"Yes, she had a grand time and wants to join," she shared. "She has read *Emma* but none of Jane's other books. *Northanger Abbey* had mixed reviews last night, but we had a good discussion. Your mother didn't care for it too much, but Sue liked how Catherine and Henry finally wound up together, after such interruptions. Sue is really enjoying her night out with the club and has become quite fond of Jane's style of writing, from what she says."

"I'm so glad," I said, the gossipy report making me smile. "Aunt Julia loves babysitting Mia, so it's a win-win situation."

"Isabella had a brilliant idea on the way home last night, by the way," Nancy said, perking up. "She heard some discussion about how some of the quilters in the group want to make some kind of block or quilt to do with Jane Austen. I know Jean has mentioned that before. Anyway, Isabella asked if I would start a Jane Austen Quilt Club at her shop. I was pretty flattered, and you know how I love projects. You'd think I'd have enough to do keeping up with those casket quilts for our funeral home. But frankly, Sue has taken on most of the production, so I don't have to worry about keeping them stocked."

"Pretty clever idea, I guess," I said, wanting to support her. "So what would they do in this club, since the literary club members are the ones reading Jane's books and having discussions?" I found the idea somewhat repetitive and confusing. What was next? A Jane Austen's singles' club or writers' club? It was interesting how Jane's life seemed to get personal with her readers. I suppose a good writer would do that. Hmmm...

"I could hardly sleep last night thinking about the possibilities, but Isabella thought making a Jane Austen quilt would certainly be a start," she began. "The shop has such a nice large classroom where we can all meet. She said she'd like to also open it up to any of her customers who are interested. Since so many of the quilters are on various skill levels, I think everyone should just do their own thing with their design. We can request twelve-inch blocks, which is standard. I think it would be quite interesting to see what they all choose. Even Sarah could really have fun with this. I'd like to see Sally and Abbey give it a try. Isabella said this could cultivate a lot of new quilters. She realizes most are new to quilting, so she would teach any techniques free of charge as we move along. That is a very generous offer from Isabella, I think."

"I should say so!" I said in agreement. "Do you think this would maybe dissolve the efforts of the basement quilters? Mother thought we should quilt Jean's quilt when it's ready, since she's done so much for me supervising the potting shed quilt. I would hate to see anything replace that, as Mother enjoys it so when we all come."

"Frankly, Anne, Isabella sees this as a moneymaker to get people in the shop, plus it's a great theme. She's a smart businesswoman. I was honored, in a way, when she asked me to be in charge, because she doesn't have the time. And well, let's face it, she knows I spend a ton of money there. I think I could really run with this idea!"

"Nancy, you're too much like me, always thinking," I found myself smiling at her excitement. "You are perfect for the task, no doubt. You've never done anything halfway." I stopped to think for a second to equal her energy. "How about you guys coming over tonight? It would do us good. No dinner, of course." We both laughed.

"I think it might work," Nancy said, beaming with excitement. "I'll call you right away if we can't. I never know if Richard will be needed at the home. Are you sure Sam will be up to it?"

"I really am," I assured her, feeling confident it was a good idea. "Frankly, I need to show him I'm okay and that some normal activity is coming back."

We hugged and said our good-byes. Nancy always had a way of cheering me up. We had such a great history together. She will just die when I tell her about Ted's e-mail, but that was for another day. Right now, I felt Anne Brown Dickson returning, as creativity and ideas started to flow through my mind.

CHAPTER 6

Sam was on the computer when I returned home. No rest for the weary describes this man. I put on a happy face and told him about my idea of an evening with the Barristers. He grinned with approval, but was also pleased it was just for a visit and not dinner. I whipped up some cocktail sauce for the frozen shrimp we had on hand and made a cheese and cracker platter, keeping it pretty simple.

"I really enjoyed your mother's soup," Sam shared, joining me in the kitchen. He kissed me on the cheek. "How was everything at the shop?"

"Well, I have to say I think they no longer need my services," I answered, half teasing. "They are doing quite well. If you don't mind, I think I'd better go in tomorrow since they have a couple of funerals. I don't think they can do it all without some help."

"By all means, Anne. I don't need to be waited on here,"

Sam said, sounding encouraging. "Unfortunately, until I see the doc again, Martingale's work will have to be run through the computer here at home. By the way, I called a contractor to do a nicer blacktop driveway from the street, as soon as the weather breaks. Also, be thinking what you want re-bricked around the house when you have time. Some of that can be done in winter mild temperatures."

I smiled with approval. "Well, you are feeling better, Mr. Bossy," I bantered, giving him a wink. "Yes, as a matter of fact, I want a brick sidewalk to the potting shed, instead of the broken concrete facsimile. I want it to lead over to the gazebo, too. Perhaps it would be nice to brick totally around it. Oh, Sam, I can't wait for spring. I have a few things growing in the potting shed, but not like I really want to grow in the future."

Now he smiled at me with approval. We were getting our old selves back to accomplishing many things at once, with our normal enthusiasm. The plans were lifting my spirits. I didn't have a regret call from Nancy, so I was prepared when they arrived at the door.

"Hey, come in! Glad you could make it," I greeted, taking their coats. Sam, looking quite normal and healthy in his handsome yellow sweater and tight tailored jeans, greeted them as well.

"You gave us quite a scare," Nancy said, kissing Sam on the cheek.

Richard shook his hand and told him his dad had the same procedure and continues to do well. We went into the living room where there was another Christmas tree to be enjoyed. Nancy brought some yummy-looking crab cakes that just needed a touch of the microwave to heat up. We left the guys in great conversation while we made our way to the kitchen.

Nancy commented she had never been in our kitchen and admired all the latest and greatest for any chef. She peered out to the screen porch and said, "Anne, it's pretty dark, but is that the potting shed quilt wadded up in the corner of the floor out there?" I wasn't sure I heard her correctly, but immediately turned on the light and opened the door to the porch to see what she had noticed.

"Oh, my word!" I gasped. "How did that end up there?" I quickly went out and picked it up. I noticed it had not just slipped off the drying rack, but was tightly rolled into a ball and tossed on the floor in the corner of the porch. "I had this all spread out on the drying rack after I gave it a good shake yesterday." Nancy quietly observed as I opened it up to examine any further damage. Poor quilt, I thought to myself. I placed it back on the empty rack, thinking I may have to plan differently.

"Was anyone else here, Anne, or would Sam think it was something else?" Nancy asked with concern.

"Good heavens, no. Sam knows I put it here and knows all about this Taylor quilt," I stated firmly, feeling disgusted.

"Well, maybe it needs to go somewhere else, Anne," Nancy suggested, shaking her head in disbelief. "I now know better than to ask any more questions, if you know what I mean."

"Good, Nancy," I murmured. "I know Nora certainly wouldn't ever do anything like this and she's the only one besides Mother who's been here of late. Let's get back to the guys. Don't say anything, okay?"

She nodded and grinned.

The Barristers were interesting to visit with, especially when it came to community affairs. Sam and Richard knew a lot of the same folks and Richard confessed it was a challenge for him to make changes at the home where his past family members managed through generations. We shared a few laughs and discovered Richard had quite the sense of humor. Their visit was short, which was good. In the back of my mind, I couldn't stop thinking about the wadded up quilt that I had just rescued. Hmmm...

I carried the glasses and snacks into the kitchen and immediately peeked out onto the porch to see if the quilt was still in place on the rack. It was indeed still there. Perhaps my disapproval got through to this unhappy spirit. It was obvious that Grandmother still had not warmed up to the quilt because Albert's wife, Marion, had made it. I'm sure it was hard for her to see us make such a fuss over the quilt. But Grandmother should be grateful it existed because otherwise, we never would have known about her daughter, Mary, who was written about in the quilt's sewn-in letters.

After I changed into my pajamas and robe, I joined my husband downstairs, near the fire in the study, where he was recuperating. He had been doing so well, but he was dozing off from all the night's activity. I kissed him on the forehead and stretched out on the couch with an afghan and one of my gardening magazines. I just wanted to be near him. My next glance showed my honey fast asleep, and I was right behind him.

CHAPTER 7

I got up extra early, thinking that if I was very organized, I could get in a brisk walk before my day at the shop. I dressed in layers, made sure Sam had everything he needed, and kissed him good-bye. I think he was somewhat relieved to see me return to my activities and to have his privacy respected.

I stopped for my usual Pike Place coffee at Starbucks and began my drive down the winter wonderland of Main Street. The trail would have too many ice patches, so the cleared sidewalks or parking lots would have to do. I parked my car near the river and began my hike to the street. Walking more cautiously along the sparsely cleared sidewalk, I felt like reintroducing myself to each building. They were so unique in architecture and I could remember so many businesses and shop owners who had come and gone in each of them. Many buildings had wonderful history that had been passed along in books and through tour guides that frequented our street. After thirty minutes, which included a couple of hills on side streets, I arrived with a smile and new energy at Brown's Botanical. I loved being the first to arrive. I put on some coffee for the others and began scanning my list of e-mails before I went home to change for the day.

Then Sally arrived. "Oh my," she said, sounding surprised. "I didn't see your car, Anne."

"Sorry, Sally," I replied, looking up. "I parked at the river and walked up from there. Coffee is on. I sure will be glad to get this winter behind us. I have to say there still is beauty in God's great hues of gray and white. It makes you realize and appreciate the miracle of spring that introduces such an abundance of color once again. You know you burn more calories in cold weather!"

Sally gave me a strange look. "I don't know how you manage those walks in this cold weather!" she remarked as she put her coat in the closet. "How is Sam doing?"

"Great!" I said, for the hundredth time since his attack. "I thought you could use some help today with those orders sitting there."

"You bet we can, if you're not needed at home," Sally reminded me, as if I didn't have it on my mind already.

"Do we have all the stock and are the stems all stripped for these two early orders?" I inquired, wanting to get to the matter at hand.

"Of course," she boasted. "Your manager has prepared ahead. Kevin will be here by ten thirty to make the first delivery." I nodded my approval.

"We got another online order this morning, but I think something in the case will work nicely," I said, walking to the front room.

"Anne, I have to ask you," she began, "do you actually realize the amount of wedding business we are turning down every day? Just doing mini weddings is fine, but you are so well-known in the community and people want to use Brown's Botanical for average and large weddings. The potential could double your bottom line, Anne, I'm certain."

"You are absolutely correct and very astute, my friend, but I'm boxed in here," I responded, putting up my hands. "I refuse to relocate from this incredible spot on the street, which adds to our charm. I have no space for a consulting room, which it would require, not to mention the extra storage and design space for more staff. It would also have to require a wedding planner to do it right."

Sally listened intently. "Any chance Gayle or Mr. Crab from next door will move on anytime soon?" she inquired. I had thought of her question a jillion times and knew exactly the answer.

"Nope. No indication," I confirmed, joining her up front. "My ideal dream would be to add on to the rear of this building, which would remove some of the parking area, of course; but I think we could have a nice consulting room and expand our designing areas as well. I may even have some luck providing a private office for myself and that great manager I hired!"

Sally grinned really big this time. "Wow, so you have given this some thought," she said, appearing somewhat relieved.

"Of course," I agreed, as I heard the door open. "If you're not moving ahead, you're behind! So, what can I do to get these finished before I go home to change?"

Sally shook her head in wonder and her face held a big smile.

CHAPTER 8

⋇

When I returned, Abbey and Jean were already in their usual chipper moods. There was wild Abbey with her pink-and-black fringed hair wearing purple polka dots on her skirt and a lime-green blouse. I always wondered if she purposely avoided any coordination in her wardrobe. Then, there was our English conservative, Jean, who liked wearing a black or white smock over her clothes. No dress code in this creative business, I told myself. At least they were being themselves.

I, Anne Dickson, however, felt I had to be dressed the most businesslike of anyone, so they could easily figure out I was the one in charge. So many of the businesses on our street had trouble getting the respect they so deserved, as many thought we were playing with our craft and didn't work that hard, since we primarily entertained the tourist trade. They expected a woman to own a flower shop, of course, as it was a feminine sort of hobby in their eyes. If a woman wanted respect in the business world, I learned very early on you had to play and look like one of the good ol' boys. I knew I was working harder than some of my corporate friends for a tenth of the money. I, for one, refused to gather around the ladies at business affairs. I sought out the male movers and shakers, who gladly accepted me. I didn't want them to think twice about where to order flowers for their wives, significant others, and for business affairs.

"Tally ho, Miss Anne," Jean said as she arrived, giving me a tight hug. "We missed you so last night, and from what I gather, your spouse is about as good as new!"

Not quite, I thought to myself. "Yes, he is," I bragged. "If he does what he's told, he should be just fine." Why I had trouble believing any of this myself, I didn't know.

"I heard you had a great literary club meeting," I said directly to Jean. "I'm sorry I had to miss it. By the way, you guys, Happy New Year! I guess you know it's inventory time, so when there is time, I'll need some help with that."

They all happily responded back with their New Year greetings.

"We had a jolly time, with new ideas popping from Miss Isabella," Jean happily shared. "I'm sure you may have already heard about it all from your mum, right?"

"Oh yes," I answered, as I kept moving back and forth from room to room. Abbey continued to comment to Sally what a dud of a guy she went out with on New Year's Eve. A few minutes later, Sally got them all on track with their assigned responsibilities.

Kevin came in on time and was elated to see me. I told him we would need his assistance to remove our Christmas tree and he said to just say the word. I had started on the Kiwanis centerpieces when Gayle from next door peeked in the door to see what anyone knew about Sam. She came into the back room and I did what I could to be polite as I chose colorful flowers to use in the pieces. She was such a sweet neighbor and would do anything to help any of us. She never mentioned a man in her life, so I assumed she had none. She was as cute as a button, but she was probably too busy like the rest of us to think about it. Who was I kidding? We all thought about it. If I could fit a man in my life, so could Gayle.

When we stopped to share a sub sandwich that Sally brought for lunch, Jean asked, "Miss Anne, I guess your mum or Nancy told you of the new Jane Austen Quilt Club that'll be starting at Isabella's? Quite a clever idea, but what's your spin on that?"

"Well, it sounds as if Nancy is going to run with this, so it'll be fun and well organized, knowing her." I truly tried to sound enthusiastic.

"I agree," said Abbey as she was making a stunning black and white bow. "I know nothing of the business of quilting, but Isabella assures me I will learn."

"Who from our club will join, do you suppose?" I asked, interested.

"It is my observation that every single one of them may, Miss Anne," announced Jean. "I have to say I am the guilty one in this matter, as I have learned to love Jane so much. I may have planted the idea in her head. I don't muck around and always want to express my fondness for Jane in the best way I can. What better way than with a bit of a quilt square, I say?"

I had to laugh at the thought. "Even the nonquilters like

you, Sally?" I asked in disbelief.

"When I heard Isabella say the word free on her quilt lessons, I figured why not?" she said, shrugging her shoulders. "I don't want to miss anything. You all are a hoot! Now, we'll see if Paige will join me."

"So, was there a date to begin meeting?" I asked with interest.

"Isabella wanted to advertise it for a couple of weeks and see what day the classroom is free," said Sally while arranging roses in a huge glass vase.

"If I can do my own thing with this quilting bit, I'm in," chimed in Abbey. "I'm not for many rules. What do you think, Anne?"

"It sounds great, but right now I can't seem to think what the next day will be like, much less in a couple of weeks," I confessed. "Sam's recovery will dictate how much freedom I have. I will do well to get to our literary club."

"Why sure, Miss Anne," Jean said softly. "You and Mr. Dickson are such a blessing to each other. This will all be a toss in no time and all will be jolly good again." We laughed and I thanked her for her support.

In late afternoon, I checked in with Sam on the phone and told him I would be stopping by the deli at the IGA for our dinner. He said to just get fixings for a salad because he was making chicken divan, one of his favorites. This was my Sam. He was so versatile. He could be a great stay-at-home wife. I prided myself in not feeling guilty about not looking like most wives.

What I hoped would be a quick in-and-out visit for lettuce was a big mistake at the neighborhood grocery. Even the clerks heard had about Sam and wanted an update. I did the best I could not to look anyone in the eye and get on my way. When you owned a business, many faces were familiar but not their names. I always acknowledged them all, figuring they either knew me from my shop or knew my family members. It was one of the charms of a small town, but forget trying to hide!

CHAPTER 9

Later that evening, Sam and I stared at the top of the staircase, as he was about to embark on the real test of his progress. "Why did you have to choose the widest and longest staircase in Colebridge?" I asked, teasing him. "You don't do anything normally, do you?"

He looked at me with a grin that answered any question I might have had. I should have reminded him that he was the one that found this house and all would be well. "You don't think I can do this, huh?" he teased. "I have plenty of inspiration to do this, believe me! I want you to climb with me, okay?"

I grinned. "You've got me, baby, but you won't need my help," I encouraged. "Just take it slowly and don't show off for my benefit!"

He laughed, knowing himself so well. He took the first few steps slowly, and then proceeded with a normal pace

41

all the way to the top! He smiled at his success, and as I listened for his breathing, it seemed perfectly normal. I gave him a big hug and he planted a very passionate kiss on my lips. "I had other intentions getting you here, Mrs. Dickson," Sam said with a twinkle in his eye. "If you recall, I was told about a saying that if you can do the stairs, you can do...," he stopped to get my reaction. I couldn't believe this guy was now steering me into our bedroom. Hmmm...

The next weeks flew by with some normalcy as Sam returned to driving and started delegating some of his business travel. Sam reluctantly chose to walk with me on a few of the mornings, which was encouraged by his doctor. It was nice, but not normal for me. I wasn't used to having the communication, nor the pace of someone else's walk. This was my alone time that I cherished. I knew he would be doing his own thing soon, like lifting weights and walking on the treadmill, so I remained patient.

Today, Mother and I decided to meet at Donna's Tea Room for lunch, just to catch up. She looked happy. Why I thought she would miss me after I moved out of the house was beside me! She was doing things on her own that I had not witnessed previously. She loved writing the newsletter for Pointer's Book Store and doing some of their book reviews. We both had the love of the pen, no doubt.

"Oh, the first meeting of the Jane Austen Quilt Club is Thursday night, Anne. Do you think you can make it?" she said excitedly.

"I haven't been going out much at night with Sam home," I shared. "I would love to go and see everyone. Is Aunt Julia going to join us?"

"The last time I talked with her, she felt she should since

Sarah was pushing her to do so," Mother said, taking her last bite of spinach quiche. "Can you believe that Sarah? She loves anything to do with the arts, so she is pretty intrigued with this quilting thing. Unusual for a teenager, don't you think?"

I nodded in agreement. "Do you know Aunt Julia only called once to check on Sam?" I remarked, showing my disappointment. "I miss her, but I'm afraid she isn't as comfortable with Sam and me since Sam fired Uncle Jim. It's bound to affect her financial support too, since he still doesn't have a job. Are you picking up on that too, Mother?"

"Nonsense." Mother dismissed my comment and then I saw her face perk up. "Not to change the subject, Anne, but I have been thinking about that Jane Austen quilt project. After giving this some time, I think I know what kind of quilt block I'd like to do for the club's quilt, and I think it suits my interests." She smiled, waiting for my response.

"Oh, pray tell, Mother dearest, what would that be?" I asked, humored by her changing the subject on me. We were then interrupted with Donna's complimentary coconut cream pie brought to us by a new server I had not seen before.

"Thank Donna for us, will you?" I asked her as I looked at Mother, urging her to continue.

"I will," the server happily responded. "Today's her day off, but Donna told me she always gives you some pie when you come in, so you can thank her."

"How nice," Mother said. "We will be sure to do that. Now back to my block," Mother continued. "You know how much I love books, so I thought I would piece strips together like books standing between two bookends. I saw this once in a magazine. Then on each end, I'll embroider each one of Jane's book titles. However, one extra book will be titled differently." She paused and I waited for her to finish. "It's going to be called *My Book*. I always wanted one of the books in the library to be one I had written, so this may be my only opportunity to do so."

I nodded and gave her a big smile for a pretty clever idea. "What a creative idea, Mother, but I think you should be able to come up with a better title than that," I suggested on a positive note. "How about naming it *The Mysterious Librarian* or *The Saga of Sylvia*?" We both laughed so loud the table next to us gave us a funny look.

"This is pretty revealing about you, Mother! I love the idea. You are so clever! You may have to help me with mine if I decide to do one. Right now, the thought of having to do that task is not exciting me in the least." She nodded like she understood.

It was a great visit that reminded me how much I missed her. Her energy and positive attitude taught me so many things through the years. I thought it so interesting that she still had that dream of someday writing a book, as do I. Would I still be yearning for that at her age? Maybe this was normal for a lot of people. Everyone wants their story told, I suppose. After all, the written word is one of the best legacies one can leave.

I told her I would pick her up on Thursday night unless I was needed elsewhere.

CHAPTER 10

✦⋺⋵✦

I was glad to get the month of February behind me. Our Valentine's Day business was always crazy, but welcome. It was getting to be our best holiday of the year. Everyone worked a little faster and longer than usual. Mother's Day was the next busiest day, but we found the orders to be more generalized. On Valentine's Day, the customer definitely had something in particular in mind.

I loved the winter picnic Sam had planned for us under the gazebo on Valentine's Day evening. It was such a simple yet romantic idea. I was glad he could be so creative. I never once saw that from Ted. He was always cut and dried on whatever the instructions said to do on any particular matter. Traditional, steady, and dependable, he was for sure. I had to give him credit there. Some lucky lady out there would love that!

Our new brick sidewalks were done and Sam's addition of a fireplace enticed us into the outdoors more often. It would be perfect for tonight. I rushed home from a hectic day and there was Sam under the gazebo preparing our dinner table. He kept it simple by roasting hot dogs and corn on the cob, with marshmallows for dessert. I loved them burnt and he loved them barely touched by the fire. Sam's snuggled embrace was all I needed at the end of this day. Earlier, we agreed to only exchange Valentine's Day cards. They were special, but I had the real thing next to me. I remembered so clearly how I had personally written a suggestive card to Sam last year. Now we were married and were happy with a card from the rack. Was this a good or bad sign?

Light snow trickled as we huddled together, but it could not have been more romantic. The fire kept us warm and the gazebo kept the flakes away. When we shared moments like this, we didn't have to force conversation. Our individual thoughts brought us closer instead of apart. I could agree with enjoying this kind of Kodak moment forever. Hmmm...

March, despite its determination to stay cold, was always a sigh of relief for me, knowing spring was just around the corner. Sally and Abbey had already stripped the red from the shop and pastels in all colors took over the decor.

In retail, you had to be ahead. My little plants in the potting shed were doing nicely, thanks to Sam letting me keep a small heater in there to keep them thriving through the winter. The few seeds I planted in the eggshell cartons were peeking out like hatching eggs. With the anticipation of spring, I was already spending more time in the potting shed, dreaming how I might improve it and add to my gardens and flower shop.

I could only dream of having my own large greenhouse. Having poinsettias bloom before your very eyes near Christmastime had to be a "high" for any floral merchant.

Red geraniums in the spring and red poinsettias for winter was right up my alley!

I had not furthered my conversation about any shop expansion with Sally. She knew I had my hands full with Sam and seemed to respect my situation. The Jane Austen Quilt Club was now the new hot topic at the shop and consumed most of our conversation. It was something unique and we knew Nancy and Isabella would make it fun. I just enjoyed hearing them get excited.

Sally and I were standing next to each other arranging bouquets when she announced her quilt block idea. "You're going to think my idea for the block is pretty dull, but I thought I would title it Sisterly Friends," she shared. "Jane really was best friends with her sister, Cassandra, so thought I would do something of the two of them. Even though my sister lives in another state, she really would still be considered my best friend." She blushed as she put more baby's breath into the planter.

"Well, at least you have an idea," I said, clipping more carnations for her to use. "You never mentioned your sister, Sally," I said, feeling curious. "I think it's a sweet idea. I wish I had a sister. Mother and my aunts were and are so close. Perhaps years ago their best friend had been a sister, especially if they were close in age. How far apart in years are you?"

"Just a couple of years," she casually said. "I am the oldest. I was jealous of her for some time, being the baby and all, but then when I later discovered she was jealous of me, we became very close. Isn't that something?" She grinned with pride that showed all over her face.

"That is wonderful, Sally," I said. "I'm glad you and Paige have a good friendship, since your sister isn't here. She's been good for you. You need some kind of social life. All work and no play, ya know!" We laughed.

"Paige is nothing like my sister," she immediately clarified. "Paige sometimes has a one-track mind, and it's usually guys. We really do get along well, despite our different tastes. I figure she'll be married within a few years, and that is not in the cards for me!"

"Oh, never say never, Sally. Look at me!" I pointed out. "I always had some kind of boyfriend, but never wanted to get married—until a Mr. Sam came along and changed everything."

Sally shook her head like she wasn't identifying with me. "No way. Plus, I have to finish my degree and help expand this business," she admitted sincerely. "Now, if a rich fella comes along and wants to pay all my debts from school, I might consider the possibility!"

This was some interesting information about Sally's life that she had never shared with me before. She was always so quiet and focused around me.

"I hope Isabella will like this idea," Sally said. "I have a feeling most folks that have a sister will like it." I had to agree. "She'll have to help me to decide what medium to make this in. I can't imagine where I would even start. This probably won't be that easy to do."

"Well, that would be difficult for me, I know," I said in wonderment. "I think you may have just inspired me to give a little more thought about this challenge than I was planning. Coming up with an idea is one thing, but producing it is another!"

We had just gotten back to more serious work when I got a call from Nancy asking me to meet her after work at Charley's. Richard was out of town, and since Sam would be working until at least eight, I told her I thought I could arrange it.

Nancy arrived looking really good, even hot, compared to the usual conservative suits she wore each day at the funeral home. She was always so beautiful all through school and was always one of the most popular students. She still was catching people's attention as she joined me at the bar. After Brad took our order, she didn't waste any time asking me how I thought the Jane Austen Quilt Club idea was going over. She obviously needed more approval and knew she could always get it from me. I gave her the deserved compliments and then shared Sally's idea for her quilt block. To my surprise, she loved it.

"Cassandra should be somewhere on this quilt, because she was so important in Jane's life," Nancy noted as she sipped her drink. "I may be the only one who is stepping out of the safe zone with my block. I have my own statement I want to make and the Jane Austen police just might come after me if I do it. Isn't that the beauty of artistic expression, Anne? We are using fabric and quilting techniques, but like any art, it should cause a reaction. Everyone's going to react differently, like to any art. I told Isabella that if we wanted participation here, we needed to let everyone do her own thing. "

"I hear ya. So what are you thinking about?" I hesitantly asked.

She took another swallow and then began a giggle I hadn't heard for some time. She took a deep breath. "My vision of Jane is that she is pregnant, maybe about five months along," she intimated, beaming with eyes wide open and a big grin on her face. I mimicked her look before she continued. I think she would look adorable, don't you? That popular style of dress with the high waist is perfect for a little bump." We did our usual giggle that Brad had heard many times from us. "So, okay. I'm thinking how I would like to be and look. So there."

"Nancy Marie Barrister," I said slowly, absorbing the very thought of the visual. "You have a one-track mind on this baby thing, don't you? Somehow I don't think Miss Austen did anything improper, do you?"

We giggled about all the possibilities until we nearly fell off our seats. "Before you announce this, you'd better be able to divulge the father. You know they'll ask," I teased. "We could blame it on that first love she had that went bad—what was his name?"

Nancy was nearly choking from laughter. "We'll make them all guess who the father is. What do you think?"

"Well, aren't the two of you having a great time?" Ted's voice asked from behind us. I was totally unaware of his approach.

"Oh, Ted. You scared me," Nancy responded, truly surprised. "Where did you come from?" We quickly got serious.

"I was across the way and heard this uncontrollable laughter," he teased with a grin. "I guess this is just like old times for the two of you, huh?"

I wouldn't look at him and started to sober up quickly. Not many would interrupt girl talk like this, I told myself. Obviously, Ted couldn't help himself.

"Ted, how are you?" I said in a serious tone. "Nancy called me for some girl-talk time, so that's what we're doing here." His facial expression changed, knowing I had dropped a strong hint. Nancy looked surprised at my curt remark and I took a swallow of my drink.

"Well then, don't let me stop you!" he said with a smirk. "Brad, give these girls another round on me so they can get back to their gaiety." He turned around and walked away. Well, it worked, I told myself.

"Wow, Anne. Pretty harsh, I'd say," she said, trying hard not to laugh. "I didn't realize things were that tense between you two."

I shrugged. It was now the time to explain my behavior. I took this opportunity to fill Nancy in on Ted's e-mail about Sam. She wasn't surprised. She said it was just Ted having a hard time seeing me happy. I knew I should feel sorry for him, and yet part of me was angry he would still want to contact me, as I was now a married woman.

After my tale of woes, Nancy began telling me about how upset she had been with Richard not wanting to continue any more tests to try to get pregnant, nor did he want to consider adoption. She said it was really affecting their private life as a result.

Without sounding unsympathetic, I told her Richard had every right to his opinion and she should just forget about the mission itself and go back to enjoying his company, regardless of his thoughts on further fertility testing. I don't think she was expecting my answer, but she appeared to be giving it some thought as I defended her husband.

It was getting late. The evening was quite fun, except for Ted's intrusion. As we had done so many times before, we left arm in arm as best friends. It was strange how different our problems always were but we always could be honest with one another, even if we didn't agree. That was the beauty of growing up together and having the history that we shared. It was so good having her back here in Colebridge!

CHAPTER 11

At the end of the next day, I was feeling quite tired and overwhelmed with undone tasks. I found it hard to justify going to the new quilt club. How did I get into this in the first place, I wondered? Wasn't the Jane Austen Literary Club enough? I was already a basement quilter, as we sometimes joked. Quilters certainly created their own little social network, and seemed to crave more. I didn't need another task or interest to distract me from my shop as well as from Sam. Did I just list them in my mind in priority order? Shame on me, I thought. I would certainly disappoint Mother if I called to cancel or drop out of the club. I'd never hear the end of it from the girls here at the shop, as well. My thoughts then turned to my Sam. My heart still fluttered at the thought of how much I loved him. I decided to give him a call to see how he was feeling and to coordinate our plans.

"Hey, Mr. Dickson," I greeted him flirtatiously. "When

are you going to knock off work today?"

"Well, Mrs. Dickson, I was wondering the same thing about you!" he cheerfully answered. "I went by an hour or so ago. I saw your car was still there. Are you still going to that quilt club tonight?"

"I really would rather not, but it's easier just to go to make everyone else happy," I said, smiling over the phone. "Have you had dinner?"

"No, but I had a late lunch with Jim, so I'm fine for now," he said.

"Oh, did he say anything about a job lead?" I inquired, hoping he wouldn't be getting tired of me asking.

"No, not really, but he has plenty of leads on lady friends!" Sam responded. "Let me put it this way. I think he is cheating on his married girlfriend!"

"No way, Sam!" I was not able to tell if he was teasing. "I sure hope Aunt Julia doesn't know all this."

"Well, according to Jim, Julia is not letting the grass grow under her feet," he shared. "Jim says Julia has been out several times with Harry Sims."

"Seriously?" I was now starting to believe him. "This is interesting, because she has not said a word to any of us. She and he did seem to have quite a bit of conversation at our Christmas party. I'll see what I can find out tonight at the club. See you at home, Mr. Dickson."

Harry was older than Uncle Jim or Sam. He looked distinguished with his early gray hair. Martingale used him for years as some kind of consultant. I wasn't quite sure what his small company did, but Sam always spoke kindly of him and wanted to invite him to our party. I guess we all needed to prepare ourselves for Aunt Julia starting a new life of her own. She certainly talked about it often enough when we quilted in the basement.

When I pulled up in the driveway, Mother was anxiously waiting to see me and came running out to the car so I wouldn't waste time coming in. She scolded me about being ten minutes late and then went into her latest chatter since I saw her last.

The interesting mixes of Austen fans were filling the large classroom. I certainly did not recognize a lot of the faces. Isabella welcomed everyone and announced that to her surprise, some members had already declared what they wanted to make for their quilt block. She briefly explained there were no rules, but the block size would be important for assembly. She said she was encouraged when she realized there would be many new quilters to participate; however, some may have good intentions but may never completely finish a block. That could easily be me, I thought. There were many questions from the group. Isabella put them at ease, telling them that club members need not feel pressured to complete a block. That was good news to my ears.

She said tonight's lesson would be a basic appliqué stitch because so many of the blocks were going to require appliqué. This did not ring well in my ears because just watching Mother appliqué was not enticing to me.

Nancy was in the back of the room pouring tea and offering assistance to anyone needing help with their stitching. I chose to stay seated next to an attractive redheaded girl I guessed was in her early twenties. She was sketching designs on a tablet and looked up to greet me when I sat down.

"I see you like to draw," I commented with a smile. "Are you designing your quilt block?"

She looked at me as if I had discovered something she did not want me to see. "Oh, I'm just playing around trying to come up with something unique that everyone won't make fun of," she said shyly. "I have always loved Jane Austen, but I'm not a very good quilter, so this is a real challenge for me."

"Welcome to the club. Many of us don't qualify," I said, shaking my head. "This Jane Austen has a way of bringing folks together, doesn't she? I heard she made a quilt on her own, so guess she'd be pleased with this whole idea. I helped quilt on a quilt, and did okay, but that's it! I do happen to know, however, that many of the quilt blocks I have heard about are going to be pretty much out of the box, so I wouldn't worry about what the others think."

"Really?" she whispered, not wanting to disrupt Isabella's instructions. "I'm not so sure Jane would think all this fuss about her is a good thing. I don't think we should exploit her, to be honest. I would like to think, instead, that we are honoring her with putting ourselves into this quilt." This girl was serious, I thought to myself.

I paused. "Your opinions and ideas are safe with me," I assured her. "By the way, I'm Anne Dickson. So, what are you thinking about for your block?"

"I'm Roxanne Harris," she whispered, not looking up. "Oh well, the design I'm not sure about; but I am a true romantic like Jane, I'd guess you'd say. I feel close to her in a strange sort of way. I love weddings and I want Jane to fall in love and get married. I know Jane did not wish for that openly, but what woman does admit she wants that? She helped others achieve their happiness, but wouldn't let herself come to matrimony. I guess that's how I personally feel, if I really analyze this. I think she would make a beautiful bride and I can just see her walking down the aisle with a simple white dress and veil. I see her carrying a simple nosegay and being married by her father, who was a preacher at one time. Oh, I'm just fantasizing. You know she had a proposal once in December of 1802 from Harris Bigg-Wither. She had known him most of her life. He wasn't attractive, and even stuttered, they said, but she thought it was time and there were many practical advantages in accepting the proposal. He was the heir to extensive family estates in the region and she knew her family would be well provided for."

"Oh, I didn't know that!" I said, somewhat surprised. Was there anything about Jane this girl didn't know?

"Well, the next morning Jane knew she had made a mistake and withdrew her acceptance. How about that?" Roxanne said in a proud manner. "I read where sometime later around 1814, Jane wrote to her niece, Fanny Knight, and said that in personal relationships, 'Anything is to be preferred or endured rather than marrying without affection.'"

"How wise and insightful," I said, thinking about my former relationship with Ted. "My goodness, Roxanne, you certainly know a lot about Jane! I think if that's how you'd like to visualize Jane, then you should make it so. It's your block, after all, and besides, I happen to know that Jane is going to turn up pregnant in someone else's block so you would be doing her a big favor by getting her married first!"

"Holy cow! That is quite shocking!" she said, trying not to laugh too loud. "That's out of the box, all right."

I knew I made her feel much better. "I can't wait to see what you'll come up with, Roxanne," I said, putting my hand on her shoulder. "It was nice to meet you, Roxanne. I'm getting some tea. Care to join me?"

She pulled her long hair to one side and graced me with a broad smile as she followed me to the back of the room. I had to admit I met a real Austen fan tonight. How did she seem to know so much about Jane? She made it seem like they were the best of friends. Mother soon joined us and told me she had my small beginner's appliqué kit that had been made available.

"Am I going to have to do your quilt block for you, Anne?" she asked with that warm smile, holding up the kit.

"Maybe not," I returned, kidding her back. "I haven't locked in my idea yet. I think I am, however, going to avoid appliqué at all costs." Mother laughed, knowing me so well.

Aunt Julia joined us, looking very frustrated. "This appliqué will drive me to drink," she joked. "I'll never be able to do this. Whose idea was this anyway?" We laughed and Mother hushed us into silence.

"Aunt Julia," I cried. "Do not leave here without telling us about Harry."

She looked startled and shook her head in disbelief. "Honestly," she whispered. "How did you all get wind of this? Was it Sam or that ghostly grandmother of ours?"

We giggled and dropped the subject for now, as others were starting to acknowledge our little party and give us strained looks. I watched as some members desperately tried to create their stitches as if their lives depended upon it. I kept looking at my watch, wondering what Sam was up to and how early I was going to have to get to the shop tomorrow to make up for my social activities tonight.

The meeting was brought to a close when Jean announced the next meeting of the Jane Austen Literary Club. What was this Jane Austen common denominator here? Everyone seemed to love Jane, but everyone seemed to want to turn her into something she wasn't. Was it as simple as everyone interpreting her differently? Or, did we just want to make her more like us? Hmmm...

CHAPTER 12

S am was sound asleep when I arrived home at nine thirty. So, would this be the new schedule of Sam with a heart condition? He used to stay up late and get up before me each morning. His sexual appetite had understandably faded, too. He likely feared becoming too excited and bringing on an attack. Even though the doctor had reassured him, he was not taking many liberties. I knew he needed time. I looked at him lying peacefully with one foot out of the covers. He often slept that way. I teased him about always wanting to be ready to hit the ground running when he awoke. He was even gorgeous when he was asleep. I still found it hard to believe this young, strong, handsome man had limitations.

I prepared for bed but felt wide awake, so I quietly crept down the stairs to get a drink. I then realized I had not had dinner. As I headed toward the refrigerator, I looked onto the back porch. Once again, the potting shed quilt was wadded up and thrown into a corner of the porch. What was such a big deal that Grandmother felt the need to continue to abuse this quilt? How else could this happen? Tomorrow, I will have to fold it up and put it away in a chest before it gets totally destroyed. I was in no mood to deal with her spirit tonight.

When I opened the refrigerator, I saw a nice plate of spaghetti staring at me. It was likely the other half of Sam's dinner. It looked mighty appetizing, so I pulled it out to give it a microwave zap. I sat down at the kitchen table to take a drink and hash over in my mind the evening's chatter at the quilt club. I thought about the young Roxanne Harris who confessed to being so like Jane herself! Were all her fans like that?

I was beginning to ponder ideas for my block when the microwave sounded. After my addition of Parmesan cheese, I savored each bite, wondering if Jane had experienced spirits in her life after loved ones passed away. Would they have openly talked about it back then? I recalled how Jean said one night at literary club that Jane's biggest promoter for her as a writer came from another writer she knew named Anne Lefroy. That was kind of cool to know another Anne had been an influence in Jane's life. I had to think for a second who influenced me to write. I know Mother reminded me how, at the early age of six, I wanted to write books to use while playing school with my imaginary friends. When I looked at books or read them, I wondered who got to write those words that must be important enough to put into a book. I knew they had to be important people, because their names would be on the books forever and ever. Hmmm...

"Is there room for two at that table, Mrs. Dickson?" Sam said as he entered the kitchen wearing his plaid robe.

I jumped in fright and answered, "Oh, Sam, did I wake

you?" I got up quickly to greet him with a kiss. "I was pleased you saved me a bite to eat. I just discovered I was famished. This is delicious."

"I thought you might enjoy it," he said, pouring a drink. "I took some sauce I froze out of the freezer. I'm afraid I ate more than my share. How was club tonight?"

"It was lots of chatter, hormones, and tea," I quipped, making fun of it all. "I love getting to see Mother and some of the others, but I think the literary club will suffice for that. There were so many people there that I think the focus on Jane got lost and it turned into a marketing event for Isabella."

"Well, like you said before, if you enjoy their company, that's all that matters," Sam said, putting his feet up on the chair next to me. "I meant to stay awake for you, but somehow, I felt the need to just crash. I've put in long days before, but when I came home tonight, I was exhausted. I know this isn't me. I hope my energy comes back soon."

I looked at him with true understanding. "I'm just so happy you recognize the needs of your body, sweetie," I said encouragingly, kissing him on the cheek. "I love when you take time for yourself for a change. Don't be so hard on yourself. Just take it one day at a time and listen to your body instead of that overactive mind of yours. Do you want some of this spaghetti?"

"No thanks, but I'd love to have some of you," he murmured, kissing me on the back of my neck.

With all I had on my mind, I was not in the mood for any romantic play, so I needed to distract him immediately. "While I have your personal and undivided attention, I want to tell you that Sally and I continue to discuss the possibility of adding onto the flower shop," I said. His look became stern as he stood back from me. I now knew this may not be the time to bring it up. Was there ever going to be a good time? "She has really been spending time proving this will be a good investment for us. I'd at least like to have a professional seek out what is possible with what little land I own there." Sam remained silent and unresponsive as I kept talking. I wanted him to at least hear me out. "The hardest part would be getting permission from the city's Landmarks Board. There would be no doubt I would also have to go to the Board of Adjustment to get a parking variance. I hate the thought of being locked in forever with this space, but I know I never want to leave that spot on the street. This may not be the time to discuss this with you, Sam, but with the time that these things take, I don't want to shelve it until who knows when." Okay, I had spelled it out. There was a huge gap of silence.

As he sipped his drink, I watched for his reaction to my words. He was now standing back from me and leaning against the kitchen counter. He had a serious look on his face as he stared at me. I knew my timing was completely off, bringing up such an adventurous project when my husband hadn't quite recovered from a serious procedure. I guess I also killed any romantic response as well. What was I thinking?

"Miss Annie, your wheels never stop, do they?" he began, critiquing me with his eyes. "I knew this would be on your bucket list, but where on the list is starting a family and finishing up the restoration and decorating here at 333 Lincoln?"

Oh no. What can of worms had I just opened? He was not smiling. I hesitated before speaking. Sam was not in the mood for any cute answers. I knew this could potentially heap more stress onto his plate. "I guess my answer is that I want it all," I said, surprising myself. I looked down embarrassed. I did not want to see his reaction.

"Then I suggest you take some advice from a VP who manages hundreds of people," he said firmly and in a loud tone. "You'd better give some order to your priorities, or you will accomplish none of them. I have no intention of telling you what to do and when to do it. I knew of your ambition when I married you. However, some decisions affect our marriage, which I do care about. Promise me you will give this more thought. I had to give myself this same little talk after I had my surgery. Being here for you was the number one priority for me, before work and this house. I told myself I could enjoy it all if I prioritized." He paused a bit, knowing he had frightened me. "I love you, Miss Annie."

"I love you, too," I managed to whisper with my head down. "I know you're right, as usual. I need to give more thought to it all. Thanks for understanding my crazy ambition. It has always been the monster inside this blonde, blue-eyed physique!" We both laughed.

"That's what is so attractive and mysterious about you, beautiful," he said in a low voice, coming closer again. "Now, will you please come to bed with me so I can let you know how really special and beautiful you are?"

Now that was an offer I couldn't refuse.

As we walked up the stairs hand in hand, I was reminded again how lucky I was that I had a man who understood my mechanics and loved me for it.

CHAPTER 13

I shall be exceedingly pleased if your mum still would like to stitch up my quilt," Jean said, approaching me the first thing the next day.

"You're done with your top?" I asked, looking up to her from my computer screen.

"I am, indeed, Miss Anne," she said, gleaming. "It's a splendid piece, if I have to say so myself."

"Well then, I'll contact Mother soon and arrange a Sunday quilting together," I assured her. "I miss our quilting in the basement and I know Mother would love having everyone again."

"Jolly good," she said, joining her hands joyfully.

"I'll have you know, I had to put the potting shed quilt in a chest upstairs this morning," I revealed to Sally and Jean. "Grandmother is determined to destroy it, I think. I had it airing out on a rack on the sun porch, and the next time I noticed, it was crunched in a ball in the corner on the floor. Imagine that!" They both had startled looks on their faces.

"I don't believe it," chimed in Sally, sweeping up the latest cuttings on the floor.

"I dare say that naughty lady needs to belt it up a bit if you ask me," Jean added in disgust. "After all that fuss and such care you gave it. You'd have to be a very sad, wretched soul for such behavior, don't you think?" Jean was right.

"She means well, I suppose," I said sympathetically. "I still feel she loves us in her crazy way. It's just that we are living in her lover's home that he shared with a wife instead of her! How would you feel? I wonder who she haunted when the house was empty. Maybe she pretended it was just her and Albert living there.

"I say she needs to get over it!" Sally stated loudly from the back room.

I couldn't agree more. "I have tried to do things that please her, like plant more lilies in the garden," I explained. "Speaking of lilies, Sally, did you order plenty of lilies for Easter? I want to put some on both Grandmother's and Albert's graves."

"Well, I went by last year's order, but I didn't factor in the graves of the not-so-dearly departed!" she said, sarcasm evident in her voice. "Our cooler is so crowded. I'm not sure how far ahead we want them."

When Jean left to go to the front room to wait on a customer, I shared Sam's response with Sally when I told him we were moving closer to forming a decision on the expansion. By the look on Sally's face, I could tell it was not what she was hoping to hear, but I assured her it would happen in time.

"Well, why don't you tell him one of the rooms in the

expansion will be a nursery for any children that may come along in time? That should score some points!" she teased. The very thought forced me into a giggle. I could just see what a disaster that would be.

"What's this I hear about a nursery?" Jean asked, peeking around the corner. So much for having any privacy in this place, I said to myself.

"A plant nursery," I clarified as I got up to say hello to Katie Maxwell, who owned the knitting shop on the street. She wanted my opinion about a group ad that was being solicited on Main Street for a new magazine. I quickly responded that it may be a good thing and that I had signed up. She was fairly new on the street and had not figured out who was who and what was what. Her shop was adorable and knitting was quite the craze, from what Jean shared. Jean was a knitter and had nothing but raves about Katie and her shop. I left her chatting with Jean and got back to my desk.

The weather was simply divine all day, giving us a sample of what an early spring might bring. While it was still light, I wanted to get home to spend a little time in the potting shed before Sam got home. On the way, I called Mother on my cell to set up a Sunday afternoon quilting. She was very eager to do so, as I thought.

"Be sure that it's a day when Aunt Julia can come," I noted. "I want to hear all about this Harry she has been seeing."

I picked up some stir-fry and egg rolls to satisfy my craving that day. With such milder temperatures, I pictured a candlelight dinner under the gazebo as it turned dusk. I rushed to change into my jeans and my favorite white sweatshirt that said, "Take Time to Smell the Roses," and made my way toward the front door. As I passed the living room, something different caught my eye. I slowly turned to enter the room and noticed the Taylor vase had been shattered on the Oriental rug. How could this happen? How could it be in so many pieces after falling on a padded rug? Falling from the fireplace mantle was not an accident. No, it couldn't be, I told myself, feeling anger increase inside me. Grandmother was being mean, just like Aunt Julia had claimed over and over. Sam or Nora would have cleaned this up, had they seen such a mess. Darn. My dearest keepsake from the Taylor family was now destroyed! I could feel my temper rise.

"Okay," I said in a very loud voice. "You have gone too far, Grandmother! I loved that vase and it was one of the few things we have from the Taylors. How could you be so mean? I have tried so hard to make excuses for you. Sam and I love this house and I thought you loved us being here." I held back the tears before I continued. "You need to move on and let us live our lives! Do you hear me loud and clear?" My voice was loud and angry enough to scare myself! I took a deep breath to calm myself. There may be a logical excuse for this, I told myself. Had I made Grandmother a target for all unfortunate incidents?

I stumbled to the kitchen pantry to get a broom and vacuum so I could begin cleaning up the mess. I brought a plastic bowl to keep the pieces in, as if it could still be repaired. I knew it would be impossible, but I couldn't just throw it all away! I had to keep the pieces as a memory of the Taylors!

I went outdoors to the potting shed to collect my thoughts and calm down as I watered my cherished plants. I sat down by my workbench and tried to think of anything rather than the broken vase. I thought of the unique Jane Austen Quilt Club and how it was affecting everyone. I revisited what I needed to create my quilt block. Knowing me, it had to be something to do with flowers, but how could I relate flowers to Jane? I didn't remember reading about any flower she particularly liked. Hmmm…

I heard Sam pull into the garage. I came out of the shed to surprise him with a warm greeting. It was about dusk. After I kissed him, I asked if he was up to a little candlelight dinner in the gazebo. It was chilly enough for a jacket, but the air was refreshing. He offered to pour us a drink and bring it outdoors as soon as he changed clothes.

We made small talk during our delicious dinner. I didn't tell him about the vase until we finished our meal. He listened intently and did not advise me as to how to handle Grandmother's behavior. His complete silence and the chill in the air sent me into the house to put on some coffee. When I entered the house, the lights began to flash off and on.

"Stop it," I yelled. "You have hurt my feelings enough and there is nothing you can do to change my mind, so please stop and go away!" By the time I got to the kitchen, they did stop flickering. I was surprised Sam didn't notice and come in to check things out.

I put the coffee on and when I went to pull a tray from the cabinet, I noticed the fresh smell of lilies. I turned to find a vase full of them on the kitchen table. Good heavens, now what? She was attempting to please me again, no doubt. How dare she, I thought. I did not respond, for I had experienced similar behaviors before. This time, it wasn't going to work. I picked up the full vase and poured out the water. They were going in the trash where no one could enjoy them but her. I went out the front door, and in my anger, gave it a hard slam. I did not say a word to Sam about the events of the previous minutes when I joined him for warm coffee and more pleasant conversation of the day.

CHAPTER 14

❖

Spring was close, but it was not comfortable enough to stop wearing a jacket and sometimes ear coverings on my walk each morning. After I finished the hilly neighborhood walk, I went to check on the potting shed. Sure enough, the winter residents were peeking out and wanting to say hello. I pictured these early blossoms in colorful pots that I could sell in my shop. I beamed at the thought of growing my first inventory! My first thought was to show Sam, but I then remembered he had left in the very early hours to go out of town for a couple of days.

I felt more at ease now that normalcy was returning for Sam, but the added worry of something happening to him out of town was a new worry for me. After a little more watering and talking to my plant friends, I went in to shower, looking forward to my free Saturday.

Since the shop closed early on Saturdays and Sally and

Abbey anticipated a light day, they covered for me. Abbey had moved into an apartment right on Main Street. I had put a good word in for her to her landlord, Donna Howard. Happily, that sealed the deal and Abbey got her wish concerning living downtown. Many envied those living on Main Street and openings were hard to acquire. With Abbey living so close to the shop, it was easy to use her at the last minute and she was happy to have the extra hours. At times, I envied her being just blocks away from the shop. The very early and the very late hours were some of the more cherished on Main Street. It was like a movie set that was waiting for its next performance.

As I poured my coffee, my cell rang. It was Mother. "Good morning," I said as I cleared my throat.

"Have any plans for lunch today?" she quickly asked.

"No, and I'd rather I not," I answered with a sigh. "I plan to stay put here today for a change. Nora is coming over this afternoon to do some extra cleaning while Sam is out of town. I don't know if I told you that she won't clean here by herself. She says there is too much unexplained activity in this house. I frankly think she's not imagining most of it, because I am dealing with a lot of our spirit's mischief myself. My garden is crying for help, my laundry is piling high, and my book is being ignored, not to mention that I am exhausted."

"Well, I have made too much chicken salad and thought I would drop some off for you," she offered. "I don't have to stay, but is there anything I can do to help you, Anne? You sound a bit overwhelmed."

"Well, the chicken salad sounds great since I have to eat and have nothing in the house. If you wear your grungy clothes, I'll have you weed the herb garden and cut some of them back. How's that? Aren't you sorry you asked?"

"I'd love it, honey. Look for me around eleven thirty," she said before hanging up.

I was putting clothes in the washer when Nancy's number rang on my cell. "You got a day off, my friend?" she asked, hopefully.

"You know what these days are like, Nancy. It's a day where you cram ten pounds of chores into a one pound bag," I responded. "I'm overwhelmed, as my astute mother just heard. She's coming over to help me. I'm still not sure what hat to put on when I'm not at the shop as I try to fulfill the role of Mrs. Dickson!"

She laughed. "I understand, Anne, but you must get more help with that place of yours," she instructed. "Doesn't Sam know you can't possibly do it all with your shop responsibilities?"

"Don't even go there, Nancy," I said, taking in a deep breath. "I asked for all of this, now I need to face the music and quit whining about it."

"Have it your way then, Miss Powerhouse," she teased. "Now I feel bad for the main reason I was calling. I don't suppose you decided on your block for the Austen quilt, have you? You are going to want to participate, aren't you?"

I took a deep breath. This is just what I need to be thinking about right now. How do I not yell at her? "You will be the first to know, my dear friend," I said sharply, taking another deep breath. "Perhaps I should make a block of Jane pulling out her hair. That would be me, all right." There was silence. What was wrong with me? Nancy now knew it was bad timing for checking on me. How could I fix this?

"Okay. Maybe I'll have a more pleasant idea by the literary club meeting this week. By the way, Nancy, we're going to start quilting on Jean's quilt tomorrow afternoon at Mother's. You are welcome to come. We could certainly use the help!"

"Oh darn, my dearly beloved in-laws are coming over for dinner and I have tons to do," she shared. "I do want to help put stitches in that, so keep me in mind the next time, okay?"

"How do you do it all, Mrs. Barrister, if I may ask?" I asked, sounding jealous of her ambitious endeavors. "If my mother-in-law planned on coming over to dinner tonight, I'd have a nervous breakdown with all I have to do."

"Hire, my girl, hire. You can afford it!" she boldly stated. I laughed, made my work excuses, and told her I would see her this week at the literary club. I sat for a moment, thinking about her magic suggestion. If I were wearing my shop owner hat, I would hire. Why not engage the thought of hiring here at 333 Lincoln? Can we afford it? Hmmm...

I decided Mother's lunch idea would work out very well and I was becoming hungrier as I went from one flower bed to another. So many of the beds needed leaves and winter weeds cleaned out before mulching could be done.

Mother had packed a delicious lunch in our old picnic basket from home. Despite the cool breeze, we sat under the gazebo, where food always tasted better. When I brought out the lemonade, she asked if we needed to toast the maker. I didn't have the heart to tell her right now that I was on the "outs" with the lemonade maker. If I told her about the vase, she would likely be as upset as well, which wouldn't accomplish anything. I simply responded with humor and continued to eat heartily. After we finished off our lunch with some of Mother's tasty brownies, she went right to work in the garden and told me to do the same.

When Nora arrived, I gave her my list of things that needed attention. I told her about the leftover brownies on the kitchen counter and that she was welcome to take them all home. She always loved any treats and refreshments I offered her.

I went back outdoors to check on Mother, who was weeding away at a good pace. We discussed what herbs needed attention, and before I knew it, I was weeding alongside her in the next flower bed. How did weeds know to grow earlier and stronger than any other plants? They thrived in the worst of weather, as if to prove something.

When I told Mother that Nancy called to check on my quilt block progress, she admitted she had just about finished her block. I figured as much, knowing her. I didn't share my frustration with her as I did with Nancy. I would likely be the last to participate in the quilt, and right now I didn't care. We weeded along in silence until I felt I could approach her with what was on my mind.

"I have been giving some serious thought to adding onto the flower shop, Mother," I began. She stopped weeding to look at me. I continued, "Sally has done a great deal of research on our needs, especially concerning weddings. She showed me how we are losing business every day and how an addition can improve our bottom line." I gave her time to respond, but she continued to stare at me, just like Sam. "I don't regret buying that building, Mother, because if I hadn't, my rent would be out of sight right now. Now, I can use the building as collateral. The larger building would take away some parking, but customers have options in other places, like the public lot down by the river. I at least want to have an architect look at the prospect. Sally agreed that if we aren't growing, we're dying." She now was sitting up straight with eyes squinting at me like I may have lost my mind.

I knew that look. Was it the same look I got from Sam? I kept going. "It would mean going before the Landmarks Board and the Board of Adjustment, but I think it may be worth the horror of it all! I want to do it in my name only. I don't want Sam to be financially involved in my business side of things. I only have rough estimates at this time that Sally threw together. I have nothing professionally done. There isn't a downside to this, Mother! You may now jump in if you like."

She moved to one side to get more comfortable and I knew the body language and the look of interrogation I was about to receive. "I have many questions, Anne," she began. "How long have you been thinking about this? Do you really want to add more work and responsibility at the shop? You know more is not always better. You can overextend yourself here real quickly. What about Sam? Does he know about this? How does this fit into your personal life? Didn't you say Sam wanted to start a family someday? What about all the work this house requires? What if Sam should become ill again? He depends on you. Should I go on?"

I knew it all was coming and I was ready. I knew she wouldn't like some of my answers, but thought I would give it a go. "When I made Sally the shop manager, her wheels started the process," I explained. "She wants this as a career and is willing to take on the added responsibility. She knows my limitations personally and knows how limited the business is with the size of the shop. I firmly believe you have to capture the moment. I have tried to do this all my life, Mother. I have approached Sam. He knows I will do as I want and understands my ambition. Yes, he wants a family, but we still have some time. The house is getting closer to being finished, but this old house will always be a work in progress. You know that. This project would be much harder once we start a family. I feel the time is now." There. I said it all pretty well, I thought.

To her credit, she was listening to every word I was saying. I continued, "I would even love to expand my little potting shed here. Do you know I have some seedlings that are starting to pop up? I plan to take some to the shop in colorful little pots and sell them this spring. How cool is that?" She wasn't amused with my cleverness and kept a serious face.

"Don't get off on another subject, Anne," she scolded. "You know in your heart that I would never talk you out of your ambitions and dreams, but I am getting concerned about you. Remember I told you that when you married Sam, it was no longer about you anymore? You both now have to make these decisions together, or it will begin deteriorating your marriage. I know how sweet and understanding Sam has been and can be, but my advice to you, my young daughter, is don't push it. Promise me you will not decide anything on this until you and Sam are both comfortable with a plan."

She made her point and I reluctantly agreed with her. However, what if both could not agree? What if both didn't even try? Did I not learn what both really meant, growing up as an only child? I did want both to include Sam. What could be better? Now, I would just have to figure out how to get both.

CHAPTER 15

After a weekend without Sam to worry about, Nora and I managed to accomplish many chores at 333 Lincoln. In my busy schedule, I added a few hours in the afternoon, quilting in Mother's basement, plus hours of hard physical work outdoors, so I was ready to get back to a simpler schedule at the flower shop. Depending on Sam's arrival time, I could perhaps attend tonight's literary club meeting.

The next morning I skipped my walk because it looked like a rain shower was about to arrive. Instead, I took my coffee in the kitchen. If Sam were here, he would have had it ready for me. I sat down and looked out onto the sun porch where Grandmother's mischief had taken place. With thoughts of the broken vase, I still wanted to punish someone. What if I didn't really understand what she was trying to communicate?

I walked out onto the porch and closed the windows

in case it rained. I stared at the vase of beautiful jonquils I had picked behind the potting shed. The smell of a fresh new day told me I must forget and move on. Somehow, I felt Grandmother's warmth again, which I had felt before. I knew I was the only one who was giving her any time and attention, whether it was love or hate. I picked up the vase of yellow brightness and carried it into the kitchen. Then, something made me pick up the bouquet and walk it into the living room where the fireplace mantle had previously displayed my Taylor vase that was now broken. I placed it on the mantle and said aloud, "These flowers are for you, Grandmother, so now behave!"

Sam's plane would not arrive until around eight this evening, so I picked up Mother for another night of Jane Austen folly at Jean's house. She had the best English tea that made us head straight to the sideboard in her dining room. Aunt Julia was ready to pour me a cup and she seemed to be in great spirits. When I glanced up at her, I noticed she had cut her hair! It was a darling shaggy French cut that changed her entire look.

"Aunt Julia! It's you!" I said admiringly. "Wow! What a change this is! I love it! When did you do this?" She grinned from ear to ear. By now, Mother noticed her as well.

"What brought this on?" asked Mother. Her tone sounded like Mother thought her sister had made a mistake.

"You don't like it, do you, Sylvia?" she asked, putting Mother on the spot.

"Actually, I do, dear sis," she replied. "I just can't get over how different you look. It is very becoming and a change is always a good thing."

"Is this because a new leaf has turned and a certain Harry

guy has tickled your fancy, as Jean says?" I teased. Aunt Julia blushed and we laughed, waiting for an answer. Before she could respond, Sarah came to join us.

"Doesn't she look cool?" Sarah bragged. "I'm trying to give her some wardrobe advice, too!"

"All very cool," I agreed, as I gave Aunt Julia a little squeeze. "We're anxious to hear how everything's going, Aunt Julia. Whenever you're ready, of course!" We all chucked, as we had now made her blush.

"I know what you're all talking about," teased Sarah. "She's looking hot for that new guy she's been seeing." Aunt Julia looked at Sarah sternly.

"Sarah, that's not true," Aunt Julia responded firmly, denying any such suggestion.

Jean got everyone's attention and we found our seats.

"My Janeites, can everyone hear me?" Jean announced above the crowd. "Tonight, we are not going to take notice of a book discussion, but instead enjoy a bit of Jane trivia from Sue Davis. She has so grandly accepted my request to start us out tonight with the topic. These tidbits can be quite jolly, I dare say. We'll go roughly ten minutes or so. Please give her your openness of heart. We also want to acknowledge Paige Beerman. We all want to thank you for bringing the scrumptious pound cake. The orange glaze is divine!" Paige blushed as she received many compliments from the others.

"On the tea table are brochures for you to obtain, regarding information for the next Jane Austen Society Convention that is taking place in Brooklyn, New York. It's been observed that their seminars are most informative, plus they have a jolly good time with social activities, which includes a formal ball. It appears some go to great extent to dress in the appropriate time period. I should only be so lucky to take part, but I shan't, I'm afraid. Let me know, by golly, if anyone would want to seek this out. I shall be delighted to help you achieve the image of that time." We all had to snicker at the thought. It wouldn't be for me, but I could see Roxanne, the redhead, dreaming of such an occasion.

"On another note, Nancy, do you have any announcements from Jane's quilt club?"

Nancy set down her teacup and picked up a sheet of paper. "We still have some folks who have not committed to what their block might be in the quilt," she announced with disappointment. "By the way, we don't hold you to your choice if you change your mind along the way. You still have lots of time to complete them. We just want the title of your block, so there are no duplications. It will also help us plan the number of blocks that will go into the quilt. I have lots of ideas if you cannot think of something. Isabella could not be here tonight, but she has grandiose ideas for the quilt when it is finished!"

Everyone started responding, which filled up the room with "women noise," as I called it. No one could resist chatting with the person next to them, as if no one else in the room mattered. It was an impulsive trait that all women seemed to have, which included myself. If Nancy wanted to make me feel guilty, she succeeded. How could I even think about Jane's quilt when I had my plate so full? Should I just pretend that it would appear on its own, in time? Should I just say no? Have I ever said no to anything that I might want to do? Oh please, let someone control this women noise and get to the program at hand. This was making me nervous.

Finally, Jean knocked on the table to get our attention. "As

I leisurely plow through all of Jane's books, I always jot down a phrase or word that delights me so," Jean began. "I thought Jane's words quoted by Mary Crawford in *Mansfield Park* were thought provoking, so thought I would share it with you. 'Selfishness must always be forgiven, you know, because there is no hope of a cure!'" Everyone chuckled and agreed.

"Okay, Miss Sue, I've held you up a bit. Please carry on!"

Finally, Sue stood up and took a deep breath as she began by telling us about Jane's fondness for dancing. She appeared rather shy in her manner when she began, but livened up as she continued. "Dancing was the only way for young people to meet and converse with one another in that day and time," she explained. Learning to dance was part of their education. A gentleman would first have to be properly introduced to a lady before he could ask her to dance. How about that?" Everyone snickered. "The dances would consist of sets of five to eight couples. There would likely be a country dance, such as a minuet, a quadrille, a cotillion, or a Scottish reel. We know all of these, right?" More laughter filled the room.

"Ladies, ladies. Please settle down and let Sue finish her report," Jean instructed.

"Each dance would last about a half hour, so you'd better like your partner," Sue explained. Oh no, many responded. Sue continued. "A couple could not dance together more than twice or folks would think they were engaged. If a gentleman persisted with his lady partner, the gossip would spread immediately. This follows suit in Jane's novels and those times. Think about how little they knew each other before they married. Today, we now can Google a person and know more than we want to know!"

"Sue, did you read much about prearranged marriages?"

Paige asked.

"There certainly was talk of it happening, but the only scenario that rings clear is in *Pride and Prejudice* where Lady Catherine de Bourgh makes it clear to everyone that Mr. Darcy had been promised long ago to marry her sickly daughter. She claimed that as infants, the two prominent families had agreed to such a marriage. Therefore, she was quite upset when she heard rumors of Mr. Darcy asking Elizabeth Bennet to marry him, remember?

"Oh yes," I recalled. "I love the confrontation with her as Elizabeth defends her position. When Lady de Bourgh begins to leave their heated discussion, she asks Elizabeth, 'Tell me once for all, are you engaged to him?' Elizabeth says, 'I am not.' So when Lady Catherine asks for her promise to never enter into such an engagement, Elizabeth answers, 'I will make no promise of the kind.' Lady de Bourgh then marches away to her carriage in an angry huff!" Everyone joined in the admiration of the scene and responded again with noisy chatter.

"Introduce me to someone, so I could get onto the dance floor!" Sue teased, bringing her discussion to a close. Again, we were amused with her humor. She did a great job and we told her so.

The evening was a great diversion for me, no doubt, except for my usual guilt trip. I now glanced at my watch to see where the time had gone. It was time for me to be back in the arms of that husband of mine. Mother and I said our good-byes and told Sue we would introduce her to the next man we would meet. Her response was, "Bring him on!"

CHAPTER 16

On the drive home, both Mother and I talked about how we wished we had more time to do all the things we loved. She said writing a book would be a far stretch on her bucket list, but then she asked how far along my book about the Taylor family was coming along.

"I'm glad you brought that up, Mother, because I was going to ask if I could have the small writing desk that we used to have in the den." I could see she was taken by surprise. "I know it's in the basement now, so you don't use it, do you? I have the perfect spot for it in that little room off our bedroom. I know I would spend more time with the book if I had all my research materials in one place. There may be times at night I don't sleep and I could just write bits and pieces. You know what I mean?"

"Oh, why sure, Anne!" she happily responded. "Are you talking about that little room Sam mentioned would someday be perfect for a nursery?"

"Yes, but I'm talking about now!" I pressed on, not acknowledging her nursery reference. "It's a perfect place to keep my research materials all in one place. That desk is just the right size. I'm also giving more thought to going up into the attic to see if any of the junk left behind would be helpful as I try to learn more about the family. I'm almost afraid to find anything because I'll want to put more time into the project."

"I know what you mean, Anne. This kind of research gets ahold of you," she related. "Just like that quilt we all took apart. Once you start something like that, it's hard to leave it. You're welcome to the desk anytime, and when my first grandchild arrives, I'm sure you will find another room in that big house somewhere, right?"

"Yes, Grandmother dearest," I said, smiling. "I think I could find several."

We parted ways having enjoyed a wonderful evening together. Maybe there was something to these clubs that brought us closer together. Hmmm...

Sam was already in his sweats turning on the fire in the den when I walked in the door.

"Well, if it isn't a Janeite! Come here and give your hub a kiss," he sweetly greeted me.

I melted mentally and physically when I was home with Sam. The release of stress and a sense of being safe was something I had not expected in this marriage. I kicked off my shoes and joined him on the couch.

"Can I get you a drink or something?"

"No thanks. I've had enough tea and that will likely keep me awake for awhile, so I think I'm fine. How was your trip?"

"Awesome, actually," he bragged. "I think I'm getting a

handle on this new position and have some pretty bright folks in place doing a good job. Oh, I brought you a little something from the airport. I was browsing in a very nice shop and saw this!"

He handed me a cute gift bag that contained a very nice red leather journal. When I opened it up, you could see it was organized to record a family tree and other information. This was my kind of gift. I have loved every form of paper supplies since my early childhood. I was never bored when I could get my hands on some paper.

"After the red color got my attention, I noticed it was more for genealogy than for storytelling," Sam explained. "There should be a nice red pen in the bag as well. It just reminded me of you and your writing. I hope you like it!" He knew he hit a home run.

I beamed. "It's beautiful!" I purred, rubbing my hand across the smooth leather. "I love it. Thanks! I think this will be a good guide for me. I was just telling Mother on the way home that I wanted to get back to the Taylor family research. She's going to let me have a cute little writing desk that I want to put in the 'nursery,' as you call it. It's just sitting in her basement, not being used. That room will be a handy spot for me when I impulsively feel like writing. I'd like to keep all the Taylor information in one place."

He gave me a somber look. "You say the word nursery like it's a bad word or something," he said, way too seriously.

"Don't be silly, Sam," I quipped. "You gave it that name the day we looked at the house, so I don't know any other name to call it! I don't think we have any little Dicksons moving in there any time soon, do we?" I tried to make it a joke, but he wasn't biting.

He took a swallow of his drink and placed it back on the table before he looked at me. "It's late, Anne, and I'm tired, but we do need to have a serious talk about when you will come off the pill."

I was silent. Good heavens! How did we get onto this subject again? "Are you ready to go up?"

"I certainly am," he declared, walking toward the kitchen.

I picked up my journal, turned off the fire, and walked into the entry hall to turn on the security alarm. The silence was heavy. What just happened? I followed him up to our room where his conversation was awkwardly polite. I, too, was exhausted from an evening of female chatter and was ready for bed. I didn't want to discuss, fight, or pretend any longer, and neither did he. We got comfortable in our snuggled positions as the light went off. I prayed sleep would come fast and all would be well in the morning.

CHAPTER 17

When I came downstairs the next morning, Sam was getting his things together to go out the door. He looked handsome, as always. He was happy to see I was going to have a walk and he kissed me sweetly.

"Hey, where is this fragrance coming from?" Sam said, walking toward the living room. "I see we have some fresh flowers on the mantle. Did you pick those from our backyard?"

"Yes, I did," I responded proudly. "There's a nice patch of jonquils behind the potting shed. I brought them in here for a reason. It was a peace offering to Grandmother after I became so angry with her. She broke the Taylor's vase, Sam." There. I told him. Sam looked at me like I was crazy. I continued without letting him speak. "I came in the room and found the vase on the carpet shattered into pieces. No one else but her could have done this. I threw quite a fit with her I'm afraid, so instead of carrying a grudge, I put flowers there instead." Sam's look was making me feel absolutely insane! Maybe I was! "Don't look at me like that," I scolded.

"Are we still amused with this behavior, Anne, or is it really becoming a major issue in this house?" he asked in an angry tone. "Frankly, I am no longer amused. When our property is being damaged, we should not be amused. Do you not agree?"

He was as serious as the night before. I stayed silent, looking down. He obviously wasn't seeing the humor any longer and was making his feelings very clear. Was I going to have to hide these paranormal occurrences from him from now on?

I kept ignoring his reaction and grabbed my jacket. What did he expect me to do about her, anyway? "To be honest, Sam, I think it's going to be what we make it. Right now, I'm going for my walk." I kissed him on the cheek and took my coffee in hand to go out the door without a formal good-bye.

As I walked, showered, and changed, I had plenty of time to think about the heavy topics piling up in my life. With all the things I had to do, I wasn't going to let Grandmother absorb any more of my time nor my marriage. Driving to the shop made me have to prioritize every day with what had to happen first at the shop or at home.

As soon as she walked in the door, Sally greeted me with frustration, which meant our day was already getting slammed. This was not normal behavior for Sally, so something serious must be eating at her. I should have gotten to the shop earlier, which used to be my usual practice until I made Sally the manager. It was easier on me to know that Sally would tackle the challenges of each day on her own. She was letting off steam with Kevin as I headed toward the computer to see what we had committed to for the day. It all looked like a fairly normal day. I guess I would find out soon enough what might be eating at her.

I heard Aunt Julia's voice out front, so I got up to say hello. She said she had just come from the spice shop and thought she'd stop in to say hello to everyone. "I have a dinner guest tonight, I'll have you know!" she announced excitedly.

"Anyone I know?" I teased, giving her a look of approval. "Does his name start with an H, by chance?"

She beamed and nodded her head. "I almost invited you and Sam, but I think it's a little premature," she explained. "He fixed dinner for me and Sarah one night, so thought I would reciprocate. It was a darn good Italian meal of his family's own spaghetti recipe, which Sarah loved, of course. He's Italian in so many ways. He talks with his hands." She laughed at herself. "I'm pleased how much Sarah is enjoying his company."

"Well, sounds like things are moving along!" I hinted.

"Yes, and no, you could say," she stammered. "It's just nice having some attention. Since Sarah thinks he's pretty cool, it makes it fun for both of us. He's a good guy, for sure."

"Yes, I thought the same thing when I met him," I shared.

"Do you think we'll all have Easter brunch at Donna's again this year, Anne?" Aunt Julia asked. "It's coming up and I thought maybe I'd ask Harry, since Sam knows him and all!"

"Well, sure. I'm glad you brought that up!" I said, motioning her to come back to my desk. "It's a great solution for me and Mother, I think. I have no clue whether Sam's mother will come again. He hasn't said. I hate the thought of it, but I guess I'd better suggest it as a good daughter-in-law should, right?"

She shook her head and smirked at me. "See what you get into when you get married?" she teased. "Yes, Miss Anne, you probably should and include his sisters as well, even though they may not come. It would make Sam feel good. By the way, our little Mia Marie Davis will be turning three next week. Has Sue said anything about a little party?"

"She didn't last night, but yes, I think ice cream and cake will be in order," I said, feeling happier at the thought of a coming celebration. "I'll be happy to do that at our place, if it's okay with Sue. I know Mother mentioned she already had some things for Mia that she picked up at Pointer's Book Store. I'll call her today and at the same time arrange the brunch at Donna's Tea Room. Thanks for keeping me on my toes. At this little shop, it's all about everyone else's holiday. When I'm done with that, it's hard for me to plan my own."

"I guess you might have to check with that ol' man of yours about all this." Aunt Julia's teasing was etched with a subtle reminder. I shook my head, not giving her an answer.

We said our good-byes and I watched her bounce happily to her car. Things were changing in her life, and I couldn't help but to be happy for her. I wondered then about my Uncle Jim and how he was doing. Was he with Brenda now or with no one?

Jean wasn't coming in until after lunch, so I tried to get Sally to open up about her bad mood. I started talking about last night's literary club meeting and that gave her the opener.

"Paige and I really got into it last night," she finally announced as she was making a large yellow-wired bow. She waited for me to respond.

"Well, there must have been a full moon!" I joked. "Sam and I didn't do too well when I got home either, but no big deal! You both seemed fine at the meeting."

Sally took a deep breath. "She's dating this guy who's trying to control her, and she doesn't see it at all," she blurted.

"Now he's insisting she move in with him, and she hardly knows him. When she agreed to be my roommate, I didn't do a lease or anything, but she knows I need the money and it puts me in a real bind. Actually, the part that really bothers me is how subservient she has become to him. Why can't some women see that?"

"Well, I suppose she cares for him enough to overlook some of his controlling behaviors," I said sympathetically. "Did you make her feel it was just her rent you wanted or that she was too good to take orders from this guy? There would be a difference regarding how she would react to your anger."

Sally shook her head like she really didn't want to talk about it any further. I decided I was going to drop the subject in hopes the two could work it out. I didn't blame Sally for being upset.

"I'm sorry to dump all this on you, Anne," Sally said after some time went by. "I just hope we can keep our friendship, whatever she decides to do. I really hate trying to find another roommate. Besides, she may move back in if she sees this guy is a jerk."

She had a good point. "I know one never gets very far by judging someone that someone else loves," I said, trying to make light of it all. "They have to find out for themselves. You might try and apologize to her. Tell her you are there to support her but that you are just afraid of her getting hurt by the way he treats her. She may not want to admit it; but now that you have pointed it out, she may think about it." She finally smiled.

I know it gave her a sense of relief to talk about it. Good heavens, I thought to myself, the human spirit is sure complicated when it comes to feelings for one another!

CHAPTER 18

Spring in Colebridge was like no other place in the world! It was such a reward after a cold winter and it demonstrated the hope of things to come. This year, if nothing else, I was determined to do more with my potting shed, which took on more and more meaning for me. It was becoming my little refuge from the shop and from the large home for which I was now responsible. I could control and manage this little place, unlike the 333 Lincoln estate standing staunchly next to it.

Easter plans were shaping up at Donna's Tea Room and, to my shameful delight, Helen was not joining us this year, due to her failing knees. She was scheduled for some surgery next month, and Sam promised he would be there with her. That was perfect reasoning in my mind, as she preferred to have him to herself, anyway. Sam's sisters all had plans, so my wifely duty was done and our family could move ahead with our plans.

Easter morning was clear, bright, and sunny. When I came out to the front porch, there were nature's reminders of the season. There were clusters of bright red tulips here and there and splashes of white crocuses sprung up along the driveway between rocks and weeds. In early spring, I always looked for green moss growing near the trees. As a child, my nest for the Easter bunny had always been shaped from grass and moss; Easter morning was always a treat, and I knew I would find hand-colored eggs, jellybeans, and chocolate bunnies tucked neatly inside the nest. I told Sam that learning there wasn't an Easter Bunny was much more disappointing than finding out there wasn't a Santa Claus.

Sam and I picked up Mother at her home. When we arrived at the tea room, Mia and Sue were already waiting for us. Mia seemed to be entertaining the crowd. She was dressed in pink and black finery, which complemented her dark skin and hair. A pink polka dot hair band made her look even older than her actual age. There was no doubt that this little gem would be a knockout one day as a grown woman. We got her settled in her booster seat and in walked Aunt Julia and Sarah with Harry Sims. I was now giving him a closer look than I had before. Yes, he was handsome and very polite. He remembered meeting everyone at our Christmas party, so he wasn't a total stranger. Aunt Julia blushed in the early conversation, and Sarah seemed perfectly at ease with his presence. When we began to take our places around Donna's nice, big, round table, I noticed baby pink roses from my flower shop were placed in some of Donna's antique teapots. Donna's favorite color was pink and it was perfect for remembering this special day. Also, it was such a creative touch from Donna and her staff. I made a note to remember the idea myself. So many times at flea markets and garage sales, the lid to a teapot was missing, so it could be a perfect container. I had used teacups before for smaller gift arrangements, which reminded me I needed to repurpose more of them. I sat down next to Sue, and Sam sat down next to Aunt Julia.

"So, when can we celebrate this big birthday that's coming up?" I asked Sue.

"How about all of you come over next Sunday afternoon for cake and ice cream?" she suggested.

"I am happy to have it at our house, Sue, if you'd like," I offered. "The date would be fine with me."

"Thanks, Anne, but I have it at all planned and goodies purchased," she described. "This is about as much fun for me as it is for Mia, I'm afraid. I have been looking forward to this!" We all knew what she meant. All of us agreed on the date, although we knew Sam may already be gone to see his mother.

Mother quietly asked us to take a moment for an Easter blessing as we held each other's hands around the table. Mia took to the request and Sue grinned with pride as she held one of her hands.

The delicious baked ham was just like I remembered from the year before. Donna always personally served each guest baked carrots with brown sugar with all her entrées. They melted in your mouth, as did most of her menu items. The choices of pie for the day were always trumped by the option of her coconut cream.

Since Sam was sitting near Harry, they chatted away like he had been a family member from long ago. Mother said she felt badly not having William and Amanda with us but she said they had other plans. I told myself to remember their birthdays and try to remember to include them when I could for any of our family gatherings.

"So, Anne, have you decided what your Austen block will be?" asked Aunt Julia between bites. I sighed, not wanting to think about it.

"No, and stop bugging me about it," I kidded. "I had one suggestion: Jane pulling her hair out. But I don't suppose that would go over too well." Mother picked up part of my response and gave me a dirty look.

"Hey, I kind of like that, Anne," Aunt Julia said, laughing. I was glad Sam did not hear me or he would have asked for an explanation, I'm sure. "Sarah's decided to design some stick drawings for embroidery. She recalled Jean telling her that Jane had eight siblings, so she wants to do something with that idea. It could be kind of cute. She's picked up the outline stitch beautifully. I am not an artist, so I want to keep it simple, but everything I think of is going to be hard to do, I'm afraid."

"I decided to do an image of Jane with a dog—Muffin, to be exact," interrupted Sue, excitedly. "I don't know if she ever had a dog, but I would like her more if she did, so I put Muffin in it. I don't think anyone else is doing that, right?"

"That's a darling idea," I said with delight in my voice. "I doubt if that idea has been taken. Isabella said we should put our personal touch on it, so that sounds perfect for you, Sue. Aunt Julia is right, though, these ideas will be hard to pull off, especially since we are not artists. Isabella said she is doing the medallion center with a silhouette of Jane, which will be the focus of the quilt anyway, don't you think? Perhaps our blocks won't get that much attention."

Mia had just spilled her milk, so the disruption ended the quilt discussion. Mia's face puckered before she broke into tears. Sue and the waitress jumped to clean up any spilled milk on the floor and Sam quickly got up to remove Mia from her chair, wiping what wet milk he could from her pretty little dress. She stopped crying as he took her by the hand to walk toward the patio door. She was delighted to leave us and Sam was delighted to play daddy for a while.

"Sam appears to be a natural with kids," Harry said directly to me as we watched Mia and Sam walk away. What was I supposed to say, I asked myself, as others were listening?

"Yes, everyone loves Sam," I proudly replied. "He is a natural with children, that's for sure!"

"You'd better start thinking about filling up that big house of yours," Aunt Julia teased. Her look was waiting for my response and I wanted to kill her. If Harry had not been listening, I would have ignored her comment.

"We need some time," I said softly. "Sam has a new job and I'm contemplating an expansion at the shop. I still have things I need to finish up on the house, as well." It sounded like a rehearsed response, which it was!

"There will never be the right time," Harry said. "I have two children that have grown up so fast. If we had waited for the right time, I'm telling you, they wouldn't exist today."

"Oh, how old are they?" I asked, not realizing he had children.

"I have two sons who live with their mother," he said in a sad tone. "One is a senior in high school and the oldest one started college last year." I wanted to learn more, but everyone was getting up and starting to say their good-byes. Sam had not returned from the patio with Mia.

Donna had a lovely long-stemmed pink chrysanthemum for each of us when we left. I remembered seeing her order come in for dozens of pink chrysanthemums. Now I knew why. She always gave away something special to her customers on a holiday and they never forgot her kindness I could learn many things from this charming businesswoman. We all thanked her for a lovely experience and I went to find Sam.

Sue was trying to get Mia to say good-bye to Sam, and Mia started crying again. She cried aloud that she wanted to stay with Unkie Sam. Oh how cute that was, I noted. I never heard her call him that before. I guess Auntie Syl, Cuzzy Anne, and Unkie Sam needed to be on their way. We kissed her good-bye as Sue guided her away with a cookie bribe.

"Will you please take us home, Unkie Sam?" I asked sweetly into his dark eyes. He gave me a full grin and a kiss as Mother joined us to leave.

"You really must get yourself one of those little cutie pies, Sam," Mother teased. I acted like I didn't hear her.

"I couldn't agree with you more, Grandma Brown," he quipped.

Oh please. Get me home, I thought. These two together were dangerous.

CHAPTER 19

Early in the week, we planned a night after work to rearrange in the shop. It was good to do this now and then. Also, Sally was determined to make some changes. We had pizza delivered and utilized Kevin for any heavy lifting. Sally took advantage of the opportunity to share with the others what she was thinking for the shop expansion. Their excitement was boxing me in to listen more intently.

"I have the perfect architect for you to talk to, Anne," Sally announced. "He's done a lot of retailing rehab and has experience dealing with the Landmarks Board with other buildings he's done in the area. I saw him at Starbucks the other day and he gave me his card. I put it on your desk. It doesn't hurt anything to just talk to him, Anne." They all looked my way for a response.

"I wish I had as much support on this idea from my family as I do from you guys," I shared. "All I get is a reminder of a whole list of reasons as to why I shouldn't add to my list of headaches. I just haven't had the energy to take on this battle right now."

"My, my, Miss Anne, that has to be a sad wrench for you, when you have such a collection of ideas for this shop," Jean responded. "Just don't give it a toss that easily, my dear. Can any of us chaps be of help?"

I smiled at all of them—friends who wanted to help make this shop part of their own. It was easy, of course, for them to spend my money and have me juggle it all. It would be easy for me to give in, but I felt there would be a price to pay if I didn't time this right. I wasn't sure I was ready to find out what it would be.

"You really are helping," I complimented them. "You all see the potential, I know that. Sally is right on with her analysis. I will talk to your friend, at least. It cannot hurt, right?"

With that confession, they all were inspired as they worked another hour or so before calling it a night. I felt I had taken a step, also. How could I make an intelligent decision when I really didn't know what was possible and what I might be up against? I had their support and I owed them that. I was at least going to make an effort to hear some facts and figures.

I arrived home just minutes before Sam. He said he talked to his mother about the surgery and he would leave Thursday to be with her. He then shared how he could actually take care of some business in the area as well, making it all rather productive. I liked hearing all about it and felt his energy return as well as his positive attitude. He was good at planning many things at once, so why couldn't I share my plans quite the same way? He certainly wasn't going to ask me if this was a good plan. That was not my Sam, whom I admired. I didn't expect that hesitation on his part, so why did I have to ask everyone else if my plan was good? Hmmm...

"Maybe you can get some writing done with me gone," Sam suggested.

"Good idea, honey," I agreed. "I'll have plenty to do, for sure. You are going to miss out on Mia's little birthday party on the weekend, I guess you know."

He grinned. "Sorry about that," he said sadly. "Be sure to take pictures. She is such a cute little tyke. It's amazing how quickly she is growing up, isn't it? You think Sue's mom and dad will come in for the party?"

"I doubt it, but I really don't know," I answered. "It would be nice to see them again. I thought about getting her a savings bond or something like that, Sam. What do you think? She has so many toys and clothes."

"Fine by me, Cuzzy Anne," he said, giving me a wink. "Be sure to tell her it's from Unkie Sam, too! Did you get a lot done at the shop tonight?" Sam asked, arranging some papers in his briefcase.

"Yes we did, as a matter of fact," I answered boldly. "We had some good discussion on expansion ideas too. They really are trying hard to get me to move on the idea. I treasure their support and enthusiasm. I'm lucky to have such a crew." I walked out of the room, not giving him a chance to respond. I didn't need a lecture tonight, plus, I was beat from the evening's physical activities. I told him I was going on up to bed. "Will you turn off the lights and set the alarm?"

No answer. There was stillness in the air as I walked up the long stairway. If he wanted to stay there and stew awhile on my news of the evening, he could just do that. I reminded myself of Mother's words of warning about being selfish. Yes, it was no longer going to be about me, but it wasn't going to be just about him, either!

CHAPTER 20

I was determined to give Sam a loving send-off the next morning. He seemed to be in a pleasant mood, despite how our evening ended. I knew he would miss me as much as I would miss him. There were unspoken words, however, that we kept to ourselves. He was a good son to be with his mother and I praised him for that. I knew the first time I met him that he was all about family.

"I sent flowers off to your mother, Sam," I said as he got closer to the door. "Please give her my love and keep me posted on your whereabouts, okay? I am going to miss you."

He hesitated, gave me a smile, and was about to speak when I interrupted by asking if he had all his medication. "Anything else, my dear wife?" he asked in a tone I wasn't sure about.

"Sorry. Sometimes I don't know what this role of wife is supposed to entail," I said apologetically. I suddenly felt crummy and embarrassed.

Sam walked over to me and brought me into his arms. "I think we are both trying to figure that out," he said reassuringly. "I'm glad we're doing it together, my sweet Annie. I love you!"

"I know you do and I love you, too, so off you go!" We kissed again as he went out the door.

I really needed my walk today to begin sorting out many things. The weather was perfect, so, to save time, I decided to walk in the neighborhood. As I walked down the hill, my thoughts turned to that of our neighbor, Mrs. Brody, who lived alone. I wasn't being a very good neighbor neglecting her loneliness. I hoped she was all right. I'll never forget how tickled she was when I brought her blackberries from the patch she could no longer manage to pick berries from in her old age. I think I could possibly remember to regularly send her some flowers from the shop. That surely would please her. I made a mental note to tell Kevin. Sometimes there were perfectly good flowers that we tossed out for one reason or another. What a surprise that would be for her to receive! It would only take him a second to run up the hill when he was out delivering in this direction of town.

On my think tank list as I walked along, I added Mia's savings bond and a reminder to pick up the writing desk at Mother's house. With Sam not being home for dinner, I could get organized on the Taylor book. I wanted to keep walking and walking, but knew I still had to go back up the hill and get ready for the day. As the hill brought huffing and puffing, I reminded myself of the heart problems on my mother's side of the family and that this was a smart and healthy exercise for me. No matter how busy I may become, I must keep walking and walking.

When I finally arrived at the shop, Jean and Abbey were engaged in conversation as they tied raffia bows on twenty animal flowerpots for a zoo-themed event. Sally was on the phone, writing as fast as she could. I sat down at my computer. Staring me in the face was the business card of Alexander King, Specialized Architect of Historical and Contemporary Structures. His address was on the north end corner of Main Street. I knew of the office building in my walks because the historic building had a corner door entrance, which was unusual. Hmmm...

I put the card in my wallet for another time. It would have to be a conversation on my cell, outside the shop. Reminded of my list, I went outside to catch Kevin. I told him about Mrs. Brody and that he could just leave flowers on her front porch without having to knock on the door. He laughed and said he would try to remember. After a briefing with Sally, I told her I was going to the bank and post office. I got as far as the bank and sat in their parking lot. Somehow, I knew that making this phone call to Mr. King would change many things. Was Anne Dickson second-guessing herself? Anne Brown would have never hesitated for a moment. I got out my cell and pressed in the numbers.

To my surprise, a man's voice answered the phone. I stumbled as I pronounced my name and said I wanted to speak to Mr. King. He said I was speaking to him.

"Yes, Anne, Sally has told me all about you and your charming shop on Main Street," he said in a pleasant voice. "I already knew of you both because I have used your florist on many occasions and I've been quite pleased. Please call me Alex, by the way."

I paused. "Great. Well, I take it Sally has told you about

me having some thoughts as to future expansion here at the flower shop," I explained nervously. "I am aware of the many hoops I'd have to go through at this location, but I'd first like to have a sense of how this could look, cost, and, of course, how it would address my needs."

"I can certainly help you do all that, Anne, if I may call you that," he said. "One has to start somewhere. Are you free this afternoon or for lunch tomorrow?"

Oh dear, this was not the eager response I expected. Wouldn't he be too busy for such an appointment so soon? "Well, I suppose after two o'clock when everyone is back from lunch, I could run to your office to see you," I found myself responding quickly, unlike myself.

"Great. You know that I'm just down the street from you?" he wanted to confirm. "How about two thirty?"

That was quick. "Fine," I responded. "Are you sure? I'm in no hurry about this."

"It's perfect for me," he quickly said. "After we meet, I'd like to see your layout of space and property at the shop. I'll need that before we can get any real numbers."

"Oh, sure. I'm just exploring the idea right now," I stated again, wanting to make sure he knew I had not yet decided to expand.

"Sure. I'll see you this afternoon then," he said as we hung up.

Why was I shaking at the thought of taking this step? The excitement of expansion was taking over any negative thoughts. I could not believe I actually talked to someone who could really make it happen. What would Sam say if he knew I jumped at this inquiry just as soon as he left town? For now, it would have to be a secret, perhaps from everyone. Hmmm...

CHAPTER 21

It was hard to concentrate as the day's business progressed. I wondered if I should have included Sally in the meeting. The answer was no. She already had wrapped herself around the idea. I still needed to be convinced.

Knowing Sam was gone, Mother didn't skip a beat inviting me to dinner. I told her a quick bite could be arranged because I wanted to pick up the little writing desk that was in the basement. Sam called from the airport telling me of his arrival. He was pleased his little wife was having dinner with her mother. Little did he know what his little wife was really up to!

Nancy came in the door with her spice shop purchase that we could all smell. We guessed what was in her bag of goodies and why she purchased them. How she managed to cook with her busy life was amazing to me. Nancy loved to cook, which is why she was making time for it. She wasted no time reminding us of the quilt club meeting next week.

"You know, Anne, if you can just decide on your block, we can get others to help you make it or they can make the whole thing for you," Nancy suggested. She wasn't about to let me back out of this. "Thanks, Nancy, but if I am going to be in this quilt, I have to do at least part of it," I claimed. "Mother said she'd do any appliqué if it required it, so that's very helpful. I think I'd go crazy trying doing that myself, and frankly, I have no desire to learn how."

"Well, that's jolly good, as Jean would say," she mimicked. After she asked about Sam, she was on her way.

I couldn't eat a bite of lunch, knowing what the afternoon had in store for me. When they all returned, I told them I had an afternoon appointment and then would be heading to Mother's for dinner.

I walked into Mr. King's attractive office, not knowing what he even looked like. A nice, attractive older lady greeted me at the front desk. She said Alex was expecting me and walked down the hall with me to his office. I looked briefly at all the framed photos on the hallway walls. They were all black and white and mostly of historic buildings right here in Colebridge. From what I observed, he had impeccable taste. Plus, it was a unique building on the street, anyway.

"Anne, please come in and sit down," he greeted me in a most pleasant voice. I became almost speechless taking in his handsome, fifty-year-old appearance. His sandy colored hair and light blue eyes complemented a wonderful smile. I certainly didn't remember seeing this man before. Hmmm...

I sat down in a comfy leather chair that blended with the very contemporary-style room with brick walls. There was no question that his impeccable taste was also expensive.

My eyes then glanced at a prominent photo on his desk that appeared to be a wife and two children. Somehow, that made me feel more comfortable.

"I first have to tell you, Anne, that I am quite envious of you owning the Taylor house on the hill. I went to look at that when I heard it was for sale, but my wife put that to a halt rather quickly. It would have been quite an undertaking and she had her mind set on a new house."

"How did you know I live there?" I asked curiously.

"I think the whole town knew when the Taylor property was sold," he shared with a big grin.

"Well, believe me, I had no idea I would be the owner of it someday," I modestly said. "It has been a huge undertaking, but Sam, my husband, fell in love with it and had to have it. I fell in love with the gardens and a darling potting shed, so we both were hooked."

"Of course, it had to be right up your alley!" he said with a big smile. "So tell me, Anne, what can I do to fulfill your needs and wants at Brown's Botanical?" I had to pause and recapture his words. He was charismatic, that was certain!

I didn't know where to start, especially when I looked directly into his eyes. I started rambling, repeating some of the points Sally had made about how much business we were turning down because we were too small to accommodate large events like weddings. He was taking notes as I talked, agreeing with me now and then. After he heard my list of challenges, he interrupted.

"I've worked with the Landmarks Board before, Anne, with pretty much success," he said reassuringly. "If losing most of your parking is not one of your concerns, I'm sure we can design something appropriate for the age of the building and get it passed. As soon as I can take some photos inside and out, I could have conceptual drawings to you very soon."

"Oh Alex, I'll have to call you when I'd be ready for the next step," I replied slowly, beginning to feel anxious. "Neither my employees nor my husband know I am visiting with you. I suppose there's no harm in taking a look at the exterior sometime after the shop closes, but I'll have to call you and let you know when you can see it inside."

He looked at me with a questioning look on his face. "Sure, that is no problem," he responded, consoling me like a child. "Try not to worry so, Anne. These steps are always scary when you first dive in. Your location is wonderful, and, if you should ever sell, you will easily be able to get your money back on your investment."

"I think I know what you must think; I'm not used to having to include others in my decision making, but on this expansion, I must," I stammered, trying to explain as he gave me an almost flirtatious grin.

"It's that marriage thing," he said teasingly. "I know all about it, Anne."

I couldn't look at him because now he made me feel like I needed permission from my husband. Okay, then. I made a mental note of all his comments. I needed to leave. He was insistent on walking me out the door. I'll bet he was wondering if he would ever see me again as I walked out the door saying good-bye.

When I got in the car, I resented his reference to "that marriage thing." It was more than that, but I really didn't feel it was his business. This total stranger did not know me, nor my circumstances. His confident attitude was nearly arrogant and chauvinistic.

CHAPTER 22

Mother was thrilled to see me and I was welcomed with a nice little pot of homemade chicken and dumplings cooking on the stove. The smell reminded me of growing up with Mother rolling out the noodles on the kitchen table and then cutting them up into squares. I could never do this, nor would she likely have a recipe to tell me how to do it, either. I let her chatter away as she caught me up with the news at Pointer's Book Store. She was pleased she had to fill in a day last week because of inventory. I was amazed at her energy and I noted how some of the interior had changed in the house after I moved out. I think she was enjoying some of her independence since she hadn't lived alone for a very long time. I passed on apple crisp for dessert so we could move right along to the basement where I knew the desk resided.

We both managed to unscrew the legs to make the transport easier. Mother insisted I take the little chair that was always with the desk. I don't think they came together, but I would need a chair to sit on and it appeared to be the same wood as the desk. As we talked, I noticed Mother had set up the quilting frame again.

"Is that for Jean's quilt top?" I asked.

"Yes, she said she'd bring it over soon, so I wanted it to be ready to go," she explained, putting the four legs of the desk in her arms. "It will be fun to help her with the quilting, and from what we saw at club, I don't think it will take us long, do you?"

"No, you're probably right, unless we talk too much," I kidded. "I personally want to do that for Jean. She and her husband have helped us in many ways. Just let me know when you think everyone can make it. Right now, I just want to get this desk home to 333 Lincoln! You are a gem to let me have this, Mother."

We managed to get everything in my car, plus my dessert she insisted on sending home. I kissed her good-bye and thanked her for the yummy dumplings.

Driving home with a tight fit in the trunk, I had much to think about. The dusk-to-dawn lights greeted me as I drove up our hill. I opened the front door and turned off the security system to make a clear move with my desk. Feeling extra strong and motivated, I managed to slowly carry the desk pieces up the stairs. After I placed it down on the floor to attach the legs, I moved it into place. Then I went out to the car to get the chair. I glanced at the inserted cushioned seat and it appeared to be a piece of needlepoint. Did someone in our family stitch this a long time ago? Oh dear. I wonder if it may have been Grandmother Davis. She'll probably let me know.

After the legs were assembled, I placed the chair in front of the desk and it looked as if the two had been there forever. I opened its only drawer and smelled the antique wood. I read where Jane Austen had a wooden lap desk that her father had purchased for her. Her desk was not near as fancy, and I just imagined her sitting there with pen in hand. Oh, if I could just have a few moments to write here each day. The only natural light from the little side room was from one window, which faced a small section of the street below. I decided the blinds in there would do, instead of a curtain, which could keep out additional light. It had a pretty oval-shaped area rug that Sam had brought with him from his loft. It, too, looked like it belonged there. Sam must not have had it long, as it looked pretty new. It nearly filled the small room and was perfectly coordinated with the yellow walls that Sam had chosen for that room. No doubt he was thinking it would do nicely for a boy or girl, I suppose. I think it shall do nicely for Anne Dickson!

I sat in the chair to get a sense of how it felt. The desk was the right height and the size of the room would be perfect as a writing room for me. The room across the hall from our bedroom would be much better suited for a nursery. It was larger, had more windows, and was fairly easy to get to, which would be convenient.

Now, where would I begin writing about the Taylors? Would it be when I discovered the quilt in the potting shed? I'm sure there was much to discover, but where and from whom? A sudden thought made me remember the attic. Sam told me there were a few things left behind up there and I had refused to explore there yet. I would have to be a big girl someday and attempt the mission when there was daylight.

I showered to relax and thought about getting a glass of wine to help put me to sleep, but got lost in all the thoughts of the day. I stayed in bed with the lamp still on as hours passed away. I thought about every word Alex told me. He made it all sound so easy. I turned off the light and tossed and turned as I reminded myself none of this could happen without the support of my husband. When in the world could I share everything about this with Sam or Sally? How this would all evolve was still a mystery. I mentally revisited my list for the day and realized I had not taken care of Mia's birthday present.

I intended to call Sam back to tell him good night, but I forgot and I supposed he had forgotten about me as well. Was he fast asleep in his old bedroom at Helen's house or tossing and turning? Was he complaining to her about me? Was she asking Sam when we would start a family? Tomorrow was her surgery, so I added to my list on the bedside table a note to remind me to call them. Perhaps if I fell asleep, my dreams or nightmares would reveal all my solutions. Pray. That's what I need to do. Would I have God's support with all I wanted to accomplish? I remembered one of my Sunday school teachers saying we should not ask God for specific things, but, rather, we should ask him for help in finding solutions and making good judgments so those good things could happen. Yes. Good judgment. Was I making good judgments? Hmmm...

CHAPTER 23

The next morning, I was awakened early by a call from Sam. Half asleep, I answered the usual questions. He was already at the hospital with his mother. She was due to go into surgery. They had already put her under for the procedure. He said she was so happy he was there with her. He then remembered I was having dinner with Mother and wanted to know how it went.

"She had chicken and dumplings, Sam, one of my favorites!" I told him as I became more awake.

"Maybe you could learn how to make them someday. It sounds delicious," Sam suggested.

I smiled to myself trying to picture the scene. "We managed to take the desk apart and get it in the car," I boasted. "It now has a place at 333 Lincoln. It fits perfectly, and I put the journal you gave me in the middle drawer. I am really anxious to get started writing on something that will inspire me to keep writing. It has a cute little chair with it that I brought home as well. I can't wait for you to see it."

"That's great, but that had to be a handful for you," he noted.

"We unscrewed the legs and it barely fit in the trunk," I described. "When do you think you will be home, Sam? Do you have any idea right now?"

"I want to see how she does before I decide and then I want to call on a company forty miles from here," he explained. "I'll rent a car or take Mother's, I suppose."

"Well, I miss you. Let me know when you think you may return," I said sweetly.

There was a long pause. "Pat is here with me and said to tell you hello," he finally said.

"Please tell her the same," I responded. I could easily visualize the two together.

"Got to go, Annie. Call you later and love you!"

"Love you, too!" Hmmm...

Sam is such a good man, I thought to myself. How did I manage to be so lucky? I looked at the clock and realized there was no time for a walk, so I hurriedly jumped in the shower. On my way out the door, I checked on the plants in the potting shed and realized they needed water. I could never stand the thought of a living thing not being able to have a drink of water to sustain its life. As I did some quick watering here or at the shop, I found it was always such a calming process.

When I went to my car, which was parked on the driveway instead of in the garage, I glanced back at 333 Lincoln. I realized I had gradually fallen in love with our home. Yes, I suppose I was like Elizabeth Bennet when she married

Mr. Darcy. He had a marvelous estate called Pemberley where he brought Elizabeth to live. Little did she ever imagine that she would fall in love with such a rich and prominent man! She was perfectly content to remain single. This was my surprise Pemberley, I told myself. Despite Pemberley's grandeur, it couldn't have been lovelier than 333 Lincoln.

When I got in the car, I was struck by an idea. I now had a vision of what I wanted my quilt block to become. I wanted a sketch of 333 Lincoln that would be entitled, My Pemberley, 333 Lincoln. I did enjoy embroidery, and if I had a drawing of our home, I could possibly embroider it all myself! I felt as if a rock had been lifted off. I had a plan, and a practical one, I thought. A sketch of 333 Lincoln could be imprinted on stationery and even framed and hung on the wall. Now I would have to think how to accomplish the task. I was not an artist, nor did I have any talent when it came to drawing, so that would be my next challenge. Nancy would be so happy to finally have my verbal commitment.

On the way to work, I stopped at the bank to take care of Mia's birthday present. As pleased as I was about the monetary gift, I felt I still needed her to open something from me. I didn't know much about children, not having siblings or being around children much. Maybe this was why I was hesitant to get pregnant. Hmmm...

Before I could change my mind, I stopped by Isabella's Quilt Shop to tell her of my idea and to ask if she had any suggestions as to how I could accomplish my block with my level of skill. I was the only customer in the shop when I walked in, but I was surprised to see quilt club member Roxanne Harris behind the counter as if she worked there.

"Well, Roxanne, I didn't expect to see you here!" I said

without thinking. "Are you working here now?"

"I am, Anne," she smiled. "I haven't been here long, but I'm so hooked on quilting since our club began that I practically begged Isabella to hire me."

Just then, Isabella came to the front from the stockroom and seemed very pleased to see me. "Anne, so good to see you," she said in a friendly manner. "I asked about you the other day when your mother was in here getting some thread."

"Well, Isabella, you'll be pleased to know I've made a decision on my block, but I may need some help from you to accomplish it," I admitted.

"Great! Can't wait to hear all about it!" she responded. Roxanne and Isabella waited patiently for me to describe what I had in mind.

As I described the block, my excitement showed and I watched the excitement build in their eyes as well. They loved my idea. No one had committed to make my idea. They now were both ignoring a lady who had just walked into the store. They were giving me their full attention and Roxanne was the first to respond.

"I love it, Anne!" Roxanne said, quite loudly enough for all to hear. "Can you imagine what it was like for Elizabeth to first see Pemberley and then later discover she would be the lady of the house someday? Jane describes it so well, as if you are right there, doesn't she? I wish every story would have an ending like that!" I watched her overreaction and looked for Isabella to respond. Roxanne was no doubt a devoted Janeite! Isabella just shrugged before she told Roxanne to cut fabric for the other customer.

"It's a grand idea, Anne," Isabella said. "No one loves Jane

Austen like Roxanne, I must admit. I guess you know her block is Jane, the Bride." We both laughed with approval.

"I don't know if this all will be possible. First of all, Isabella, I cannot draw," I confessed. "I like to embroider and I love red, so would it be terrible to stitch it in red like the redwork patterns I've seen?"

"Goodness, no. It would be darling," Isabella's tone calmed me a bit.

"Anne, would you like me to try to draw that for you?" Roxanne asked as she overheard our conversation. "I was an art major, and if you gave me a photo of your house, I could probably manage the artwork part. If you don't like what I come up with, you don't have to use it on your block."

Praise the Lord, I thought! "Why sure, and I will pay you, of course," I said, appreciative of her graciousness. "That would be such a help."

"What are Janeites for?" she said, giggling. "I'd love to do it. You don't have to pay me."

"All I can say is that you both need to get on the ball here," reminded Isabella. "We need to gather and assemble these blocks soon. I guess I have to set a deadline or everyone will procrastinate forever! Frankly, Anne, I'm just glad you didn't choose to draw Jane pulling out her hair!" We all laughed, as did the lady paying for her fabric.

"I will get a photo to you really soon, Roxanne," I said. I felt very fortunate. "I really appreciate it and am so pleased you like my idea."

"Now see what you can do about your Aunt Julia's block," Isabella noted. "Also, we need Jean and Abbey to complete theirs. Could you remind them when you get to the shop?"

"I will," I said. "They will be shocked that I beat them to

submitting their choices. I'm running late, as usual, so I'd better be on my way. Thanks again, Roxanne. I will drop a photo off here at the shop as soon as I can."

Off I went, feeling pretty relieved and even clever about it all. My next plan was to get a really good photo of my Pemberley.

CHAPTER 24

S ally and Jean were scheduled and busy getting ready for the prom weekend in Colebridge. Parents and boyfriends spared no expense on this occasion. I asked to see how I might be of help and they just pointed me to the messages that were left for me at my desk. The first one was from Nancy saying to call her back, and the second one made me pause. It was from Alex King. Why would he be calling when I told him so clearly that I would contact him next? It was Sally's handwriting that took the message, so she probably was connecting the dots on my perusing the expansion. Now I felt bad for not yet telling her and would have to think of a way to communicate the obstacles so she wouldn't get her hopes up so high.

She then came over to my desk with a grin. "Guess who was outside poking around when I got here this morning?" Sally asked in a joking tone. "It appears as if someone dropped some hints to Mr. King." Oh, dear. This information was not good.

"Oh Sally," I began shaking my head in disbelief. "I wasn't going to say anything because I'm running into difficulty with Sam about this idea. I did go to Mr. King's office and agreed to let him take a look at the outside. That was probably a bad idea. I'm sorry for not saying anything, but Mother and Sam both think I have no business pursuing anything like this right now, so I'm treading very carefully." Inside, I was feeling angry over Mr. King's aggressiveness.

"Hey, Anne," she started, "you don't owe me any explanation. You know my heart is in the right place, and you have to feel good about this or it will fail. I'm just pleased you like the idea. Rome wasn't built in a day and I think Sam will eventually come around. I guess you may have to do what my mother always did with my father. She would eventually make him think it was all his idea." That would never happen, but I knew what she meant. We grinned at the thought.

"I think she was pretty smart," I concurred. "Now I just have to figure out how to do that." We were still laughing when we were interrupted by the UPS driver delivery.

When we got a quiet moment toward the end of the day, I told whoever was listening in the shop about my block idea and they were delighted, saying it was quite clever. They were surprised to hear Roxanne was now working at the quilt shop and equally surprised Roxanne had offered to draw my house.

"I am almost to the mark," chimed in Jean. "I figured a teacup would be a nice coming out from myself, I supposed, but that doesn't sound as fancy or as clever as what other

Janeites are drumming up."

"I think that's a wonderful idea." I wanted to encourage her. "What if you did a teacup with Jane's silhouette on it? You are a tea connoisseur, Jean. I think it's perfect."

"That's a sweet idea, Jean, but you are from Bath, England, for heaven's sake," Sally reminded. "Isn't there something about when Jane herself lived there?"

"Jane did little writing in Bath," Jean said. "Some said she was a bit out of sorts at that time, but others say she was just too occupied to enjoy herself. She and Cassandra, her sister, were attending dances, going to the theater, and visiting those pump rooms there in Bath, so I don't think she was too out of sorts."

"Maybe you could make a block of her in the pump room!" Sally said in jest. "That was what they called the Roman Bath House, right?"

"Right," Jean said, laughing. We all broke down trying to picture Jane there. "I don't want to make fun of my dear Jane, ladies," she said in defense of Jane Austen. "I want a pleasant sort of idea for her."

"Well, if you put her in a bath house, she would have on a pleasant face, for sure, Jean," Sally teased. "It could say, 'Come Clean with Jane'; or maybe it could say, 'Jane has a Bath in Bath.'"

"Oh, that is really tacky, Sally," I said, trying not to laugh. "Don't they show the house where Jane once lived in Bath, Jean?"

"Yes, it's nothing fancy, but is shown on a tour, for sure," she noted.

"I would embroider the house and simply say, 'Jane's House in Bath, England' and be done with it," said Sally.

"The house would be a bit of a bore, especially when they see Miss Anne's Pemberley block," Jean teased. "So you think Life in Bath is a better idea than Tea with Jane?" Jean asked, sounding a bit confused and lacking direction.

"Having tea with Jane sounds a lot happier and more appropriate as to her activities, if you ask me," I admitted. "I vote for a fancy teacup or tea set!" Jean seemed convinced when we gave her nods of approval.

"I'm locking the door, Janeites, just so you know," yelled Sally from the front door. "It's Paige's birthday and I want to catch her before she goes out tonight."

"How nice," I responded. "Please take a flower basket out of the cooler for her, Sally. Tell her happy birthday from Sam and me. I'm glad things are okay with you guys. Is she still going to move out?"

"So far, she's put him off concerning the idea, so I'm happy with that," Sally shared. "I think she convinced him that she was locked into a lease with me or something like that, so he wouldn't think it was all her fault."

"She's a special one, that Paige," Jean also bragged. "Tell her happy birthday from her English mate."

"I will, you guys," Sally said with a gleam on her face. "You are just like family, ya know that? Thanks so much!" Off she went and Jean and I smiled at each other.

As the chatter and noise went out of the door, I thought about the rest of the evening. I remembered I had not yet returned Nancy's phone call, but frankly, I was tired of talking and wanted to go home to my potting shed and writing desk.

CHAPTER 25

I stopped to pick up chicken fried rice to take home. It was always a comfort food to me and I didn't feel like fixing myself something. My mission for the evening was to decide which photo of the house to give to Roxanne and to start the introduction to *The Taylor House*. The thought of stitching 333 Lincoln excited me a great deal. I may not want to give it up for the quilt!

I checked for messages and there was just the reminder from Nora that she would be coming first thing in the morning to clean. She insisted I be there. Later in the day tomorrow, I had plans to have cake and ice cream at Sue's to celebrate Mia's birthday.

The mild temperatures took me to the south porch to enjoy my dinner. The peace and quiet and the view of the gazebo were just what I needed. I had pretty much decided the best place to start my adventure of *The Taylor House* was to describe my memory of seeing its rooftop from Lincoln Street many years ago. I envisioned something magical instead of something scary, like so many others. I found it fascinating that it took someone outside of the community, like Sam, to discover its beauty and potential. Now that I'm here, it is still magical to me.

It was dark before I finally went upstairs to change into my sweats. I sat down in my writing chair and went through my digital photos in my camera to decide what would be a simple view for stitching 333 Lincoln. My decision was quickly made and I found myself grinning.

I decided my introduction to the book would be written in longhand as I scribbled my thoughts. I thought this would make editing easier. I opened the drawer to reveal the lovely red pen Sam had given me. I positioned my empty tablet. A vision of the attic interrupted my train of thought. What if there was something revealing that was waiting to be discovered? What if there were letters or photographs in the left-behind pile? Why was I so hesitant to look? What was there to be scared of? I lived with a ghost every day of the week, so what was the big deal? Wouldn't Sam be proud of me if I approached the attic without him?

I got up from my chair and went to make sure the lamp was on in the hallway. It was something I insisted should stay lit at all times in case of an emergency. I decided in a moment's notice to just take a peek at the top of the stairs. What harm could that pose? As I remembered, there was a light switch at the bottom of the stairs. I made a mental note to tell Nora to be sure to clean the narrow stairs, which were heavily coated with dust and a few spider webs.

I made my way, step by step, remembering how brave and

independent Anne Brown used to be. I was nearly to the top when, all of a sudden, the lights began to flicker off and on before they went totally dark.

No, not now, Grandmother, I thought to myself. I remained still, knowing it was her practice to then turn the lights back on. Nothing but total darkness engulfed me. How could it all be so black? I couldn't even see the door that I had left behind with the hall light still lit. I took both hands and pushed them against the walls of the stairs to support my balance. What if the lights didn't come back on? I had to get down the stairs in some way, so I turned around and slowly felt each step as I held my balance. Breathe and keep calm, I told myself. I finally found the words to ask Grandmother out loud for some help. After what seemed like an eternity, I could feel the frame of the door I entered. There was no light from any direction, but I managed to walk carefully across the hallway. I felt my way following the hall's Oriental rug and finally felt the entrance to my bedroom. The only light was a dim glimmer from of one of the windows that I knew looked out onto Lincoln Street. I made my way to get my cell phone on my bedside table and dialed my mother's number. The streetlight below was still lit. Did I blow a fuse? Maybe there was a power outage in Colebridge. Or was it just my ghostly house?

"Mother, sorry to bother you so late, but do you have electricity?" I said as calmly as I could.

"Why yes, what's wrong, Anne?" she asked, quickly sensing there was a problem.

"Everything here went totally black," I quietly explained. Did she think I was afraid of the dark? I never was as a child. Darkness here at 333 Lincoln meant something, I'm afraid.

"Oh dear, Anne. How about I call in to report it for you?" she said reassuringly. "I keep those emergency numbers right by the phone." Of course, why had I not done that?

"Would you call them, Mother?" I heard myself talking like a little child. "Thanks so much. I was going to do some writing, but I guess I'd better just call it an early night and crawl into bed!"

"That's probably a pretty good idea, Anne. You could use the rest, and with an early rise, you can make up for what you planned to do," she encouraged.

"Thanks. I guess I'll see you tomorrow at Mia's party." That sounded like pretty normal conversation, considering I was actually very concerned.

"Oh yes. That'll be nice," Mother said in a comforting tone. "Sleep well. I'm sure they'll have the power on in no time."

I hung up, thinking about how foolish I was to have to call my mother at this stage in my life. She was talking to me like I was six years old and afraid of the dark.

I folded back my covers to climb into bed and pull them over my head when suddenly, on came the lights. So what really was this about? I quickly got out of bed and went to the attic door to switch off the light. I slammed the attic door as if it would never be entered again. I turned off the floor lamp near my desk and went back to my bed. Perhaps I would have to think about another introduction to *The Taylor House*, or not think of it at all.

CHAPTER 26

I awoke early from a surprisingly good rest. Summer offered such great light in the morning, which made the thought of my walk so much more appealing at an early hour. I quickly put on my shorts and T-shirt, wanting to accomplish a walk before Nora's arrival. I made a quick glance at my desk waiting in the other room as I headed toward the kitchen to make coffee. That other room will have to be named something other than the nursery.

It was going to be a beautiful day and many wildflowers were appearing on the hillside landscape as I walked along. Queen Anne's lace, one my favorites, was blossoming in various stages. It was such a complicated blossom that could survive in the most primitive soil and weather conditions. The unfortunate memory of the flower told me it was once again going to be my birthday. How I used to look forward to June 17. This year, I just wanted to celebrate with Sam, who knew me better than anyone else in the world. I had barely returned back up the hill, huffing and puffing, when Nora pulled up in her pickup truck.

"You're up quite early, Miss Anne," Nora greeted. "Is Sam still home?"

"No, he's out of town to be with his mother for some surgery she's having," I said. "Help yourself to some coffee, Nora. I'm going to check out some things in the potting shed."

I turned around to see the lawn service pulling up to do some mowing. The weeds were starting to get ahead of me, especially with the last rain. I entered the shed and wondered how in the world I could expand this little piece of heaven. It really wasn't big enough to grow anything substantial. It was fine for filling pots and starting seeds, but not near enough space to do much in my little patch of raised soil in the corner. I thought of Alex King and how he could take a look at this and tell me which direction to expand and what part of the worn structure could be saved. It had become so special to me that I wasn't sure expanding its original charm was the answer. Why couldn't I just leave well enough alone? Should I leave Brown's Botanical alone as well? What if I ruined what so many had admired about the shop, myself included? It was getting hotter and hotter inside the shed, so when I left, I opened the few windows and kept the door ajar for more air.

"Anne, Anne," Nora shouted above the lawn mower noise. "Your mother is on the phone in the kitchen." I brushed myself off and went in the back door where Nora had already wet wiped the kitchen floor.

"Did you get your power back on, Anne?" Mother asked.

"Yes, it came on shortly after we talked," I said, reliving some of the fear inside my stomach.

"Great! So, do you want to go together to Mia's party?" she offered. "I'll be happy to pick you up."

"No thanks, Mother," I told her. "I have so much to do and don't know the exact time I can get there." Cutting the call short, she agreed and politely accepted my answer.

"Nora, before I forget, would you be sure to clean the attic steps for me?" I asked as I got myself a cup of coffee. "I'd really appreciate it. They haven't been cleaned in decades."

"Sure, as long as you don't ask me to clean that attic, Miss Anne," she said with conviction. "I don't ever want to go up there."

I ignored her comment and took my coffee upstairs to shower. When I was dressed for the day, I came downstairs to make sure I had everything I needed for the rest of the day.

Nora was coming down the stairs when I asked how much longer it would be until she completed her tasks.

"I'm doing fine, but I have to tell you that I'll have to clean the attic steps another day. I got as far as the first two steps and the light went out. I couldn't see a thing. I'm sorry, but Mr. Dickson has got to be the one to change the bulb at the top of the stairs. It just feels plain creepy when you open that door, Miss Anne. It's just me, I'm sure. Please don't make fun of me. I'm just a big chicken when it comes to the unknown in the dark."

"Well, don't worry, Nora," I said calmly. "I'll have Sam take care of it when he gets home and maybe he'll be kind enough to take a mop to the steps. Everything looks great, so whenever you're ready, you can go on home." I didn't have to tell her twice before she headed out the front door.

On my way to Sue's, Sam called to give me an update on his mother and said that he would be leaving the next day to meet up with a client just miles away. It was very good to hear his voice and to hear the loving messages he was so good at expressing. I was feeling a tad guilty about some of my thoughts and activities while he was gone. Did he have private thoughts and ambitions without letting me know? How much I would tell him when he returned, I wasn't sure.

CHAPTER 27

When I arrived at Sue's, Mia was running around with package ribbon on her hair as I picked her up to give her my kiss and hug. Wow, she was getting a bit too heavy for me, I thought to myself as I put her back down. She wiggled away as she headed for more cake and ice cream that awaited her at the table.

I looked around to a nicely attended party. Everyone loved Mia and wanted to support Sue and her little family. I walked over to Sue, Paige, and Sally, who had just gotten their cake and were sitting at the kitchen table.

"Glad you finally made it, Anne," Sue greeted. I hugged her. "Please join us for the best part of the party!"

"Happy Mom Day to you, Sue!" I teased. "I got a little delayed I'm afraid, but here's a little something for Mia from Sam and me," I said as I handed her my birthday card. "She doesn't have anything to open, but from the looks of things, she is being pretty entertained with plenty of goodies!"

Sue laughed in agreement and was very pleased when she opened the envelope. "I was hoping Mom and Dad would come in for the weekend, but they are even busier than I am," she said, shaking her head. "Did you see that Amanda came? She fits into the family so nicely and adores Mia, of course. She made her a teddy bear with a little matching quilt. It's darling. I guess she's got that quilt thing going on, too!" We laughed.

"Sally and Paige gave her that little table and chairs over there. She will love that! Jean couldn't be here, but she sent a darling antique child's tea set. Mia is royally spoiled, I'm afraid. Just wait, Anne, someday you'll know what I'm talking about!"

I could see Paige and Sally were nudging themselves with that remark. They knew it would rattle my chain. I just smiled. I got a cupcake and a glass of punch and went back to the table as Isabella joined us.

"Did you see the cute quilt that Isabella brought for Mia?" Paige asked.

"No, I'm just trying to take it all in," I said among the chatter and Mia running around for attention.

"It was on display as a shop sample that had Mia's name written all over it," Isabella said as she sat down to join us. "I knew Mia was all about pink, so she did react with a smile when I gave it to her."

"Oh, Isabella, would you give this photo to Roxanne for me when you see her?" I asked, handing her an envelope. "I was so surprised to see Roxanne working at the shop."

"Well, she was pretty determined that I hire her, I have to say," explained Isabella. "She is quite taken with Jane Austen.

She never stops talking about her, which gets annoying at times. Your idea about stitching your house is a clever one, Anne. Now if we can just get Paige, Aunt Julia, and Abbey to commit to their blocks. Two blocks came in yesterday, all finished. Some are more inventive than others, of course. Our time is running out and I'd love to see all your blocks in the quilt. It can't be that hard to think of something!"

"Hey, now wait, Isabella. I've decided I cannot do this, nor do I really want to," jumped in Paige. "I don't have time, nor am I quilter. Maybe I'll give Sally some help, but count me out. Do you hear me? Out!" Wow, I think she really meant it!

"That's fine, Paige," Isabella said, backing down. "I didn't mean to pressure you. I'm sorry. I have to tell you that there are some strange blocks coming in, so no one should feel intimidated here. One block today had Jane as a beatnik with braids and black stockings. Quite a sight, I have to say. One that I thought was clever was Jane holding a microphone singing I Wrote It My Way!" We were all laughing when Aunt Julia came to join us.

"What's all so funny over here?" Aunt Julia asked, smiling.

"I was just telling them about some of the blocks that have come in that are pretty entertaining." described Isabella. "Did you figure out what your block will be, Julia? The topic is wide open, I assure you!"

"I'm still thinking," paused Aunt Julia. "I can't decide how far I want to go, if you know what I mean. I'll think of something."

"I just have to make sure we have the time to set it together and have our machine quilter quilt it," explained Isabella. "I know you're all very busy."

"Better not let Mother know you are going to have it

machine quilted," I threw into the discussion. "She still dislikes the look of it."

"Oh, it'll be fine," Aunt Julia said. "I've seen the custom designs they do with the shop samples and in some quilts. You cannot tell the difference. I just have no time to concentrate on this silliness." This time, I couldn't have agreed with her more.

"It's all that dating that takes up time, right?" I teased.

"Well, you're right, it doesn't help," she blushed. "I promise, Isabella. I will have it turned in next week for the meeting. I'll keep it simple. My skills are limited. I actually thought about just a plain tombstone with her name and dates on it. It sounds a bit morbid, though, and I hate to be that way."

"Well, you certainly cannot put all the writing that read on her real grave, I hope," commented Isabella.

"Nope. I read that, and people were all surprised it never mentioned her as a writer, so I thought at the bottom of her name, I would put 'writer.'"

"I love that, Aunt Julia!" I said. "I can't imagine why that was not mentioned. Leave it to you to pick up on that, Aunt Julia. I think you really need to do it, and it will be simple enough!"

"Okay, Isabella, consider it decided!" Aunt Julia gleamed with pride. "I'm tired of thinking about it." Again, I knew how she felt.

Isabella took a pen out of her hand and wrote down Aunt Julia's decision. Good thinking, girls. This is going to be quite the quilt and it will get a lot of attention at the quilt festival. We may even win a prize! When you see Abbey, please encourage her like you did Julia today!"

It was time to sing *Happy Birthday* to Mia. She clapped

her hands and danced around, still full of energy. After that, I kissed her on the forehead to say good-bye. I went to say a few words to Amanda, whom I had neglected during my visit. She and Mother were engrossed in happy conversation when I said I was leaving. It was a grand little party and put me into a sentimental mood, which caused me to miss my husband.

When I came home at dusk to my empty but clean house, I noticed the freshly cut yard and manicured trimming that made the Taylor house blossom. "My Pemberley" was now my pride and joy. Not feeling hungry from my afternoon party refreshments, I went into the house feeling dinner would not be needed. The house was quiet without Sam. When he was home, the TV would likely be on with sports or news. I looked into the study at his chair and wished he were there to greet me as I arrived. I glanced at our wedding picture on the mantle and beamed with pride.

I had to tell our story of 333 Lincoln, whether I would capture its original history or not. I headed up to that room again, where I saw the empty pad of paper waiting. It was, in fact, a waiting room, I thought. It was there waiting for my words, or it could even be waiting for a little Dickson someday. I shall call it the "waiting room," I decided. That should be satisfactory for all concerned, right?

CHAPTER 28

I slipped off my shoes and positioned myself in the empty chair. I had pictured this scene many times. I was always a visual person. So, before most tasks, I would often have to picture them in my mind.

The pen moved quickly in my hand as if it had been waiting to spill out the words that had been locked inside the pen. Were Marion and Albert watching me as I wrote? Was their daughter, Miranda Sue, who died so young, watching to see if she would be included? Was Grandmother Davis standing by with her hands on her hips, making sure she was mentioned with Albert? Surely there had to be more to The Taylor House than this love triangle. Did the attic hold further information to these questions? Why was I such a chicken to make sure?

My pen kept writing, not giving any thoughts to editing or time. I kept flipping to another blank page, and finally I gave in to my yawns of an exhausting day. I got up to stretch and walk into the bedroom and noticed the light flashing on my bedside phone. I had forgotten to check messages when I got home.

I pressed down to hear the first message of a somewhat familiar and pleasant voice."It's Alex, Anne," he began. "I just wanted to let you know I had a chance to get a pretty good look at the exterior of your shop. I'd like to discuss it with you soon. I went ahead— on my own time—to draw up some preliminary sketches that I think you'll like. I'll call you tomorrow at the shop. Hope you had a good weekend and talk to you soon."

Oh no, why did he call my house when I told him my husband did not know about our meeting? Why did he continue to pursue this without my consent? So there were sketches? How could I not be interested in them? I had only envisioned my own designs in my mind. He didn't have a clue about what I wanted. Now what?

The second message was from Roxanne at the quilt shop. "Isabella gave me your photo when she came back to the shop today," she went on to say. "It will do nicely and I should have it done in no time. I'll drop it off at the shop on my lunch one day. Nice house, by the way! See you then!" This means now I will really have to do this embroidery block! When will I have time for that?

The third message was Sam, which always brought a smile to my face. "Hey, Annie, guess you're still out partying with the three-year-olds!" he teased. "Call me when you get in. Miss you!"

I grinned inside and out. I looked at the clock and it was almost midnight. Sam was likely asleep, and I was still up thinking about the Taylors. Where had the time gone? I then remembered it was spent writing in the waiting room! I smiled as I undressed and put on my white cotton gown. I turned the lights out and slid into bed with thoughts of what a larger and more beautiful Brown's Botanical Flower Shop might look like. If I didn't know any better, I would think that Mr. Alex King was taking a little too much interest in this idea. Was he interested in me or was he simply trying to muster up business for his company? He sure wasn't worried about getting me in trouble with my husband. How was I going to tell Sam that this pipe dream of mine had already made its way to paper and pen?

Now wide awake, I still had so many questions as the Taylor family took over my thoughts again. Did Albert's affair with Grandmother Davis go on for years and years or was it only a one-time fling? How could he have been so insensitive to her having his baby? What was he telling her the whole time the affair was happening? Did she think they would marry someday? No wonder Grandmother would not let go of his memory. Was Grandmother ever in this very house? He must have given her lilies, her favorite flower. Oh my, now my imagination was getting away from me.

I knew I could probably get more information at the historical society archives as far as the house was concerned, but certainly not the affair. The archives staff there already knew to keep their eyes peeled for anything on the Taylor family. How could I squeeze in another visit with them with all I had to do?

All the characters were dead, I reminded myself. Grandmother Davis didn't seem to realize her state at times. Come to think of it, she was the only one I could still talk to about the history. I knew she heard me when I spoke to her. She just didn't always choose to listen. Perhaps she could help me with this book more than I thought. There was no doubt that she wanted to communicate. How would I know what she revealed was really true and wasn't a biased opinion? I sure would like to hear both sides of this story. From what her daughters said about her, she was very strong willed. It was her way or the highway. Do I really want her help? Hmmm...

CHAPTER 29

Sleeping later because of a late night meant no walk and a quick drive through Starbucks to get coffee before getting to the shop. The flowers on Main Street were now in perfect bloom before the summer heat would hit the Midwest. Kevin did a great job planting my geraniums and ivy in the flower boxes. The merchants group took care of the other plantings along the street. All the light posts had full blossoms of red begonias in hanging pots every year that looked their best in the middle of the summer. The street was alive and happy, ready for visitors. I was about to get out of my car when Sam's number came up on my cell.

"Are you at work?" he asked.

"Yes, just drove up." I kept moving toward the door. "It was late before I saw my messages last night, Sam, so I didn't bother you. I got some writing done, for a change, and the time really got away from me."

"Well, good for you," he said, making me feel better. "I should finish up here this evening, so I will likely be home tomorrow. How about that for good news?"

"It's about time, Mr. Dickson," I teased. "Don't you know you have a lonely, beautiful wife waiting for you?"

"Right, Mrs. Dickson. I do have a beautiful wife to come home to, but I doubt if she is lonely." We both chuckled. "By the way, you surely don't have to be reminded that your birthday is this weekend."

"Oh, don't remind me," I stammered. "After seeing true joy and happiness at Mia's birthday party, I cannot compete. I really just want something low key, Sam. Mother has already been hinting that she'd like to have us over for dinner on my birthday. How would you feel about that?"

"I feel terrific about that idea, if you do!" he responded. "Would you rather go out to eat?"

"No, not really," I said. "We really don't see her much, and you and I can always go out after we leave Mother's place."

"I've been giving some thought on a subject I want to discuss with you, if I can manage to have your undivided attention soon," Sam said. His tone was suddenly serious. "I'll save it for when we go out after we leave your mother's house."

Hard telling what Sam had on his mind. Whatever it was, it sounded like he would need time to make his argument to state his case. Please don't let it be about me coming off the pill. I wasn't in the mood to pry into that subject.

"Fine. It's settled. I'll tell her," I offered. "She'll be thrilled. Your mother is still doing okay? Did she like the flowers?"

"She sure did and she had many nice things to say about you," he bragged.

"I've got to get to the shop, Sam," I felt badly cutting him off. "Let me know if you'll be home by dinner tomorrow, okay?"

"Yes, boss lady," he joked. "I think you can count on it."

When I walked in and set my things down on my desk, I overheard Sally telling Jean we had just turned down another wedding request. That was just what I didn't need to hear right now. I had to slow this train down, starting with Alex King. I glanced over at Abbey, who was wearing an outfit resembling a bumblebee. I could hardly look at her face without laughing as she spoke.

"I just took a message from your friend Nancy, Anne," she said, handing me the written message. "You are to call her."

"Sure, thanks," I responded.

"Kevin is looking to speak to you, too, but he said he'd catch you when he comes back for the next delivery. He's got his hands full today."

"Sure hated to miss that little party, Miss Anne," Jean added to the chatter. "Did you get to see that bit of a tea set I gave her?"

I smiled, remembering it was very delicate. "Jean, it was precious, but it looked antique. Am I right?" I questioned. "I'm not sure Sue is going to let her touch it just yet."

"Yes, I've housed it for years," she stated. "I purchased it from a flat mate many years ago who was down on her luck. It is dear, to say the least. It is most fitting for that snazzy Mia as she grows. I'm sure Sue will teach her to be a real lady!"

"I just remembered you are doing something with tea with Jane for your quilt block, are you not?" I asked as I rolled through e-mails.

"Yes, and I have it nearly finished, by golly," Jean bragged. "I'll be taking it to Miss Isabella at the next meeting."

"I'll be kicked out of the club when Miss Isabella sees my block," Abbey said, overhearing our conversation. "Everyone is so prim and proper with our dear Jane, but I simply cannot go there! The Jane I want to show is trying to become liberated. She is going to be picketing for women's rights. I may dress her all in black or all in bright pink, I don't know, but she will be seen and heard with her picket sign." We all stopped what we were doing to try to picture the sight.

"Good for you, Miss Abbey," chimed in Jean. "I have to say, the black would get my attention and would make the proper lady a bit more daring, don't you think, Miss Anne?"

I really liked Abbey's idea. There were many rights to fight for back then. I was about to give my added approval when Alex King walked into the shop! I couldn't believe it. Sally was already looking suspiciously at me, like I was keeping something from her. I got up to greet him, in hopes that the others would carry on with their prior conversations.

"Good morning, ladies," he said with an overconfident voice. "I thought I'd just drop these sketches off, Anne, as I have to go out of town for an unexpected meeting." I remained quiet, not knowing what to say. "I would loved to have had lunch or a drink to explain them, but rather than put you off, I'll hand these preliminary sketches to you personally. As you said, it takes time to wrap yourself around an idea." He stopped and noticed Sally. "Sally, I think we have your boss starting to think outside the box here, so thanks again for the introduction." They shook hands. I stared blankly at them both, not knowing what to say.

"Well, I'm glad you've had some luck," Sally said with sarcastic humor in her voice. I sighed, looking at each one of them without offering any words. I did not want to encourage further conversation. I solemnly thanked him, wished him a safe trip, and stated I would be in contact with him.

Jean then announced I had a phone call. So, I excused myself, not missing Sally's bewildered look. I took the plans and put them on my desk. I'm sure Sally was anxious to see what he brought.

"Hey, girlfriend," Nancy said when I answered. "My calendar reminded me my best friend has a birthday this weekend!"

I switched gears, now needing to contemplate a completely different subject. "Leave it to you to remember, since I'm three months older than you," I joked. "At least I am saying it before you cleverly remind me."

She laughed. "I must also remind you that you are wiser as well, sister," she joked back. "I have a situation here. I'd love to celebrate with you tonight at Charley's, if you're free. We are leaving tomorrow for Boston. It's a family gathering for his parents' anniversary. I can't remember what number it is, but I'm told we have to go. That means I'll miss the quilt club, so Isabella is filling in for me. Darn it! So, will Sam care if we meet up?" Why did she always talk so fast?

"No, he won't," I said, thinking about my free evening. "He's out of town and comes back tomorrow, so it should be no problem. What time?"

"Well, if he's not home, let's make it dinner for the two of us," she cheerfully suggested. "How about we meet at Charley's around six o'clock or whenever you can get there?"

"Sounds great, Nancy. I can't wait." I said, hanging up the phone. There was always so much to discuss with her that I couldn't share with anyone else. She was always the one to make the contact, which sometimes made me feel guilty. She was a walking social calendar. I was a terrible friend when it came to keeping tabs with friends and family. I hardly had a moment's time to myself, much less for others. My special treat was to be left alone for a second or two. Would I still have time to write a few pages tonight? Now I had to face Sally with an explanation regarding the plans Alex just delivered. I couldn't pretend they were not here. Hmmm...

CHAPTER 30

When I hung up the phone, I looked up to see a grin on Sally's face. She deserved some kind of reaction, but she also knew her place as an employee who should not become too nosey.

"Okay, Sally, I'm thinking about all of the expansion stuff, so we'll talk, but not now," I told her as I moved the sketches aside.

"No problem, Anne," she said, smiling as she got back to putting fillers into an arrangement.

"Hey, Anne, before you leave, can we talk somewhere?" asked Kevin. He was coming in from his last delivery.

"Oh sure, Kevin. The girls said you were looking for me," I said, giving him my full attention. "Let's go outside. It's such a beautiful day." We walked to the edge of the parking lot where I had a park bench and two potted flowers on each side. "So, what's up?" I asked as I sat down.

"I need some help," Kevin said, getting to the point as he paced back and forth. Without giving me time to respond, he went directly into an obviously rehearsed explanation as to why we should hire another delivery person. He felt the hours were getting too long for him and our delivery range was expanding. So far, I was nodding with approval regarding his reasons until he muddied the waters by telling me the delivery van consistently needed maintenance of some kind and that we may also need to update it sometime soon. I waited until he had no more words and had joined me at eye level by seating himself at the other end of the bench.

"Kevin, I haven't been totally unaware of our growing needs in every direction," I conceded. "You made a good argument and I agree we should do it. I'd like you to take charge of interviewing someone, if you don't mind."

"Are you kidding?" he quickly interrupted. "I didn't do so good the last time I recommended creepy Steve to help you in the garden!" We both had to laugh and somewhat shiver at the slightest reminder of how Steve had tried to hurt me.

I agreed to place an ad in the newspaper as well as online, but told him we absolutely had to make the van last as long as possible. He seemed to be pleased. I didn't want to lose Kevin, for many reasons. He was so dependable and helpful in tons of ways, like helping Sam and me put up our Christmas tree. He also did a great job barbecuing for Sam's birthday party. He was our muscle source at the flower shop. Was I saying it was so nice to have a man around the house? The thought of all the extra expense this would entail made me look forward even more to relaxing with Nancy at Charley's tonight!

When I had the next quiet moment, I called Mother to

tell her I would be happy to share my birthday dinner with her. I insisted it only be the three of us and she reluctantly agreed. I wanted a simple dinner in my old familiar home.

Sally was a good sport and left for the day without mentioning my sketches from Alex. I refreshed my make-up and hair as Abbey and Jean said their good-byes. As I looked in the mirror, I wondered if or how much I had changed since I became Mrs. Dickson.

Nancy wasn't there when I walked into Charley's. There were a few men across the bar that I paid no attention to as I said hello to Brad, the bartender. He responded. He was always so friendly and knew everyone by name if they had visited Charley's previously. I had just pulled out my cell phone to check messages and e-mails when a voice came across the bar calling my name.

"Well, look who's here!" Ted said in a voice I nearly had forgotten. He started to walk my way, awaiting my response.

"Meeting your drinking buddy, Nancy, again or that husband of yours?" he said with a cockiness about him that I clearly did not recall.

I looked up from my phone, wondering how curt my remarks should be as I addressed him. He really did not deserve any answer. He appeared to have had a few drinks. "How have you been, Ted?" I replied, totally avoiding his questions. He was about to answer when Nancy quickly appeared and started her apology.

"There's an accident on the bridge, Anne," she announced. "I'm sorry I'm late."

"I was just about to entertain her for you," said Ted, with a smirk on his face. Nancy didn't know what to say, giving us a half smile.

"Nancy, I have a table waiting, so we'd better go," I interjected, gladly changing the subject. "Will you excuse us, Ted? Enjoy the rest of your evening!" Whew! Close call, I thought, as we walked away to our table.

Nancy followed me as I grabbed my purse off the bar and quickly headed upstairs to the second floor of the restaurant. Why did Ted still rattle me? When we took our seats, Nancy looked at me strangely. "Now, what's up with Ted?" Nancy asked as she lifted the menu. She wasn't really expecting an answer. "I'm starved. I've been in the doctor's office most of the afternoon, and then this darn wait on the bridge."

"Yeah, it was peanut butter and crackers for me at lunch, so I'm in the mood for something hearty like their French dip sandwich, how about you?" I asked, looking at the menu that I had pretty much memorized. "I have no idea what Ted was doing here, but he was drunk, that I can tell you. I was praying you'd appear before I had to have a conversation."

"I really don't care about Ted unless you want to talk about it," Nancy offered. "How is Sam? I'd rather hear about him!" We both smiled and I was glad she understood.

"He's good," I nodded. "He's working harder than ever, but he is working out a little more at the gym at work and I think he's eating better too! He looks great!" I blushed.

"I hardly see my hubby, especially since he took an office position with the Funeral Directors of Missouri," she shared. "It makes it even harder for me to get pregnant. He just doesn't have it on his radar screen, and he is getting to dislike it when I bring it up."

"Oh, Nancy, I'm sorry," I lamented, feeling her pain. "You know, this is really ironic, because Sam wants to interject wanting children every chance he gets and I guess I'm ignoring his messages like Richard is avoiding yours. Crazy, isn't it?"

We ordered and continued chatting nonstop about our husbands, Jane Austen clubs, the funeral quilts, and even the new eyeliner Nancy had just purchased and loved. She hadn't changed since grade school. She was always prettier and more popular, but she never once let that show as our friendship grew. Then I got up the nerve to ask her if she knew Alex King.

She looked up like I said something notable.

"Alex King?" she asked. "I sure do! He just recently got divorced. I know his former wife, Beth. I met her at the country club and played tennis and golf with her on several occasions. She took the breakup really hard."

"We're talking about the architect, right?" I asked with curiosity.

"Oh sure. He has quite a business right here on Main Street," she confirmed. "I really don't know him like I know Beth, because the divorce had already started when I met her. He's a darn good-looking guy—I'll say that much for him. Why do you ask?"

"I just met him after Sally recommended he look at expansion ideas for us at the shop," I said. I heard a hint of hesitancy in my voice.

"Expansion at the shop?" asked Nancy, like she had just been told big news.

"Not now, of course, but Sally said he's the best architect in Colebridge," I replied, wanting to play down the comment. "I can't handle that right now, plus the red tape that goes along with it. Sam and Mother nearly have heart attacks when I even mention the thought of adding on, so keep this between you and me, okay?"

She looked stunned. "It's a perfectly reasonable thought, Anne," she added. "I can see you are all falling over each other in that little shop and I also know about all the business you're turning down. The Anne Brown that I know would not be second-guessing this expansion one bit! So, you're just going to throw in the towel because they don't see the value in this?"

"It's not exactly like that, Nancy," I began, trying to calm her down. "They feel I'm in over my head with 333 Lincoln and the shop." She crunched her face like I had fed her something distasteful. "There's certainly some truth to what they say, and Sam's health is a worry."

"Mrs. Anne Dickson, may I remind you that you have a great business head on your shoulders. You always did," she firmly stated. "You always could multitask better than anyone I know! We all have homes and husbands! What's going on here?"

I didn't have the words to respond and express the way I felt. What was going on here? Hmmm…

CHAPTER 31

When Sam arrived in town about noon, he stopped by the shop to say hello and give me the great kiss and hug he does so well. The girls were glad to see him as well and we all quickly asked about his mother.

"She's doing pretty well, thanks!" he said convincingly. "She sent a pretty big package with me for your birthday, Anne." Wow, I was impressed. This was a first, I told myself.

"Oh yes, Miss Anne," Jean jumped in. "Your birthday is soon, and I collect we'll choose a time to celebrate, right, Sally?"

"No, not necessarily, so forget about it!" I responded.

"We'll have to celebrate without her then, huh, Jean?" said Sally. They all laughed, knowing the staff would welcome any reason to stage a party at work. We were interrupted when the door opened and in walked Roxanne Harris.

"Oh good, you're here," she announced when she saw me.

"The design is all done and I think you'll be pleased." We were all caught off guard with her bold interruption.

"Great. You're quick, Roxanne!" I said, pulling out the drawing from a manila envelope she handed to me. "Oh, Roxanne, this is quite nice and pretty darn accurate." I gazed at a rather simplified sketch of what appeared in most of the photos of 333 Lincoln. The perspective was certainly its best, showing the south porch from an angle, as if one were driving up from the hill. The south porch was really the front of the house because it faced south. There were other porches on the house, but this porch was the one Marion Taylor referred to as the south porch. It was where she and Albert shared their lemonade that she referred to in her letters. It was a tradition I wanted Sam and me to continue.

"Look, Sam. This is a drawing of 333 Lincoln that I am going to embroider for our Jane Austen quilt," I said, holding it up for Sam to see. He barely observed the piece of artwork and the girls went back to their work. "Sam, meet the artist Roxanne Harris, who also works for Isabella at the quilt shop. She is quite the dedicated Janeite and she belongs to both Jane clubs."

"Well, you're quite the fan, aren't you?" Sam said, reaching to shake her hand. "It's nice to meet you, and this appears to be quite nice work that you do."

She blushed. "You have quite a home there, Mr. Dickson!"

"It's not as grand as the real Pemberley, but we love it, don't we, Sam?" I bragged, giving him a big smile.

"Yes, and I'm hoping to see it soon," Sam said in jest, indicating he was anxious to leave. "It seems as if I've been gone longer than usual and I miss Mrs. Dickson here," he teased. I looked down, feeling embarrassed, and saw him to the door.

We quickly kissed each other again and decided we'd both try to be home around six. What that would really mean was dinner, I supposed. Cooking was the last thing on my mind right now, but Sam was easy to please and I knew he was so tired of eating out all of the time. Perhaps if I were lucky, he would take on the task.

When Sam left, I showed the drawing to Sally and Jean. They thought it was quite nice. Jean instructed me once again how to trace the design onto fabric and then use one strand of floss because of all the detail. I knew I could do it. I had the supplies I needed, but it would just be a matter of when I would have time. I had to admit, however, that I was a bit anxious to start. Jean said that when something is stitched, it comes alive. As soon as they all left for the day, I was right behind them to make sure I arrived home before Sam.

With the help of my fairy godmother and whatever other spirit resided in the house, I managed to have a presentable dinner for Sam when he arrived home. Broiled whitefish I had taken from the freezer combined with baked potatoes made an aroma of a warm and loving home. Sam's favorite salad of Bibb lettuce, mandarin oranges, bacon, toasted almonds, and blue cheese was already on the dining room table, accompanied with two lit candles. I picked a few red rosebuds from right outside the house and filled in with clips of ivy for a nice small centerpiece on the white tablecloth. I can do this, I reminded myself.

Sam glowed with pride as he greeted his apron-adorned wife in the kitchen. This is what every man wants, isn't it? By the look on his face, I succeeded, but how would I learn to really cook and enjoy the process at the same time like most other women?

"Nice to eat a home-cooked meal with my sweet Annie for a change," he said as he hugged me once again. "This looks great and is quite a healthy menu, I may add."

After we ate, we left our dishes for the morning and enjoyed some time on the south porch. The evening was just starting to cool off and the summer fireflies twinkled as it became darker. I asked many questions about his family and work, which he was eager to share. In this relaxed atmosphere, I really wanted to tell him that I had taken a step closer on the feasibility of a shop expansion, but I knew I would disturb the romantic atmosphere that we really both deserved.

When we went upstairs to retire for the evening, Sam noticed I had moved my writing gear into the adjoining room. I told him I now called it the waiting room. I beamed as I told him how pleased I was with myself to have finally started writing about 333 Lincoln.

He grinned and I felt his sincerity about my happiness. He went so far as to compliment the style of the desk and chair and how it would be a handy arrangement for me. His eagerness to hold me in his arms brought us together where we belonged. I do love you, Mr. Darcy. This was my Mr. Darcy at my Pemberley!

CHAPTER 32

With daylight arriving earlier this time of the season, I seldom got to relax with Sam by my side in the mornings. Today was no different. Sam typically woke early and I knew he would be making coffee, trying not to wake me. I reclined there, trying to assess my day's schedule. Tonight was Mother's birthday dinner for me, even though tomorrow was officially my birthday. It was the low-key kind of birthday I liked. Mother always said birthdays were celebrated for the moms who gave birth, not necessarily for the child. I believed that. She always was very excited about the day.

Sam came in to bring me coffee as I lounged there like a newlywed. "Almost happy birthday, sweet Annie!" he teased. "Since it's Saturday, I wasn't sure you were going in today."

"Yes, I am, for a little while," I said, sitting up. "I want to make sure no more orders came in for the Maxwell funeral. Sweetie pie, can I ask you to do a little something for me

155

this morning while I'm gone?" He looked puzzled and didn't smile. "When Nora went to clean the attic stairs for me this week, the light bulb went out and she wouldn't go up to change it because she's afraid of most everything around here, remember?"

"Yeah, and she's not the only one," he said, grinning at me. "I don't suppose you've been up there to look at any of the remains, right?"

I took a deep breath. "No, but I will go up during the day sometime soon," I assured him. "We need that light on the steps, regardless. I wanted her to clean the steps for us."

Okay, my dearest, I'll do it right away," he said, going back downstairs.

I quickly put on walking clothes for what should be a beautiful walk down by the river before I stop by the shop and make sure all things are taken care of before our noontime closing. I took one more sip of my coffee when Sam walked into the bedroom and said, "There's nothing wrong with that light bulb, Anne. I think she just didn't want to do the task! It works fine, but you're right. Those steps could use a good cleaning."

"Oh well, no harm done then," I said, heading down the stairs to leave. "I'll see you this afternoon and then don't forget dinner at Mother's tonight!"

It looked like Nora and I would have to tackle the attic at our own risk. Hmmm...

Some things never change, even when you leave your childhood home. That evening, Mother had the dining room table set just as she did for any of the family birthdays. In the center was my favorite two-layer chocolate cake that I knew she baked herself from scratch. Beside my plate were a few birthday cards that were sent here from those who did not know my new address since I got married. The first one I noticed was from Amanda and William, which was quite touching.

"You should have let me bring something, Mother, or we could have easily eaten out, you know!" I told her.

"And deny your very own mother the joy of treating my only child on her birthday?" she said, laughing. "It is all my pleasure, sweetie."

"Sylvia, for my sake, I hope you keep on cooking and you can spoil that husband of your daughter's anytime and as much as you want!" Sam teased, giving her a little squeeze.

"I kept it simple, Anne," she said as she brought the salad bowl to the table. "Remember that lasagna recipe I tried some months back for the quilters and everyone went nuts over it?"

"Yes, I loved it," I said as I now recognized the smell. "I certainly remember how wonderful the leftovers were!" We laughed.

"That did not include me, so there may not be any leftovers today," Sam cut in. "I love a good lasagna, Sylvia. What can I do to get this meal started here?"

Mother had him pour the drinks for each of us. After a quick prayer and a birthday toast, we enjoyed a delicious salad with tomatoes from the farmer's market. The garlic bread and lasagna were as good as I remembered. When Mother served the cake with no candles, I thanked her.

"Would you like us to sing, Anne?' she teased, looking at Sam.

"She doesn't like it when I sing to her, Sylvia. We'd better skip that!" Sam suggested.

"Thank you, thank you," I said, applauding his suggestion.

When we started eating our cake, Mother said, "Here's your card from me with a gift certificate from Pointer's. I know it's not very exciting, but they carry so many books on writing. I thought you would like to purchase one."

"This is great, Mother. Thanks," I said, gratefully. "They have a ton of stuff I'd love from there. I'll probably spend it this week."

"Speaking of Pointer's," Mother started saying, "you know Harry Stone, of course, don't you, Anne? He's managed the store all these years for Vicki Pointer. I don't know what she'd do without him, frankly."

"Of course. Did something happen to him?" I quickly asked before she could finish.

"Oh no, he's fine," she quickly responded. "I just thought you'd find it interesting that we've had dinner a few times together." I stopped breathing, for she couldn't possibly mean like a date. "He's been a widower since the time I've known him at least, and he's been my contact person when I turn in a book review for the newsletter." I was still digesting her words. What was she getting at? "Of course, he's always complimentary of my reviews. So, like old friends, we made it a habit to have dinner on that particular night when I'd go into the store. It's no big deal, but he is very interesting and quite the charmer outside of the bookstore." She blushed. She really blushed.

Sam smiled with approval, but was waiting for me to respond first.

"He has always said complimentary things about you when you did get to work with him for a spell," I said, shaking. I wanted to respond with the right words. "You certainly don't need any approval from anyone, and it makes me happy that you have someone to have dinner with once in a while." I swallowed hard, hoping that's all it was.

Sam was just sitting there grinning, clearly enjoying what was taking place before him.

She continued on, disregarding my comments. "The two of us can talk and talk forever about all the good books we've read," she said, with her face lighting up. "He also belongs to the same literary club as I, and one night, he had some of us over for coffee. He has a small historic house on Benton Street, near the church on the corner. It was as neat as a pin and his library is absolutely amazing. I'll bet he has a copy of everything the bookstore ever had in stock."

Oh my, she was smitten. I could tell. She lit up like I have not seen her since she told me she had gotten a part-time job at Pointer's. How could I not be happy for her? Harry treated me like a father ever since I can remember. He was not real handsome, but very distinguished. Vicki certainly thought the world of him. She traveled a lot to book fairs and did the buying at all the shows as he kept the bookshop running.

"Sylvia, how nice this must be for you!" Sam finally said. "I don't know him, but know who you mean from my few visits in the store. He's always quite helpful and it's great you have all those books in common."

I just looked at him. This was my mother he was giving compliments to. Shouldn't I be saying all those perfect things? "So, is Harry pleased to have you as a special friend as well?" I awkwardly asked.

"I think so. At least he says so," she kind of laughed. "When I asked him to come to dinner tomorrow night, he seemed very pleased. I have to admit that's why I wanted your dinner tonight instead of tomorrow, because it's the only night he had available."

I coughed and laughed. "So I'm now second fiddle to this Harry Stone," I teased. Sam looked sternly at me.

I knew that was the wrong thing to say.

"Oh, Anne, you know better," she blushed. "I thought about having him here this evening, but wasn't sure how you would take to that. Tonight is about your birthday."

"You did the right thing," I assured her. "Harry would have been a bit uncomfortable, I'm sure. This way, we each have you to ourselves!" I couldn't believe I said that! "Let us help you clean up here," I said, getting up from the table.

I wish she had told me this news privately. This was a shock. I never imagined my mother seeing anyone romantically. It just wasn't her. With Sam sitting here, I wanted to react in the correct manner instead of reeling with surprise.

"I have a better idea," Sam suggested. "Sylvia, you did the cooking and it's your birthday, Anne, so the two of you go in the living room or out on the porch while I fill the dishwasher. I'm sure you can think of something to talk about!" We laughed and agreed to do so! Get a grip, I told myself.

The porch air was refreshing and I continued to listen to Mother chatter about her flowers and neighbors. My mind was still back at the table digesting the news of Harry Stone who was now in my mother's life. I was glad she dropped the subject for now. When Sam joined us, we thanked her for a great dinner.

When Sam and I got in the car, he was the first to speak about the news we had heard at the dinner table. He knew this was all unexpected for me. "I'm proud of you, Anne," he said, winking. "You handled it well. This is a good thing for your mother, don't you agree?" He was always so positive.

I nodded. "Yes, no doubt. I just hope she doesn't do something goofy and foolish," I said, taking a deep breath. "Her face really beamed while she talked about him."

"You mean like that goofy daughter of hers who jumped into a marriage so quickly with an older man that almost no one knew?" he teased. I couldn't help but giggle at the very true statement.

"I love you, Mr. Dickson!" I said, kissing him on the cheek.

CHAPTER 33

My real birthday of June 17 was as close to a normal day as could be made. I was determined to get in my walk, and other than a quick stop at the shop, I had no plans except to meet up with Sam for dinner. I was about to leave the house when Aunt Julia called to wish me happy birthday.

"You're probably booked, popular lady, but would you be free for me to take you to lunch?" she asked, with some hesitation in her voice.

"I think I can!" I answered, surprising myself. "How very sweet of you to think of me, Aunt Julia. It will have to be a quick one. Can you just stop by the shop and we'll have something quick on the street?"

"Sure, see you at noon!" she said agreeably. That was a nice little suggestion from her. There was a lot to catch up on between me and Aunt Julia. I wondered if she knew about Mother seeing Harry Stone. I wondered how things were going with her Harry. I had a salesman due this morning, so I knew I had to rush to the shop, as always.

Sam was gone for an early meeting, so he left a sweet card on the breakfast table. Sam's birthday was in July, and I knew each year I would be struggling to think of something to give to a guy who had everything. It would be hard to top last year's surprise of the gazebo. It was getting lots of use, and we would try to repeat a barbecue as we did before. It was such fun, despite a late rain. Summer rains were romantic if you were under a gazebo and if they didn't include storms, of course.

When I got to the shop, the sales representative was there. His company sold many things, but I was particularly fond of their Christmas merchandise and unique pots. He assured me they would be here by September, which I requested. It was hard for Sally and Abbey not to give their opinions regarding my choices. For some reason, today they were welcomed, unlike other days. Jean was off today, but I was curious about what Abbey thought. Her taste was usually out of the box, and I felt I could learn something from her. She freely gave her opinion and Sally's eyes rolled. To my own surprise, I went with Abbey's selections, and she was thrilled.

I finally was able to respond to the happy birthday balloon on my desk and a nice tray of cupcakes. There were cards to open and Sally bragged that she made the cupcakes. I gave each employee a hug, knowing it was meant to be like a little party, but there was no time, as usual.

Aunt Julia was punctual as usual and chitchatted with the girls in the shop before we could get away. Out of habit, we walked toward Charley's.

"This isn't a very special treat for you, Anne," Aunt Julia said as we entered Charley's. "We could have gone somewhere else on the street."

"I have to eat lightly and this will be perfect to just get a salad," I confirmed. "Sam is taking me out tonight, and I'm sure there will be courses and courses, if I know him." She nodded like she knew that could very likely be the case. We gave our order and made small talk about Sarah's new boyfriend and how his appearance was sloppy and unruly, according to Aunt Julia. She also had an update on my Uncle Jim, who finally took a job with a competitor of Martingale. It sounded as if Aunt Julia and Uncle Jim were communicating.

"I thought you may want to know that I'm not going out with Harry any longer," she divulged, surprising me. "I guess I'm just too alert to what a man becomes in time," she laughed. "I think I need more time away from men, period. I didn't like the way he was sometimes talking to Sarah like he was her father. It also seemed he was using a bit more control with me each and every time I saw him. I just don't need that in my life anymore. I was flattered, at first, that anyone would find me attractive, but that wore off pretty quickly. Does this surprise you, Anne?"

"Not at all, Aunt Julia," I conceded, shaking my head. "Don't you think we need certain people at certain times in our lives, and then it is time to move on? I guess I'm thinking of when I left Ted behind. Rather than continue, I had to move on or it wasn't fair to him. This is why we date, right?"

"Exactly," she stated. "I knew you would understand."

"I have some news about another Harry, if you are interested," I teased. She gave me a look of total innocence. "My mother, your sister, Sylvia Brown, is seeing Harry Stone from the bookstore!"

She looked at me like I was crazy. "You have got to be joking!" she said, pulling her head back in surprise. "When, for heaven's sake, and why hasn't she said anything to me?"

"I just found out last night when we went over for my little birthday dinner," I revealed. "As a matter of fact, she is cooking for Mr. Stone tonight!" Aunt Julia's surprised face did not change as I continued. "He's a wonderful man, Aunt Julia. They got to know each other when she worked there, and then later attended the same literary club. It's kind of a pleasant surprise to see this side of her. She is pretty happy right now. As soon I left the house to marry Sam, she rearranged and decorated some of the house and even fixed her hair a little differently, as you know. She and I both needed the change to do our own thing. I think I can honestly say I'm happy for her. I don't want to even think she may get hurt, which sometimes happens, as you know."

"Good heavens! Who would have thought?" she marveled, shaking her head in disbelief. "Why hasn't she said anything to me?"

"I do think she probably felt she needed to tell her daughter first," I said. "I can tell she doesn't want to make much out of this. I think they'll just keep enjoying their knowledge of books and each other's company. At least I don't have to feel guilty that she is home feeling lonely."

"Okay, this is big news, to say the least, but I'm almost afraid to ask about Grandmother Davis. Is she behaving herself?" Aunt Julia asked with a snicker.

"She does reside at 333 Lincoln, no doubt." Aunt Julia looked surprised. "She lets you know what she doesn't like, for sure. I finally had to put the Taylor's crazy quilt away because she kept wadding it up and putting it on the floor."

"What?" Aunt Julia gasped. "You have got to be kidding me, right?"

"No, and it gets worse," I began. "She broke the beautiful vase we found in the potting shed." Aunt Julia now had her hands over her mouth. "It looked so great on my mantle until I found it in pieces on the carpet one day. No one could have done it but her." Aunt Julia tried to interrupt, but I kept going. "Now, she is sending a message that no one, especially me, is to go up in the attic, where I know some of the Taylor's things were left. Should I continue?"

"Oh, for the life of me, Anne, how can you stand that?" she asked, with frustration in her voice. "Aren't you afraid? What does Sam say about it all?"

"What can he say?" I asked sarcastically. "For one thing, he doesn't get to witness what I personally do. Grandmother isn't mean, just territorial and jealous when it comes to the subject of Marion Taylor."

"Oh, yes, she is mean. I've told you that!" Aunt Julia warned. "This was always her nature before she passed on. I'm just glad she is leaving me alone. You're crazy if you think breaking and destroying things like she does isn't mean! I can hardly stand to hear about all this!"

"I know, I know, I know, but there is nothing I can do about it," I stated.

Aunt Julia sighed as she listened to me. "Okay, I am changing the subject here, since this topic never goes anywhere," Aunt Julia said as she took another sip if her iced tea. "When are we going to start quilting on Jean's quilt? I thought it was already in the basement and Sylvia had it ready to go."

"She does have it and the frame is up," I nodded. "I noticed it last night, but we can't think of a time when everyone is free. It seems Jane Austen has taken over our social lives, as well as some others." We laughed, knowing it was true.

"You're right there," she agreed. "I'm finally turning in my block this week. Will you be at literary club? In my opinion, they should combine the two, don't you think? Two nights and homework devoted to Jane Austen is a little more than I bargained for."

"I couldn't agree with you more. I don't know if I'll make the literary club, but I will be there at the quilt club, for sure," I answered. "I'm anxious to see all the blocks."

We said our good-byes and my afternoon became constantly interrupted with birthday wishes. It was a small town and a small shop—what can I say?

CHAPTER 34

❧❧

When we arrived at Stone Creek Table that evening for my birthday dinner, I was totally surprised and thrilled. This best-kept-secret restaurant was becoming quite famous and almost impossible to get reservations. Leave it to Sam to think of something so special. It was a small, stone cottage operated by a first-rate chef that designed his own courses according to available locally grown produce. I recently read about his accomplishments and elaborate cookbook. Since it was located outside of Colebridge, it did not pop up on my radar screen when I wanted to go out to dinner. The candlelit cozy room held very few tables and we were greeted and seated with open arms. Of course Sam had told the staff it was my birthday, so I was handed a darling bouquet of wildflowers. What a romantic gesture in this old, stone cottage atmosphere.

The beautifully presented six-course meal started with corn bisque, adorned with bacon and Gruyere croquette. The courses finished with a layered cake and mousse of dark chocolate and huckleberry hot pot. We were so busy enjoying each course, complete with the waiter's elaborate descriptions, that we had little time for conversation until coffee was served.

"You know, you are nearly impossible to buy for, Annie, so rather than another piece of jewelry, I thought about what you seemed to enjoy most at 333 Lincoln," he began to explain. Oh boy, this was going to be good.

"I know you have complained about that tiny potting shed, and wished you had more space to grow things for the shop. I want you to know that I totally support any expansion you want to do there at whatever expense you think is necessary."

I stared at him, knowing he was expecting a leap of joy and praise from me. "How sweet and thoughtful, Sam," I said, almost in a whisper. "That's so interesting you took the time to think about how much I love that little place. I went out there while Nora cleaned this week, and because I love that little piece of heaven so much, I realized that I don't think I want to change it." He looked puzzled.

"I know it sounds crazy, and perhaps someday I'll change my mind, but I think an expansion would change all the things I love about it." He remained silent. "Making all those changes would not increase my joy. If I ever got serious about growing indoors, there is plenty of ground on the property to build a greenhouse that would suit my needs. Right now, I'm not ready for that."

He now was looking for the right words to say. "Well, there goes my birthday surprise," he said, clearly disappointed.

"My goodness, Sam, this dinner was as amazing and romantic as one could imagine," I responded. "This is plenty, and it's the thought that counts, sweetie! I am very touched by your suggestion. Perhaps this is a good time to tell you what is really preying on my mind." I paused and saw he was now looking more puzzled than ever. "I would give anything for your approval on expanding Brown's Botanical. Before you react, let me give you a little more information than when we discussed this the last time." He folded his arms in defense of what I was about to say, but to his credit, kept silent.

"I told you Sally had done all the number crunching to prove this was feasible financially," I started explaining. "She even provided information about an architect that has done historic expansions and is familiar with the Historic Landmarks Board. He did say he has had a lot of success with them."

"What do you mean, he said he had good luck with them?" he asked sternly. "You've spoken with him, yourself?"

Here we go, I thought! "Yes, I did, but don't get all upset." I heard myself sounding apologetic. "I just felt I needed more information before I threw the whole idea out the door. He was very helpful and he knows this is just in a preliminary stage, if it happens at all. It's Alex King. Do you know him?"

Now he really stirred in his chair. "I think we'd better leave to continue this conversation, Anne," he said as got up to settle up our dinner bill.

This was not a good sign. Why did I think the lead into this whole idea was pretty smooth? Now what? Do I back down or play the role of endearing wife that stepped out of line?

When we got in the car I pretended the exit wasn't awkward, so I began the subject matter as we headed home. "What is so wrong here, Sam?" I asked, pretending I had no clue. "I am a business person and will likely continue to be a business person. Why would I turn down any feasible information that is going to improve my business? You, of all people, should understand this. Why wouldn't you be interested enough to know what I learned, knowing this has been on my mind?" I decided I was not backing down as I made my point.

"I'm not interested right now about any details you may have learned, Anne," he said calmly. When he called me Anne, I knew he was being dead serious. "I think the big message here is that you chose to pursue this topic when I was out of town so I wouldn't interfere, right?"

"No, this wasn't planned that way. However, because you were gone, I was free to spend more time at the shop," I explained. "It seemed a good time for me to do more background checking. Please don't make this sound like some conspiracy, Sam."

"Meeting up with Mr. King doesn't present a very pretty picture, Anne, especially when you could have told me on the phone that you met up with him," he said sternly. "A little background checking on your Mr. King may have been the place to start. You knew darn well I wouldn't be happy about any of this, but you did it anyway, behind my back. Correct?"

"You don't check with me when you meet with a female counterpart concerning something that is business related. Why should I have to check with you?" I retorted, raising my voice. "Oh, and I had a salesman come in this week, too, now that I'm confessing my terrible sins!" He did not respond. He just kept driving home.

I sure know how to ruin a perfectly good evening, as well as my own birthday! Silence now hung over us like a black curtain. We both had said things to each other that were hurtful and thought provoking. I couldn't cool my anger. The more I thought of having to apologize, the angrier I became. When I got out of our car, I slammed the door harder than I intended, sending a big signal of my unhappiness.

When we entered the front door, there was a large, beautifully gift-wrapped package on the center round entry table. I stopped to stare at it.

"That's your birthday present from my mother," Sam said, breaking the silence.

"I'm sorry I had to ruin your evening Anne, but perhaps Mother's gift will please you. I didn't have much luck."

I hated seeing Sam like this. He left me alone to open the gift as he went upstairs. I never saw us both react this way. I took a deep breath and tore open the package. Inside the box was a large, beautiful, red and white star quilt. The pattern looked very intricate and quite striking. His mother knew how fond I was of red and white, so, how thoughtful of her! It didn't go in our all-white bedroom, but in one of the extra bedrooms this would be the focal point, for sure. I smiled at the pleasant surprise, which revealed a side of Helen that I liked. I took the wrappings to the kitchen to dispose of them.

Out of the corner of my eye, I noticed a fresh bouquet of white lilies on the kitchen table. I smiled, remembering the new set of gardening tools Grandmother's spirit had put in the potting shed for my birthday last year. These flowers were large and beautiful, to say the least. She wanted me to know they were especially for me on my birthday. "How did you know I needed support right now, Grandmother?" I said out loud, as if she were really listening.

I poured myself a drink. Sitting down at the table, tears began flowing down my cheeks. I raised my glass, half smiling and half crying. "Happy birthday, Anne Dickson," I said to myself. "Here's to being your old independent self and screwing up a perfectly wonderful evening!"

After a good cry, I felt I needed to get up to bed and face the person I cared most about. I'm sure he had plenty of time to think about his terrible and inconsiderate wife. I'm sure he'd be asleep by now. I quietly tiptoed around the room to undress, hoping I wouldn't disturb Sam. I crawled between the covers and snuggled up to my friendly pillow, looking away from Sam. I suddenly felt an arm come around and embrace my body like he had done each night.

"I'm not going to sleep without telling my terrific wife how sorry I am and how selfishly I reacted," he confessed, bringing me closer. "I love you, Annie," he whispered in my ear. I stayed still and quiet, not knowing if I could switch moods and thoughts. "I had no idea how much you wanted this expansion. I'm sorry I wasn't supportive of your thoughts and ideas. Will you forgive me?" He gave me another squeeze.

"I'm too tired right now not to love and forgive you, Sam," I whispered as I turned around and met his lips. "Let me think about it while I kiss your neck, arms, and back. I'll give you an update soon." Hmmm...

CHAPTER 35

The week began with my regularly scheduled events, which took me to the Jane Austen Literary Club. Mother was not able to go, so it allowed me to go a little later. Jean didn't make a fuss when I entered and she immediately had a cup of tea waiting for me.

Roxanne had the floor and was explaining the timelines of Jane's publications. She was so into it, I found it almost humorous. When I sat in the loveseat with Sue, she nudged my arm and rolled her eyes in response to Roxanne's dramatic descriptions. Sue admired my stitching as I pulled my block out of my purse. I saw a couple of others working on their blocks as well. Later in the week was judgment day at the quilt club. Roxanne pulled out her wedding block of Jane and it was darling. She seemed to be really proud of it. The tiny beads sewn in Jane's bridal headpiece were clever and so dainty.

Roxanne closed by reminding everyone of the deadline for the quilt blocks. Abbey surprised us with handmade Jane Austen bookmarks that each had a different quote from Jane. Abbey was so artistic. Perhaps she could design some floral bookmarks for the flower shop. She had the talent to have some kind of creative business, but I didn't think she had much common sense at times. It turned out to be an interesting meeting after all.

"Next month is a tad close to the fire show holiday and all, so I think we'll cancel next month, unless you all think we need to give it a go?" Jean asked. We laughed at her reference to the Fourth of July as a fire show.

"I say we just enjoy the fire show and meet up the next month," Sally said, teasingly. "We'll see each other soon at the quilt club anyway." Everyone clapped, indicating agreement in support of canceling.

I, too, was relieved. I was so absorbed with my stitching and how much I was accomplishing that I didn't realize everyone had left but me.

Jean took a deep breath and joined me with another cup of tea. "You sure took a shining to this block, didn't you, Miss Anne?" Jean said as she sipped her tea.

"I suppose I have, Jean," I admitted. "I find it to be mindless in effort, and yet like a painting that is coming to life. I find the repetition of stitches very relaxing and almost addictive. I think that's why I also love digging in the dirt!" We laughed.

"You do a wonderful job with this literary club, Jean," I said, looking at her beaming with a sense of pride. "I didn't think I'd get much out of it at first, but it's been relaxing and very informative. Your English spirit pulls this off nicely."

"Thanks, Miss Anne," she said, getting up to gather teacups. "I do love it so, and Al knows it gives me pleasure and he's been giving me a helping hand now and then, by golly."

After I helped her gather things to the kitchen, I took my project and said good-bye. I came home to find Sam waiting for me in the study. He was reading the paper with some lovely classical music playing in the background.

"How was literary club?" he said, looking up.

I smiled. "It was pretty boring compared to some nights, which was good because I nearly have my quilt block done for our quilt," I shared. I just told Jean how much I have really enjoyed stitching this.

"May I see it?" he asked, getting out of his favorite chair.

"Sure," I agreed, pulling it out of my bag. "I just have some of the background to finish, but the house itself is done. What do you think?"

He took it from me, carefully examining my work. "You continue to amaze me, Annie," he said admiringly. "You are very talented in many ways. As busy as your days are, you still find time to do something like this. This is very nice and I actually do recognize it!" He laughed at his own joke and then changed the subject. "I was wondering if you'd like me to go with you when you meet with Alex King again."

"If you're truly interested, but it's not necessary," I said, trying not to react too excitedly. "Then...you don't mind if I keep pursuing this idea?"

"I don't know how I could, nor do I think I should. However, I have to be honest with you regarding how I feel about your choice of architects," he said, catching me off guard.

"Really? Why?" I asked.

"Alex and I have a little history, you might say," he said as he took a drink of iced tea by the end table. "I think we need to drop any of the details here, if you don't mind. Just trust me that it will complicate things if you continue to meet with him."

"What on earth could this be about?" I sat nearby to hear more.

"Some of it involves ethical information that I'm not at liberty to discuss, and the rest is personal, which I'd rather not mention." he responded.

I looked at him in total confusion. "Fine, honey. I have no attachment to him in particular, I just took Sally's recommendation," I explained. "He's already done some sketches, which I already have."

"Did you request he do those?" Sam asked, sounding like a businessman.

"No, not really," I commented, shrugging my shoulders.

"That figures," Sam winced. "That's how he does things."

I took the hint and dropped the subject, knowing I had made progress on the expansion idea. I didn't care who my architect would be, as long as the job was done. Now, I would have to figure out how to handle the handsome and mysterious Mr. Bad Guy.

I went upstairs too tired to figure it all out. I walked by the waiting room and saw my paper and pen. At some point, I needed to begin entering what I had written in my notebook into the computer. Before I could think twice, I sat in my chair and picked up the pen to continue my next thoughts starting from where I had left off. It all seemed to flow easier by handwriting the words. I had a relaxing evening that put me in the right frame of mind. Somehow, my mind wasn't on the Taylors tonight. It was on Jane Austen who had taken over my friends and family, both in time and in thoughts. I kept thinking about that quilt we were making and what Jane would think about our members creating something else. Before I knew it, these words came out of my pen:

IF JANE WERE SITTING HERE

If Jane were sitting here, with all her books and fame,
Would she grin or grimace if we make her not the same?
If Jane were sitting here, would her fingers stitch or sew?
Would she approve or question the methods she'd not know?
If Jane were sitting here, would her spirit just be still?
Or would she make a scene or shadow to let us know her will?
I wish our Jane would be sitting here; I'd like to make it so.
I'd wish to ask her many things a writer wants to know.

A good half hour passed when Sam came up behind me and kissed me on the neck. I had lost myself in the moments with Jane. Is she here with me now, as other spirits sometimes are? Somehow, I felt close to her tonight.

"My sweet Annie continues on into the night!" he

whispered. "Come to bed so I can whisper sweet nothings into your ear. You may want to use them in the book."

We laughed and I turned around to meet his face. "You are quite the distraction, Mr. Dickson," I teased. "If you were not such an important character in my book of life, I'd tell you to leave me alone. But since you are so very important, I must obey and take notes along the way! You are my Mr. Darcy that Jane wrote so eloquently about. Mr. Darcy was strong, very mysterious, outspoken, and so very handsome. It is no wonder that women are still enamored by him today. Yes, Sam, you are my own Mr. Darcy. I will love you for the rest of my life."

Sam looked at me as if I were an actress in a play. He took my hand and kissed it. "Yes, and I love you so, Mrs. Darcy," he whispered.

CHAPTER 36

The Jane Austen Quilt Club was well attended when Mother and I walked into Isabella's Quilt Shop. Even I was interested to see this unique quilt take shape. Isabella, taking the place of Nancy, was already instructing us where to place our blocks. Roxanne was running around like a drill sergeant giving directions on this and that as if she were in charge. I put down my pressed block and compliments were coming my way. Practice had certainly helped to improve my stitches. Mother was especially proud of my accomplishments—as mothers should be, right?

Roxanne finally got everyone to sit in their chairs in an effort to get their attention.

"Thank you all so much for these wonderful blocks," Isabella began. "They will come together nicely. By next month, you will see the finished quilt before it is sent off to the quilt competition in Florida. It will compete in the group quilt category. I think we will do well with this clever theme. It certainly will not be like any other quilt there!" Everyone laughed in agreement. "As a thank you from the shop," Isabella continued, "I am giving a twenty-five dollar gift certificate to everyone who finished a block." The group clapped to express its delight. Isabella was smart to make the generous offer. "Now, with your approval, I'm going to show you the appliqué of Jane's silhouette that will be in the center," she announced, holding up the familiar black motif everyone recognized.

We again reacted with approval by clapping our hands. It was a very good copy of the silhouettes I had seen. Her appliqué was perfect and neat. Seeing some of the other block designs was quite interesting. I wondered if they all had a story behind them, as did mine and some of the others.

From the back of the room someone yelled, "What will we work on now?" This person needs a life, I thought to myself.

"I have some ideas and we'll discuss them next month," Isabella answered. "I've heard some of you say you need a break." Voices of approval came from the group. Yes! A break, for sure! "Paige and Sally brought refreshments tonight, so please thank them and enjoy." Applause erupted once more. Sally was certainly getting into the baking thing. Her lemon bars and cookies were delicious!

I got up to take a closer look at the blocks and was amazed at everyone's creativity. As crazy as some were, there were none that presented Jane in a distasteful way. One block was a birthday cake with Jane's birth date written with icing. Some very clever artist created Jane's writing desk. I wished instantly I had thought of that. The one that really caught my fancy was five little sunbonnets in a row, each representing the five Bennet sisters. The maker must be as taken with *Pride and Prejudice* as I. Frankly, why we hadn't decided to create an entire *Pride and Prejudice* quilt was beyond me. Perhaps that could be our next endeavor. Oh dear, what was I thinking? I did have a life. Hmmm...

"Oh, before I forget, Alex King called the shop after you left today. He was looking for you," confided Sally, who was now sitting next to me.

"Thanks, I'll call him tomorrow," I responded, wanting to change the subject for now. I would have to handle him without offending Sally.

"Will I get to see those sketches sometime soon, Anne?" she asked, grinning.

"I haven't even seen them myself, but I'm sure we can take a peek tomorrow," I replied, ending the topic. She seemed to be satisfied.

On the way home, I asked Mother if she had seen Harry Stone lately. She said she had not seen him since he came over for dinner. "His literary background is so impressive," she bragged. "He studied to be a professor, but didn't like what came with it all. Interestingly enough, he would have liked to have opened his own bookstore, but his wife became ill and then died. He seems to be very happy, however, working for the Pointers all these years." She had really taken an interest in this man, I noted.

"I was talking to Sue earlier and she is free tomorrow night to get started quilting on Jean's quilt," she continued. "Would you be able to come over for a while? Jean will be there, of course, and I'll call Julia in the morning."

"I'll try. I want to help with that," I said, thinking about Jean. "Nancy will still be gone, I think. We should have been doing this sooner. Sam is going out of town just for the night. I'd like to think I'll use that time to write, but there's always an excuse to do something else. I certainly want to help Jean with her quilt."

"If you'd rather not, Anne, it's no big deal. You are so busy," Mother sympathized.

"I'm neglecting the gardens, too!" I said, taking a deep breath in frustration. "The good news is I don't have to drag paperwork home as much since I have Sally to manage the shop."

"I figure if we all come early enough, it will give me an excuse to make that hot chicken salad recipe," she said, thinking about food again. "I'll whip up a salad and serve some warm bread. How about that? Tempted, my dear?"

"You know what buttons to push, Mother dear," I teased. "I'll do my best. You haven't made that dish in quite some time! I love it! How will I ever learn to cook for myself when I am still being spoiled with your good cooking?" She smiled.

Sam was sound asleep when I got home. His deep breathing meant I didn't have to be very quiet. I changed and slid in the sheets beside his body. So many thoughts were running through my mind. Tomorrow, I would have to face Alex King and somehow explain to Sally why Alex was not going to be the one to help us with the expansion. What was really the problem with Sam and Alex? Did I really want to know? Perhaps when I tell Sally I got a green light from Sam, it would not matter to her that Alex was not going to do the plans. I would have to find someone new.

After some thought, I decided I should bring this expansion news to the entire staff when we were together, so there wouldn't be hard feelings about whom I may be close to. We really were in this together, even though it was my pocketbook. They would be delighted, so perhaps we could have a meeting one night at the shop to share ideas. Why couldn't I just go to sleep to forget about all this tonight? As I gazed the room with my eyes wide open, it seemed unusually light. I moved out quietly from the covers and walked over to the window facing the street. There was a bright full moon smiling at me. No wonder it was so light. It was beautiful and romantic. I felt I was closer to the moon at 333 Lincoln than at my home on Melrose Street. I felt I belonged on this elevated piece of heaven on the hill.

The quaint town of Colebridge was down below by the river. Everyone else was at rest or asleep as the town below looked dark and silent. Was anyone else up besides me? Was Isabella up planning the Jane Austen quilt? Was Mother wide awake thinking of Harry Stone? Was Aunt Julia feeling lonely without her Harry? Was Nancy awake thinking of how she was going to entice Richard to want to start a family? Was Sally feeling underappreciated with Brown's Botanical? Was weird Roxanne fantasizing about being Jane? Did Colebridge really have some homeless folks like I read about in the paper this morning? Okay, it was too much for my simple little mind. I went back to bed and hoped my dreams didn't turn into finding Jane Austen homeless on Main Street! Hmmm...

CHAPTER 37

A fter seeing Sam off the next morning, I took my coffee to the south porch to plan my day instead of taking a brisk walk. I was dragging from lack of sleep, so I just needed to think. The morning was glorious. June was the perfect month in Missouri. It wasn't too hot and the mornings and nights could still be a little cool. Mark Twain was quoted as saying he thought October was the perfect month for Missouri. He said the goldenrods would be blooming and harvesting would be over. He had a point, but October was too much an introduction to winter for my taste.

I wanted nature's clear colors and perfect temperatures. Did I love pearls because the pearl was June's birthstone and did I love roses because the rose was June's birth flower? No doubt the Gemini sign fit me perfectly. My two personalities continued to conflict and yet came in handy at times. At least I had a choice, I humorously told myself. My independent business side confronted the romantic little girl in me all the time. I think I even noticed two different tones of voices as I lived them out. Was I lucky to have two options for what was needed in my life, or was it somewhat of a curse? Hmmm...

The deep red geraniums I had planted in the gazebo's flower boxes were doing nicely. Sprinkles of the sweet potato leaves were creeping over the edges, along with a few vines of ivy. I felt their dry soil and decided they needed water, so I set down my coffee and grabbed the hose from the side of the house.

The grounds here at 333 Lincoln could absolutely be a showplace, had it the time and attention of its owner, or a professional gardener. Maybe I could talk the lawn folks into doing some extra tasks. It wouldn't be as extravagant as spending money on a professional gardener, would it? The weeds were going mad, too mad to keep up, for sure. The inside of the potting shed always seemed to be the object of my attention, however, so when I finished watering the boxes, I made my way to my little slice of heaven. I watered the herb garden and a few rose bushes along the way. I then thought of all the lilies I planted, in Grandmother's honor, at the side of the shed. They should be nurtured as well. Perhaps this was the time I should take to talk to her, to keep her calm and behaved. The lilies did make me smile, and I'm sure she knew it. I took my time to make sure no plant was thirsty at 333 Lincoln. Oh, the time was moving on and I still didn't have much of a plan for the day. I could stay out here all day, I told myself. I hurried into the house to dress and get to the shop, taking my coffee with me.

The checkout counter had a couple of customers waiting when I arrived, and Jean and Sally were both attending to them as I cheerfully said hello.

"Good morning," one lady said to me. I didn't recognize her at all. "It's a beautiful day out there!" She followed me to my desk.

"You don't recognize me, do you?" she asked with a grin.

"I can't say I do," I responded.

"That's okay," she said. "I work for Alex King as a receptionist. You came in one day to meet with him. I can't tell you how pleased he is to be helping you with your expansion. You certainly could use more room here, that is certain! I'm surprised you didn't expand years ago. My family has been a good customer of yours for years. I know your mother from the bookstore."

Well, what a busybody, I thought to myself. Who was she to say I needed more room? Was she here for Alex to seal the deal? I wasn't in the mood to fall into her nosiness concerning my business.

"Well, I guess after all this information I must tell you that my expansion plans are not only on hold, but this is also information I consider confidential with Mr. King. I'm sure your boss would not approve of you sharing his business or mine. Please excuse me. I have a very busy day." I turned and began walking away, not entirely believing what I had just done.

"Oh, Anne. I'm sorry," she quickly responded. "I only meant to give you a word of encouragement."

"Thanks," I said turning to see her face. "I'm Mrs. Dickson, by the way."

She turned around and went directly out the door. Sally and Jean were stunned and speechless. Thank goodness no one else remained in the store to hear my rudeness. Perhaps my hormones were taking over my emotions.

"Sally, please notify Kevin, Abbey, and Sue that I want to have a meeting tomorrow morning before we open to discuss the expansion of Brown's Botanical," I announced.

Jean and Sally looked at each other like I had gone mad. Sally nodded with approval, not wanting to ask any questions.

"Jolly good show, Miss Anne," Jean said. "I'd say that was a fair crack of the whip, by the way!" We burst into laughter. Leave it to Jean to break the ice on nearly any tension.

"I'll get right on it, Anne," Sally said, smiling as she shook her head in disbelief.

"Sally, just so you know, we need to find a different architect," I announced. Her look was one of puzzlement, but I could tell she wasn't going to question my decision at this point.

"Can you help me with that? Bring all the research you have done and any other items on your wish list to the meeting tomorrow so we can get started. Oh, and just so you both know, Mr. Dickson is on board." They lifted their arms as in a statement of victory and cheered.

The quilting at Mother's that night was just what I needed. The aroma of the hot chicken salad brought back great memories of my mother serving it for many luncheons years ago with her card group. Our attendance was small with only me, Mother, Jean, Aunt Julia, and Sue. Sue brought Mia and her dog, Muffin, which made it extra lively, as always. Mia pulled at the high-seated chair that she remembered sitting in for various occasions. She knew good things were tasted in that chair. We managed to all sit around the crowded kitchen table that was full of various chatter as we enjoyed the comforting food.

Aunt Julia brought an early birthday cake for Jean in case

we didn't see her in a few days when Jean would celebrate her actual birth date. The angel food cake was covered in whipped cream with strawberries perfectly arranged on the top.

"That was so sweet of you, Aunt Julia," I said, preparing to take the cake downstairs. "How did you know it was her birthday?"

"Because when she said it one night at the literary club, I took notice that it was the same as Jim's birthday," she said, with an unmistakable sadness in her voice.

"Oh, my goodness, it is," I noted. "How is he doing, by the way? I'll send him a card in the morning. I wonder if Sam remembers or knows of it?"

"Sarah said he likes his job, but that's really all I know," she shared.

"Come on, girls," Mother yelled from the basement. "We need the coffeepot down here. I have cups and plates." I quickly grabbed the coffeepot and Aunt Julia lifted the beautiful cake as we headed down the stairs.

"You all have such openness of heart. This is a gift of love, indeed," Jean said, smiling at us. "I will treasure each bite with delight!"

Sue then took a photo on her cell phone as we posed. Mia begged for more attention, requiring a few more photos with cake all over her face. Mia had a habit of dropping bits to Muffin who was running around her chair. It appeared Sue got a shot of her doing just that.

"It didn't take much persuasion to talk everyone into coming to a basement quilting, Jean," Mother said affectionately. "Your birthday just makes it extra special."

"Do you want us to sing *Happy Birthday*?" asked Sue in a teasing way.

ANN HAZELWOOD

"Please, no, no, I dare say the cake is quite enough and such a delicious surprise," Jean said with a glow. "If it weren't for Miss Anne here and my fancy for the flower shop, I'd have the misfortune of not being here at all!" They all clapped and said their happy birthdays personally. She was really such a gift to all of us!

Before we tasted Aunt Julia's special angel food cake, we caught up with what was happening in our own little worlds. Sue brought us up to date with some of the cute goings on with Mia. Mia loved books, so Mother made sure there were new ones to entertain her. Mia sat for a spell in the little rocking chair that was made for me when I was about the same age. Would that little chair ever live at 333 Lincoln? I wondered about that for a moment, watching little Mia enjoy the books.

"I may as well share with you a little secret from the flower shop, since you are all family," I began. "Jean already knows, but tomorrow morning, we have an important meeting at the shop to discuss the expansion of Brown's Botanical."

The silence was sudden and Mother, of all people, was not smiling. Jean's knowledge of the meeting and its challenges caused her to look down, not knowing how everyone would react. I could feel she was going to stay out of this conversation.

"Congratulations, Anne," Aunt Julia finally spoke. "You've obviously figured out how it can be done. Good for you!" Mother still wasn't talking or smiling.

"We are all going to do whatever it takes to make this a good decision," Sue added. "I really miss going in once in awhile to help out. When Mia starts preschool, I hope to be more helpful there. It sure will be nice to have more space." Jean was still silent.

"Mother, I know you worry I am doing too much, but I now have Sam's support," I said, looking directly into her eyes only. "He knows how much this means to me. He also has no reservations that it will be a good business move. I don't think anyone could disagree with that." Mother was still listening and looking for the right words to respond."Sally has taken the initiative here, which I give her credit for. She has invested her time, along with all of us, to make the shop successful. I'll be able to service most weddings after that, which is a huge market we have been missing." I waited for her response.

"That's my Anne," she finally responded, forcing a smile. "She takes after her father. When he got something in his head, it was impossible to change his mind. If there is a will, there is always a way, he would say." She got up from her seat and came over to kiss my cheek. "If anyone can pull this off, it's you, Anne," she said lovingly. "You have my blessing, along with your father's."

I wanted to cry, right there in front of everyone.

"Thanks. It means a lot!" I managed to say with most of my emotions intact.

"Now, we'll have some of that delicious birthday cake," Mother announced as she went to cut the slices. In the end, we made a couple of toasts, the first to Jean, our birthday girl, and then to the future success of Brown's Botanical Flower Shop. Mother then jokingly lifted her glass to toast Grandmother Davis and my Aunt Marie, who were part of the family and the basement quilters.

CHAPTER 38

Having slept like a baby, I woke with new energy, having made a decision about the shop's expansion. Before I went downstairs, I called Sam on my cell to find him in a coffee shop with a business associate. We chatted briefly and he said he'd see me later this evening. Certainly he could sense my good mood.

When I came downstairs, I saw the red and white quilt still in the box that Helen so generously gave me for my birthday. I still needed to call and thank her, which I decided to do immediately. She wasn't too awake as we spoke, but I assured her I loved it and I was going to decorate one of the bedrooms in red and white. I told her Sam loved it as well, which I knew would mean more than me telling her my response. To my surprise, she then announced that if she were up to it, she would be coming to Colebridge for Sam's birthday in July. I encouraged her to do so, despite my own reservations, but I wanted to be a good daughter-in-law. I would cross that challenge when I came to it. Today was about sharing my plans with my shop family.

I picked up some baked goods from the IGA and greeted all the early arrival faces when I came in the door. Sally had already put on a pot of coffee, which I was indeed ready for, welcoming a cup before beginning my speech.

I began the meeting by giving Sally credit for putting the expansion feasibility picture in front of me. I avoided mentioning anything about Alex King and told them the proper professionals would be hired soon. At first, they all hung on every word I said, munching on their rolls and drinking their coffee. It wasn't long before the excitement erupted with ideas and happy responses.

The most surprising suggestions came from Kevin, who had wonderful input and even suggested an architect that had done the designing at the Q Seafood and Grill. Knowing the shop would have to open soon, I told them I would give them frequent updates in e-mail, so everyone would be on the same page. They loved it and clapped at the conclusion of my meeting. Sue was the first to leave to get to her job and I asked Abbey to stay at the shop while I ran an errand.

I grabbed the sketches from Mr. King without giving them one peek. I did not want to be influenced by anything this man had suggested. When I got to his office, I was greeted coldly by the nosey receptionist who had paid me a visit at the shop. She told me Mr. King was not in the office. I handed her the sketches and told her she could tell Mr. King that his services would not be needed, but that I appreciated his interest. I then sharply turned around, feeling a big load off my shoulders. I felt a quick smile on my face.

When I got back to the shop, there was a phone message from Carl at the historical society. He said he found something I might be interested in. Hmmm...

I had the payroll to work on or I would have dropped everything to see what he had to show me. Further information on the Taylor family would have to wait.

Between waiting on customers, Sally and Jean were working on a Fourth of July display when Roxanne walked into the shop. I could hear her talking to the girls and wondered if she was giving us business or gossip. She then asked for me, so at the request, I went to the front counter.

"Hey, Roxanne, what brings you to the flower shop today?" I asked cheerfully.

"Well, I do want to get that cute little watering can I saw for sale in the window, but I also wondered if I could get an honest reaction from the three of you on something concerning the Austen quilt." We waited silently for her to continue.

"What about the quilt?" asked Sally. "Did some people not turn in their blocks?"

"Well, a few backed out on completion, which was no big deal," Roxanne responded. "I have to say that I just saw the top completed and it is magnificent! You did nice embroidery work on the house, Anne. What is a concern of mine, and some others I might add, is Isabella's decision to send the quilt off to compete in a national quilt show. It is a huge risk. You realize that if the quilt becomes a prizewinner, which it likely will, it will travel in an exhibit for some period of time. Isabella said at the last meeting that any prize money would go to a charity, and then who knows what will happen to the quilt in the future? We all have put too much into the quilt not to know that." We stood with our eyes squinted and wondered what point she was trying to make.

"First of all, Roxanne, do you honestly think we have a prizewinning quilt?" I said, employing a joking tone. "You are assuming a lot here. I certainly have no problem with prize money going to charity. None of us made it to make money, that's for sure! I'm sure Isabella would see to it that the quilt ends up in the proper place."

"Oh, Roxanne, wouldn't you be as proud as punch to have that quilt travel the countryside?" Jean asked. "It would strike the fancy of every Jane Austen admirer for sure. Right, Miss Anne? I know I'm exceedingly proud my block made the cut! Don't get your knickers in a twist over a nice deed by Isabella! It's just a silly quilt, for heaven's sake!" Roxanne frowned and was definitely offended.

"Jean's right," Sally added. "You're worrying about nothing. For heaven's sake, what do you think Isabella should do? She's showing how pleased she is with our work and wants to show it off."

"It should stay here in Colebridge where it belongs," Roxanne said, almost shaking. "We may never see it again. I think she's just thinking of the publicity for the shop. She's determined to follow her plan, so I told her to be sure to get it appraised." In the back of my mind, I wondered how much Roxanne had told Isabella of her strong feelings.

"Oh, I'm sure she will," I said, hoping to assure Roxanne. "I actually heard Isabella say she was going to do that before it was sent off. Should I ring up this watering can for you?" She knew I wanted to change the subject, even without her blessing.

"I'm pleased you think it turned out so great, Roxanne,"

Sally said as she went back to hanging a patriotic swag over the window. "I can't wait to see it!"

"That would be a jolly good problem to have if we won, don't you think?" Jean asked Roxanne.

Roxanne winced, not wanting to answer as she paid for her purchase. "Okay then, ladies, we'll hope for the best," Roxanne said, going out the door.

We all shrugged our shoulders at the interruption and worked until closing time. The payroll was done and so was my happy red, white, and blue flower shop.

CHAPTER 39

I was getting comfortable with coming home to an empty 333 Lincoln. Part of me really loved the time alone, which I didn't typically seem to have much of in my life, but then part of me saw Sam in every nook and cranny, which made me long for his presence. This was truly our house, not just mine. Sam was expected to arrive at home late, so I went upstairs to change into shorts so I could check on the potting shed, water flowers, and if time allowed, pull a few weeds.

When I went to grab a bottle of water from the kitchen to take outdoors, I saw Grandmother's lilies still remaining fresh on the kitchen table, just like they had at her lover's grave for many years. Earlier, when we all had learned of Albert Taylor's illegitimate child with my grandmother, the lilies had died.

I had to keep reminding myself that my grandmother's love for him never died, even though he married someone else and lived many years in this very house at 333 Lincoln. I found myself repeating to everyone that it was why she couldn't seem to move on and remained here all these years as the ghost of 333 Lincoln, which everyone talked about. I understood and loved her, but Grandmother's behavior was destructive at times and loving at other times. I guess she felt she was the one that deserved to live here with him and was not going to leave until she was good and ready. How patient would Sam and I continue to be with her? What choice did we really have?

I went out into the late heat of the day and opened up the hot potting shed for cooler air. With the door and windows open, the breeze on the hill was just what it needed. The thriving weeds were calling to me from everywhere. The sturdy shaded wild ferns under some of the trees had automatically returned there as they had for years, it appeared. I found them most delightful and they seemed to be independent in their nature, choosing to pop up wherever they pleased, multiplying at will. My cell phone suddenly went off.

"Anne?" the familiar voice said.

"Yes, it is," I answered, unable to quickly place the voice.

"It's Alex King," Oh no, I thought to myself. "I'm sorry I missed your visit today. I had a meeting," he began. "I was sorry to hear you had changed your mind, so I'm calling to see if we could meet to discuss this further." Before I could respond, he kept going. "Are you already home or can we just meet for a drink?"

I had to interrupt him. "Alex, there's no need to continue this conversation," I inserted quickly. "I'm sorry, but I'm rethinking the project in general and I feel badly you took it on your own to do so much work. I have to take my time with this."

Alex then took his turn to interrupt. "Anne, I think you were the one who sought me out on this project, and yes, I did spend a fair amount of time on this but it's more than that," he said firmly. "I have always admired you in many ways, you might say. I looked forward to getting to know you better through this process. I'm not going to charge you for anything so far, but I know we can achieve what you are wanting. I think we would work well together." His voice softened as if he could still persuade me.

I paused to recapture what I had just heard. Yes, there was more to this, just as I feared. I knew this was turning into another conversation that made me feel uncomfortable. He was fishing to see if I was attracted to him and if I would go for the generous free work and personal attention he might give. How did this go so wrong?

"Anne, are you still there?" he finally said, following the obvious silence I provided.

"Oh, yes, I am," I answered in a professional voice. "I'm sure I should be flattered, but, as I said, I am no longer interested in pursuing this and I'm sorry if I gave you any other impression. I need to go now, Alex. Thanks again for everything."

I clicked before I could hear his voice respond. I can't believe I just hung up on him. Sam would have a fit if he had heard this conversation. I didn't know what Sam had on this Mr. King, but I knew for certain I did not want to be part of it. I didn't know if I should have been flattered or insulted by his attempt to get to know me. Did he decide to pursue me because of ill feelings with Sam? Hmmm...

I was working up an appetite pulling weeds faster and faster as I thought about the phone call. I went in the house, showered, and then returned to the kitchen. The refrigerator offered me nothing but a quick omelet that I could throw together with onion, cheese, tomatoes, and green pepper.

I took my improvised dinner to the south porch where the full moon became my dinner companion. The temperature turned the evening into a pleasant one as I watched the sun go down. I decided to call Mother since I hadn't heard from her in some time. It seemed our calls were happening less and less. When she answered, she said she was in the basement quilting all alone. With a happy tone in her voice, she explained she wasn't quite ready for bed, so she thought she'd put in some quilting on Jean's quilt. Her topic quickly turned to telling me she had a nice lunch with Harry that day. She suggested to Harry that they take a drive over to see Amanda and William one afternoon, and he thought it was a wonderful idea.

"Mother, I feel terrible I haven't made time for them myself, but I have been a little sidetracked, to say the least," I confessed. "I have them on my invitation list for Sam's birthday party. I'm on the south porch right now looking at the gazebo, which just reminded me of it, remembering how we celebrated his birthday when I gave him the gazebo for his gift. Helen said she is thinking of coming in for his birthday, so I guess she is recovering okay. I wish I could be more excited about it. Oh, Mother, did I tell you about the beautiful red and white quilt she sent with Sam for my birthday?"

"No, you didn't," she said, surprised. "That was very generous and thoughtful of her, Anne."

"Yes, it was, and I really, really like it," I said proudly. "It's a star pattern of some kind. It will be perfect for one of the back guest rooms that I want to decorate in all red and white. So back to lunch, Mother. I take it you are still enjoying Harry's company?" I was now getting back to the subject that held my interest most.

"Yes, it's quite nice," she said softly. "Sometimes, he just stops by after work and we have a cocktail on the porch or in the den. He tells me about the store happenings of the day, knowing how much I know about it and all!"

"That is pretty cool, Mother," I admitted. "It makes me happy when you are happy." I was hoping she could feel my smile over the phone.

"Are you and that husband of yours still happy, sweetie?" she asked, taking me by surprise.

"Yes," I firmly responded. "I am going to try to stay up for him this evening, but I was exhausted from the shop and then I put in a couple of hours of yard work, so we'll see. There is so much to tend to in this yard, as you know. I'm sure Sam will be glad to still see me awake."

Mother thought that was an excellent idea if I could be up for him since he may have had an exhausting day himself. It was just like Mother to always think of the other person instead of herself. She was right. Sam would likely be as exhausted as his dear wife.

When Sam finally arrived, I was curled up on the leather couch in the den, about to doze off. The TV was on and I had draped Helen's quilt over me during the course of the evening as the temperatures had lowered. His gentle kiss on my forehead was a welcome ending to a very, very, long, stressful day. He was touched that I had waited up for him and attempted to carry me up the stairs. As I quickly became more alert, I got on my feet to avoid any additional stress for Sam.

"Let's just lean on each other to get to that comfy bed of ours," I suggested. With arms around each other, we did just that.

CHAPTER 40

When I took my walk the next morning, I tried to think of when I could go by the archives to find out what Carl had discovered for me. I was determined not to let the plans of the shop expansion take over my life now that I decided to do it. Sam and Mother would be waiting to jump all over me for that. I had a lot to accomplish for the day, which included a phone call to Jason Cunningham, the architect suggested by Kevin.

When I returned to the house from my walk, Nora was waiting for me on the south porch. She wasn't smiling when I opened the door to let us in.

"Oh, Nora, I'm sorry I forgot you were coming today," I said, feeling overwhelmed by all my thoughts. "Can you go ahead and get started? I have so much on my plate today, but maybe I can do some of my work at home this morning, like phone calls and e-mails." It was becoming a pain that she refused to clean in the house alone.

"Okay, Miss Anne," she said hesitantly. "I'll work as quickly as I can."

I took my coffee upstairs with me to shower. I passed by the room that had my pen and pencil waiting for me. Perhaps Carl would have some information I could use the next time I wrote.

I looked up the number of Jason Cunningham and made an appointment for the end of the week. He was pleased about Kevin's referral and said he'd be happy to help me. He sounded younger than Alex King. Do I invite Sam to come along with me to be courteous or do I insist from day one to handle this by myself? Hmmm...

I came down to use the computer in the study, where I found Nora dusting at a quick pace. When she saw me, she started complaining about how the windows needed a good washing.

" I haven't even thought of that," I answered innocently. "You are so right! I should notice things like that more, shouldn't I? Do you do that or do I need to hire someone else?"

"No, ma'am," she firmly stated. "I don't like heights. It's bad enough I have to do my own windows at home."

"Okay, I'll take care of it," I assured her as I realized that was another thing to put on my to-do list. "Running this house is all new to me, Nora, so please be patient. When I'm at the shop I feel guilty I'm not here, and when I'm here, I feel guilty I'm not at the shop!" She didn't seem amused or sorry for me.

"Speaking of the shop, Nora, I really have to get going soon. Won't you please, please stay to finish here today without me? I know the upstairs needs attention, so I don't want you to let that go." She stared at me like I had asked her to step in broken glass.

I didn't look at her, hoping to get a positive answer.

"Okay, just this once I guess," she said, hesitating once more. "I sure can't leave just yet. I'll change the bed linens if I have the time. You sure are always in a rush, Mrs. Dickson."

"Oh, it would be great if you could do that," I said, getting my things together. "I'm used to being rushed, Nora. There is never enough time. I still have the key I wanted you to take. I'll set it right here on the desk. All you have to do is make sure you turn on the alarm before you leave and then lock the door." I pointed out where she could turn it on and she nodded. "You can use the front or back door. Thanks so much, Nora. I don't know what I'd do without you! I'll call and get someone on the windows. I appreciate you suggesting that." I made sure the computer was off, grabbed my purse, and got the key for her before she changed her mind.

"I'm curious why you keep bringing home these lilies, Mrs. Dickson," Nora asked as I got near the door.

"I told you to call me Anne," I stated. "You know, they cheer me up and they last forever!" She gave me a strange look as I went out the door to begin my list for the day.

"Good to see you, Mrs. Dickson," Carl said when I walked to the front counter of the historical society on Main Street. He appeared to be the only one there.

"Thanks for remembering my requests about the Taylor family," I said, hoping to get right to the point.

"I really don't have that much, but I figure a picture might be meaningful to you," he said, going into the back room.

When he returned, he had a full newspaper-size page that

contained a feature article and photograph from the once-published *Colebridge Herald* newspaper. The title of the article read *Taylor Enterprises Celebrates 10 Years.*

"It says it was taken at their celebration at the Colebridge Country Club," read Carl. "I would guess these were their employees. They sure grew to be quite a large corporation since then."

I took a closer look to read the names of the people in the photograph. Albert Taylor was behind a podium and there were people standing on each side. Only one woman was included. There she was. There was Martha Abbot, my grandmother. She was so beautiful and young looking. She had hair like my Aunt Julia. No wonder Albert was attracted to her. She looked happy and innocent in the photo.

"Carl, I'm in kind of a hurry, so could you make a copy of this for me?" I asked, still wanting to read more.

"Sure, Anne," he offered. "I can probably get you a little more information on his company, but I haven't run across anything personal about his family."

"That's fine. It's nothing urgent," I said, taking his photocopy. "This is pretty helpful. Do I owe you anything?"

"Heavens, no, that's what we're here for," he said with a big smile.

I thanked him and out the door I went. When I arrived at the shop, the front room was filled and all were busy, making me feel terrible for my absence. The phone was repeatedly ringing in the background.

"Oh, Anne, thank goodness you're here," Sally said, doing two things at once. "Can you get the phone? It just keeps ringing. I guess they know we have to be here!"

I rushed to answer, ready to give an apology, but it was

Nora. She was out of breath.

"Miss Anne, I'm calling you from my house," she said hysterically. "I left your house unlocked and I didn't turn on the alarm." She was panting as if out of breath.

"You left?" I quickly responded. "Why did you do that?"

"As soon as you left, I went upstairs to clean, starting with that little room off of your bedroom." She now was nearly in tears and breathing even harder. "When I went in there, your tablet and pen flew in the air like a big gust of wind had come along. Your papers went everywhere! There was no way in God's heaven that wind could have come from anywhere. It became freezing cold and scary as all get out. I had to get out of there quick. I ran downstairs and out the front door to my truck. You've got some kind of creature in there, Miss Anne. I'm so, so sorry I had to leave the house unlocked—thought you'd better know. I'm not going back there again. I'm sorry."

"Calm down, Nora," I said, knowing my grandmother's mischievous and destructive behavior. "I shouldn't have left you alone. I promise I won't do it again."

"No siree, Mrs. Dickson. I'm stayin' away for good!" she said bluntly. "I'm sorry to do this to you, but I can't work there! You all better be careful, that's all I can say!"

I apologized once again, but she hung up as if it were dangerous to talk to me. I could tell she had reported to me out of a sense of duty, so I could lock up the house. At least I had to give her credit for calling me. This is just what I need right now. Why couldn't Grandmother help me instead of throwing obstacles my way? Why would she want to scare Nora, of all people? Why wouldn't she move out of 333 Lincoln?

CHAPTER 41

⟨✦⟩

With a thoughtless explanation to the staff, I said I had to leave right away and would call them later. As I drove quickly home in my steaming hot car, I became more and more frustrated about having to deal with this spiritual interaction at 333 Lincoln. I went in the unlocked front door and went directly upstairs to the waiting room. Sure enough, I followed a paper trail leading to the desk where papers were flung everywhere. My red pen and red journal from Sam were on the floor. I started gathering papers and told myself I would put them in order at a later time. Many unflattering words were repeated in my frustration. I had to be careful with whom I shared this incident. How was I going to explain the runaway cleaning lady?

After a presentable pick up, I phoned to check in with Sally at the shop. She was worried about me leaving the shop so suddenly and asked if everything was okay. After I said it was nothing, just something I had to do right away at home, she dropped the subject and told me I should just stay here. She said everything was under control and Kevin was taking the last delivery. The blazing heat from the afternoon had kept walk-in traffic away, so they were now just cleaning up. The good and bad news told me I had a pocket of free time. My first order of business was to change clothes and then do watering outdoors before addressing any e-mails or shop-related business on the computer. It would be three more hours before Sam would be coming home for dinner. If I hurried, I could get to the IGA and cook something for us. Perhaps there could be some normalcy and good from this crazy day.

When I went outdoors to water, I remembered the newspaper article in the car and brought it inside. My curiosity got the best of me. I wanted to read it slowly, even though there wasn't much length to the article. I went to the refrigerator to get a bottle of cold water and there was a pitcher of lemonade. Hmmm...another attempt from Grandmother to say she was sorry.

I grabbed my water and closed the door. I sat down at the kitchen table where I once again saw Grandmother's pretty face in print. She was likely so in love at that point in her life. Albert Taylor was an average-looking guy, but men with power always became more attractive. Somehow, it was hard to think of them as lovers. Her appearance really reminded me of Aunt Julia. It didn't list the titles of the people; it listed just their names, so I wondered if she worked as a secretary or more than that. Perhaps Mother would remember. The description went on to brag about the company's rapid growth nationally and internationally. I thought of the letters from London he wrote to his wife, Marion. It listed some of Mr. Taylor's organizations, such as the president of the Colebridge Citizen's Bank as well as the Progressive Pioneers of Colebridge. I wasn't sure how helpful this article was, but it did confirm that my grandmother worked for Albert and seemed pretty happy at that time. Food for thought, I said as I made my way out the back door to the potting shed.

It was like an oven at this time of day. I propped up some cardboard sheets to shade some of the heavy light from the two windows and then went to get the water hose. I should have waited until the evening to water, but convenience was never an option. I felt I was giving temporary relief to my green friends. Tempted to turn the hose on myself, I was reminded I had to get to the IGA grocery store.

In short order, by the time Sam walked in, my salad was made, pasta was cooking, and there were fresh beef filets laid out, in hopes that Sam would choose to grill. He was shocked to find such a welcome with the kitchen table set like a normal home. Beside his plate was the newspaper article. His welcome kiss was met with cold lemonade from Grandmother's fresh supply that I had already poured into a fine crystal goblet. He asked no questions as he took his first swallow.

"Why and how does a man like me deserve this, Miss Annie?" he said with a pleasing smile.

"I'm trying to turn a rotten day into a rather pleasant one," I said sheepishly.

"Tell me all about it," he said, pulling me onto his lap. "Start with the rotten part."

I took a deep breath and pulled myself back from him. "I had to make a quick trip home around noon today," I began.

"I left Nora here so she could finish her cleaning. I know now I shouldn't have, but I stayed here with her as long as I could. I had so much to do today and I wanted to go by the archives on my way to work to get the article Carl found for me. You'll have to look at that." I pointed to what sat beside his plate. He was listening closely.

"When I got to work, Nora called me, hysterically saying she left our house quite suddenly and hadn't locked the door or turned on the alarm," I confided, shaking my head in disbelief.

"And why would that be?" Sam asked with a wrinkled face.

"She said she went in the waiting room upstairs to clean, and papers started flying everywhere and it felt like a wild bluster of cold air. She said my journal and pen went flying. It scared her immensely and she ran out the door and called me when she got back home." I looked for some kind of reaction.

"So, was it true or something she imagined?" he asked very calmly.

"Oh yes, quite the mess, I'm afraid," I continued. "I hurried home from the shop and found the pen and journal you gave me were under the desk. I gathered up the papers, but I'll have to organize them later."

Sam shook his head in disbelief and took another sip of his lemonade. "I don't know what to say, Anne," he said in disgust. "Eventually, in time, she will move on, or we will have to do something to force her to move on. I just hope she doesn't hurt anyone, especially you!"

"Oh, she's not going to hurt me physically, but she's driving me nuts and making my life harder," I explained. Good luck forcing Grandmother to do anything! "The worst part is now

I have to find a new cleaning lady and a window washer on top of everything else I have to do! If she wants to please me, why doesn't she clean my house, water my flowers, and help me write my book? No, she couldn't possibly do that!"

I knew from the look on Sam's face that it was the wrong thing to say. He had been telling me over and over how overextended I might be getting, especially since I decided to add onto the shop. I jumped off his lap and changed the subject by asking him if he would grill the filets.

"Sure, I'll do it in a second, but let me take a look at this article," he said, picking it up. "This is your grandmother, right? She doesn't look very mean there."

"Yes, isn't she beautiful?" I bragged. "It's interesting that she is the only woman in the photo. I think she looks like Aunt Julia, don't you?"

"Yes, she does, as a matter of fact," he agreed. "It's rather ironic that Julia had the biggest problem with her. So, why isn't she giving Julia all the grief now instead of you?" he asked.

"She's not the one living in the house that Grandmother feels some right to." I went to answer the ringing phone as I watched Sam read the article. It was Nancy saying she was back in town.

"I'm so glad to be back," Nancy announced, sounding relieved. "I forgot how controlling the Barristers could be. Never mind my drama, how have things been for you? The last time we talked, you were thinking about expanding the flower shop. Is anything happening with that?"

She finally let me get a word in. "Yes, I'll have to fill you in," I said, perking up. "We're about to have dinner, so may I call you later?"

She kept talking. "Well, another reason I'm calling is that Isabella said the quilt is finished and she'd like us all to meet tomorrow night," she explained.

"Tomorrow night?" I responded. "Our regular meeting isn't supposed to be until next week."

"I know, but she has to get this shipped as soon as possible," she said with urgency in her voice. "She wants everyone to see it and have a little celebration at the shop. She is inviting the press in hopes of some publicity. We could catch up there. I'm helping her call everyone since it is such short notice."

I could learn some lessons about publicity from Isabella, I told myself. "Well, under the circumstances, you know I'll be there," I said, giving in to another request. "I'll pick up Mother if she's free. She has been kept pretty busy lately with Harry Stone from the bookstore, Nancy. Isn't that something?"

"Well, I have been gone too long," she laughed. "I met him, Anne, and he is a sweetheart, don't you think? Good for her!"

"Yes, it appears that way," I agreed. "I guess I'll see you tomorrow night."

CHAPTER 42

M other called me to ask for a ride to Isabella's. Sam had a dinner meeting, so I was guiltless in deciding to join the unveiling of the Jane Austen quilt.

The quilt shop was buzzing with happy quilters when we arrived and many were gathered in front of the quilt, which Isabella had hanging on the wall. Even from a distance, it was a sight to behold. A chill of pride came over me as I thought of being a part of such quilted art.

As I got closer, I could see the immediate impact of the black medallion silhouette of Jane's profile that Isabella herself had done. The narrow black sashing framed each block as if they were separate photographs. The crowd thickened as each found their block and broke out in laughter and chatter.

"Miss Anne," Jean called as she came toward me, "this turned out exceedingly well, don't you agree?" Before I could answer, Nancy joined us.

"Did you find your block?" Nancy asked excitedly.

"No, we just got here," I responded. "I haven't been close enough to find it."

"It's in the lower right-hand row," Nancy described. "You did a great job. The sketch of 333 Lincoln is quite good, I must say. I love the redwork embroidery idea. It's just what that corner needed and it's the only redwork in the quilt, I might add. I must try that someday. You surprised me, my friend!"

"You know how much I love red," I teased. "It's like taking a red pen and making the design come alive. It's nothing compared to some of the others. I enjoyed it much more than I thought I would. I wouldn't mind doing an entire quilt in redwork someday...perhaps in another life." We laughed, knowing that wouldn't happen.

"Little Miss Roxanne is up there making sure no one touches the quilt," Nancy said, her tone laced with sarcasm. "She's an odd duck, don't you think? She acts like it is her quilt, doesn't she?"

"She's not happy about sending it out to compete, I can tell you that." I added. "I wonder if she has complained to the other members as she did to all of us in the shop."

"I do say, it's none of her bee's wax," chimed in Jean. "She's been a bit out of sorts ever since Isabella began talking of the quilt contest. She's a pretty unhappy spinster who wants Jane married, by the looks of her block."

"Anne, come look," Mother said, taking me by the arm. "My block is the center here. It turned out much better than I thought." She was right. Her appliqué was so close on the set of books, and the embroidered titles were stitched perfectly. The books looked very real. That was my mother, always done to perfection!

"I particularly like the book that says *My Book*," I teased, making her blush. "You've got to admit, Mother, this is beautifully machine quilted! The custom work here was well planned. I don't know which of her girls did this, but she is to be commended. You should tell Isabella."

"You're right, Anne. I'm just old-fashioned that way," she responded. "I know they wanted it done fast. I do love the personal Jane details quilted into the quilt, I'll give her that much!"

"Okay, let's give this a go, as Jean would say," I said, pushing myself to the front.

There it was, My Pemberley, 333 Lincoln, placed in the corner. I wondered how many had read *Pride and Prejudice* in this group of quilters. If they had not, their curiosity had to be spinning as to what I meant. It did stand out not only in color, but like a pen and ink piece of art done in red. I was shocked at all the creativity displayed in each block. The outside border had all of Jane's titles quilted around the quilt. How did she do that? It was all so balanced.

"Good job, boss lady," Sally praised as she looked at my block. "I love the red in the quilt. I wish now I would have made the dresses different colors. They don't show up too well."

"Your block is very good, Sally," I said with amazement. "I'll bet you surprised yourself. You are now a quilter!" She gave me a look of uncertainty. "Your topic is perfect, and I'm glad you embroidered their names on the block too."

"That was Paige's idea," she offered. "That's her handwriting for the names, and I traced and embroidered it."

"Hi, Sue," I said as she joined us. "Well, look who else came to see the quilt. Hello, Mia Marie!" I tried to reach for her, but she just grinned and then quickly turned toward her mother. There were times I thought children really didn't relate to me, at least not like they did to Sam. Perhaps they had a second sense that said, "She doesn't want babies." Hmmm...

"I wasn't going to come, since it was such short notice, but then I really didn't want to miss this," Sue explained. "We'll just stay a little while. I made sure we found the cookies right away to keep Mia occupied. Now, if I can just keep her away from the quilt."

I was already observing messy hands that said she needed to avoid more than our quilt on the wall. Sue never seemed to be bothered about such things.

Mother started wiping Mia's hands and walked away with her so Sue could look closer at the quilt. It was fun to see Sue react when she saw her block. "My little Muffin looks like a little rat on the quilt instead of a dog, don't you think?" she joked. We giggled because she had a good point.

"That had to be hard to do, Sue," I said in all honesty. "All the blocks are so personal. Most of us are not artists and had no idea how hard our block would be. We just pulled these ideas out of our heads. I'm going to take a photo with my phone when enough people clear away. I'll take one of your block as well."

"That's a great idea, Anne," she said, agreeing. "Will you take one with Mia and me in front of the quilt?"

"Sure," I said eagerly. "Before you get Mia, I want to give you a little news. Did you know that Mother and Harry Stone have become a couple these days?"

"What?" she said, her eyes widening. "The Harry she talked about from the bookstore where she worked, right?" I nodded. "You don't say! Why is it everyone else and never me? Well, I'm sure he's a very nice man and I'll bet they have a lot in common! Way to go, Aunt Sylvia!"

"Please have some of the goodies, ladies," Isabella interrupted. "I can't believe so many brought cookies for us. One kind looks better than the other!"

We proceeded to the long table of delicacies that was centered with an antique punch bowl of lemonade punch. Various Jane Austen motifs were placed between the platters of finger sandwiches, cookies, and fruit. It was all tempting, and I wondered about the lemonade punch. Hmmm...

"May I have your attention?" asked Nancy as she clanked on her glass to quiet the crowd. "Thanks so much for coming to this exciting event, especially with such short notice. Thanks to Isabella and her staff, we have a finished quilt that we are all quite proud of. May I present to you...the Jane Austen quilt!" Everyone loudly applauded and Sally gave a whistle. "Many of us have learned a lot about quilting, thanks to Isabella's patience in giving us some guidance. Now, I have to say we don't know what Jane herself would say about this quilt, if she were here!" Everyone laughed and made their side comments. Oh dear, they should hear my poem, but I decided it was for my eyes only. "Let's give Isabella and the girls a round of applause!" Everyone clapped and cheered. "Isabella, would you like to say something?"

"Yes, Nancy," she said, beaming ear to ear. "This is a huge achievement for all of us. It was a pleasure helping many of you for the first time in making a quilt block. Jane Austen would be proud of our fondness for her, which resulted in this quilt. I thank each and every one of you who exceeded all expectations for this idea. We are fortunate tonight to have someone from the local paper here in Colebridge to take our picture in front of the quilt. Please be sure to give your name to him. I don't want to forget anyone. I will hopefully be shipping the quilt tomorrow. The deadline for the competition is getting near. It will be entered in the group quilt category, and as I told you before, I think we'll win!" Another large round of applause filled the room. "The quilt was appraised yesterday for insurance replacement, so now it's time for the international show and tell!" Another round of applause erupted. "Nancy has done a great job with this group and I thank her very much. Her persistence in getting you all to do this has been amazing. I know she is glad to be relieved of that responsibility. I have another project in mind for those who want to continue to keep quilting the Jane Austen theme!"

This time, loud chatter and laughter said many were having second thoughts, including myself. After we took the group picture, everyone started to leave. I then had an opportunity to take a photo of the quilt in its full glory.

"Too clever and unique to send off to strangers," said a voice from behind. It was Roxanne, who stood with arms folded.

"Aren't you proud of this, Roxanne?" I asked sadly. "It is so beautiful and unique."

"My point. Very proud," she said as she walked away. I somehow felt unexpected sympathy for her. She seemed to be the only one who was truly against the quilt competing, which had to make her very sad.

I found Mia sitting on Mother's lap while Sue was

visiting with Sarah and Aunt Julia. Mother was the resident grandmother, since Sue's parents lived out of town. She loved every minute of it, especially since her only daughter seemed to be reluctant to have any children.

We all walked over to get photos that Sue had requested, despite Mia's resistance to being held. We complimented Sarah on her stick people block. She seemed very proud to be included and I think we have a next-generation quilter, thanks to the basement quilters and this fun Austen quilt.

CHAPTER 43

I was much later getting home than I expected, and finding Sam had already retired was not expected. I turned off the alarm and made my way upstairs to find him snoring. I had never encountered that before. Perhaps it was because I was usually the first one to fall asleep. It was rather cute in a funny sort of way. I got ready for bed thinking about all the day's events. I hoped my dream or nightmare would not include it all. Grandmother had a way of now filtering into my dreams. I could just imagine her coming to Isabella's shop and destroying our quilt because it had 333 Lincoln on it. If anyone had reason to destroy this quilt, it would be Jane Austen herself.

The next morning, I kissed my well-rested husband good-bye to get to my walk down by the river before the predicted rain. I planned to make a quick stop at Mother's to show her the newspaper article. I knew her coffee would be on and her newspaper opened. A surprise visit from me would make her day.

"Good morning," I yelled, opening the door with my key like I still lived there.

"Hey, Anne. Long time, no see," she teased with a pleasant look on her face. "What's up?"

"Take a look at this, Mother." I said, putting the newspaper with Grandmother's photo in front of her. "Have you ever seen this before? I picked this up at the historical society."

"Well, no good morning Mommy dearest?" she replied with a yawn. "This must be important. No, but let me see what you have." She gave it a long good look. "I guess this is Mother! If I didn't know better, I'd think I was looking at Julia."

"I said the same thing, Mother!' I replied. "I don't remember many of her photos in younger years, but she was beautiful!"

"Yes, she was," she said, still staring at a person she knew long ago. "She never talked about her past to me, but she may have said more to Marie because she was the oldest. The shame of it is that we never asked. I doubt if she would have spoken of her heart being broken, much less having an illegitimate pregnancy. They didn't speak of such things back then. Why does that happen? I'm pleased you are showing some interest, Anne. As children growing up, we are always looking forward to the next birthday or what's going to be next instead of taking an interest in what was. I suppose that's normal."

I could tell I was making her sad with this discovery, instead of happy. "I was wondering if you knew what position she had with that company," I inquired, looking at her as she kept staring at the paper.

"She couldn't have been more than a clerk, especially back then," she noted.

"Do you recall seeing pictures of her at work or with Albert?" I asked.

Mother looked at me like I was about to stir up trouble. "Heavens no, Anne," she said firmly. "Remember, that was not done much then and remember her affair had to be a carefully kept secret. This is so interesting to see. She looks pretty happy, doesn't she?"

"Yes, I thought so," I commented.

"If there were any old pictures from her youth, they went to Marie," she recalled. "We have a few of our mother and father, like the one on the mantle, but I don't recall seeing any baby pictures of our mother. We did bring a box of old pictures back here after the funeral. You should go through those sometime."

"I will!" I eagerly said. "Now I need your help with something." I paused, trying to make sure I didn't sound like I was whining. "Nora quit on me and I am in desperate need of a new cleaning person. I need my windows washed as well, as Nora so bluntly reminded me. It would be nice to have someone do both. Do you know of anyone?"

She looked at me as if her child had once again done something wrong. "What's happened to Nora?" she asked, pouring me some coffee.

"To make a long story short, she refused to stay in the house alone and I'm just too busy to always be there with her." The look on her face said everything. Mother's imagination was figuring it out. "I have to have a recommendation from someone."

She shook her head as if this was getting to be an annoying subject. "Now that you've brought that up, I've been thinking about getting someone here to clean every other week," she added. "It's just too hard on my knees to do floors and hard-to-reach places. Harry couldn't believe it when I told him I was doing all the cleaning myself."

Harry could convince her of most anything, I thought. "I'm glad Harry got through to you," I said convincingly. "I've told you that for years. You can afford it, Mother! Have you found anyone?"

"Harry recommended his cleaning lady; she is only in her early fifties and supposedly does a great job," she said, pouring herself another cup. "She's going to come over this week to give me an estimate. I've never had anyone clean my things, but perhaps it's time."

"This is wonderful," I agreed, putting my hands together in glee. "Tell her about 333 Lincoln, would you?"

"You don't want me to tell her everything about 333 Lincoln, do you?" she said with sarcasm in her voice. "You may never be able to keep anyone there, if you don't get your grandmother under control."

I was shocked that she finally had accepted my explanation of her presence. "Be sure to ask her about doing windows, too!" I reminded her. "Does Mr. Carter still do yours like he used to?"

"No, and I need to address that as well," she admitted. "The Carters are getting old, too, just like me. They pretty much stay busy with doctors' appointments and going to lunch." We laughed. "I feel that way sometimes."

"I've got to get going, Mother, before it rains on my walk," I said, going near the door. "Don't forget Sam's birthday, by the way. I think Helen is coming in. I really need you to help entertain her. We're getting a pretty good e-mail response in attendance. I got one from Amanda saying she could attend and William is coming, for sure. By the way, Mommy dearest, if you'd like to bring Harry, it would be perfectly okay."

She grinned like she had already planned to do so. "Oh good, it should be fun," she said, grinning. "I'll bring my macaroni and cheese everyone liked so much last year. Oh, here comes the rain, my dear." Mother pulled back the curtain to see out the kitchen window revealing the rain pouring down. "There goes your walk. Do want your coffee to go?"

I said not to bother and headed back home to shower as I postponed my walk. I knew Mother would take care of my cleaning problem. She was always saying I needed more help, so here was her chance to find it. What would I do without her? She had become a friend as well as a mother. I was told that happens once the daughter gets married. Hmmm...

The first thing on my schedule for the day was to meet with Jason Cunningham. I checked the orders for the day and all three girls were busy working and Kevin was out on his first delivery.

"Anne, I thought you might want to acknowledge this," Sally said, coming near my desk. "Ted's mother passed away yesterday. We are starting to get quite a few orders for her funeral. They are coming from organizations and many are from out of town. I guess she was pretty well known."

"Oh my, I wonder what happened," I said sadly, thinking of Ted. "The last time I saw her, she appeared to be well. She couldn't be that old." How ironic that I just realized this morning how lucky I was to have my mother, and Ted lost his mother last night. I'm sure Mother didn't yet hear of the news, or she would have told me this morning.

"It probably had something to do with her heart, because the heart association is listed as one of the preferred charities," Sally noted.

"That's how I will respond, I guess," I muttered, thinking it through. "I will be sure to make a donation. Is she being viewed at Barrister's?"

"Yes," Sally nodded. "Kevin already took at least two pieces with him this morning. By the way, Kevin's assistant will be showing up sometime this morning to talk with you. His name is Kip Blackstone, Kevin said."

"Right," I said in a blur, as my eyes started to water. I couldn't help thinking of Ted and his family. After all, they thought the world of me and were heartbroken when we split up. His mother was always so kind to me and was not bashful about wishing that Ted and I would marry someday.

Jason arrived on time, and after introductions to my Botanical family, we grabbed some iced tea and he joined me beside my desk. He looked around, sizing things up as we began our conversation. He was easy to talk to and said his father knew my father years ago. I was slowly forgetting the sad news of Mrs. Collins as we talked about the expansion. He said my early e-mailed list of wishes for the expansion made sense, and once he could measure inside and out, he would have something back to me in a week or so. I could feel my blood circulating with the excitement of it all. He said he would be applying for a permit today as well as making an appointment with the city planning department.

Wow, it was really starting to happen! Did this mean I couldn't back out? His required deposit was more than fair, so I wrote him a check out of the business account. It was done and moving, I thought. I saw him out the door. This was so different from my encounter with Mr. King, who wanted to turn my professional interest into something personal. That experience once again reminded me that women in business still did not get equal respect. Jason had also done his homework by visiting with Sally, who seemed to be much more detailed concerning what we needed than I currently was. She was elated with our progress and gave me a sign of approval after he left.

CHAPTER 44

Kip Blackstone was making small talk out by the counter with Abbey when I greeted him. Abbey was all google-eyed as he spoke. He would indeed be a handsome match for her. I knew she could be a flirt, and a cute one at that. After I introduced myself, he responded in a gentlemanly manner. I knew instantly he would fit in nicely, unless Abbey gave him too much attention. I gave him his paperwork for employment and started to show him the process of our deliveries.

"Hey, that's my job," Kevin said, coming in the back door. "Hey there, Kip! Have you met everyone?"

"Sure did!" he politely answered. "This doesn't look too hard. I'm sure I'll get the hang of things once I can ride along with you."

"Oh, but Kip, you are not just a delivery guy around here. Didn't she tell you?" Kevin teased. "You get to cook, put up

Christmas trees, move furniture, and then try to keep the peace between all these ladies!" Everyone laughed, knowing it was true. He was the man in our house, and we took advantage of it.

"Kip is going to help me barbecue and set things up for the party, if that's okay with you, Anne," Kevin explained. "I took some things over to the house this morning, like the bunting for the gazebo. I figure if the weather is good, I can get that up the night before. Wait until you see Anne's place on the top of Colebridge, Kip. It's really neat."

"This morning, my mother told me where you live," Kip shared. "I always wondered what it was like up there. There was always a private or keep out sign posted."

I was surprised his next sentence wasn't about the so-called ghost that he heard resided there. "Well, you'll have a chance to do that," I told him. "Tell me, Kip, where did you work before? You said you were going to school at the university here? You look so tan, like you work outdoors." Kip and Kevin laughed.

"As of last week, I worked part-time at the Colebridge Country Club, working mostly outdoors," he said, with disappointment in his voice. "They laid off seven people to cut back on expenses. I feel sorry for those left having to make up for all of us who were let go. I really enjoyed it! I like working outdoors."

"I heard things weren't going well there, but I don't know any details," I said. "What did you do outdoors?"

"Most anything, Mrs. Dickson, which explains my tan," he said, grinning. "I was out all day long. I cleaned the pool, painted, trimmed bushes, planted flowers, collected golf balls, worked the valet parking when they needed it—the list goes on! They had special mowers for the course, so I never did that."

I was impressed. "You know this is a part-time job, don't you?" I asked to make sure. "Kevin will make the call regarding when you're needed."

"Oh sure, that's what he said," he happily responded. "I'm just tickled to get a little work right now. Thanks so much."

"Okay, follow me, brother, and I'll show you where I load up," Kevin instructed.

I was not only impressed with Kip, but also with how Kevin took leadership about what the shop needed. He was certainly capable of being something other than my delivery guy, I thought to myself. The girls were giggling and talking softly by the counter as I joined them.

"He's a hunk of a guy," Abbey said with a flirtatious grin. "I could keep him very busy!" We all laughed.

"A keeper, for sure! Right, Miss Anne?" Jean added.

"I'd keep him for a lot of things, but you should think about him for 333 Lincoln, Anne." Sally suggested. They all agreed, all talking at once. "Didn't you say you need a gardener to help you?"

"I suppose I did, part-time, anyway," I said, thinking mighty fast. "After that terrible Steve encounter, I don't know if Sam will agree to such help. I have certainly made him aware that the Taylor's estate needs a gardener, just as they did years ago. I'd better talk to Sam first, however, but that is a great idea, Sally. If he was good enough for that persnickety country club, he'd be good enough for me!"

The days ahead were busy with the holiday activity at the shop, which included my services for one of the best hometown parades in Colebridge. Every school band, organization, and politician participated in the Fourth of July celebration. It was quite fun and Main Street would pack the outlining sidewalks with folks wanting to get a glance at the parade as it went by. Many organizations depended on me getting them wholesale supplies and offering them advice on the Independence Day holiday float that the merchants group would decorate. I tried to avoid many of the organizational meetings regarding this holiday because it involved alcohol and there were sure to be folks upset. If there was alcohol on any occasion, there was always a negative reaction and some controversy.

The heat had been terrible the last two weeks. Supplying water for people's lawns and flowers was now a bone of contention with our city. Volunteers tried to keep the sidewalk-lined flowerpots watered, but anything else was discouraged because of the water shortage. The outdoor red geraniums were holding up well, as always, but some were turning the darker red that showed their dislike for the high temperatures. We kept a dog bowl of drinking water out by one of our benches for the many dogs that seemed to visit along the street as they strolled with their owners.

Many visitors came inside the air-conditioned shop to cool off and browse instead of making a purchase. Some shops closed early due to having no customers. That was an aggravation of mine for all the years I had been a merchant on the street. I could not believe how some shop owners were easily discouraged and closed their doors. In my business, we had to be there rain or shine for phone orders as well as any walk-ins that would occur. Special occasions and tragedies went on in everyone's lives, no matter what the weather. Even if I owned a gift shop, having just one or two sales would be better than going home with none.

Sam's outdoor birthday party wouldn't start until five in the evening, with hopes that the sun would be merciful and the night would be cooler. We had a fan in the roof of the gazebo, which would help, but I certainly couldn't and wouldn't want to entertain all the attendees inside. I will have to keep my fingers crossed that all will be well with the party, as well as my visit with my mother-in-law.

It was the day before the big party when Sam's mother, Helen, arrived. Sam picked her up at the airport and brought her to the house. We planned to take her to Donna's Tea Room for dinner as soon as I got home from work. I was exhausted from the heat and had last minute things I wanted to do at home when I got there. However, Helen was our guest and it was her son's birthday! I kept telling myself that it would all work out!

"Welcome back, Helen!" I said, giving her a hug when I joined her and Sam at home in the study. "How was your flight?" She barely acknowledged my hug and sat back down in the chair. "You look very well!"

"The flight was pretty miserable, I'd have to say," she said with a sigh. "We were late coming in and you could hardly breathe on the plane because it was so hot and stuffy. The heat here is brutal, to say the least. I don't know how you expect folks to sit out there in this heat for Sam's party!" The look on my face must have been a signal for Sam to step in and rescue the moment.

"Oh, Mother, this is Missouri," he said with a laugh. "Everyone here is used to it. One never knows what the next day's weather will be. They aren't predicting rain, so that's a good thing. It'll be fine. We'll have lots of cold lemonade and those cool, icy drinks you liked so much the last time you were here!" Sam and I smiled but she did not.

"Oh, you are always the optimist, Sammy," she bragged. "I'm looking forward to dinner tonight. It should be delicious, as always, and I'm sure I will be quite nicely cooled inside the restaurant."

"It certainly will be," I concluded as I went upstairs to freshen up for an interesting evening ahead. The cool drinks couldn't come fast enough to suit me, I thought. My night and weekend would be long and stressed. Now all I had to do was keep my cool! Hmmm...

CHAPTER 45

The next morning, Sam and I managed to get up very early and tried to be quiet so we wouldn't disturb Helen. Sam made the coffee and I kept kissing him and wishing him happy birthday in as many ways I could imagine. He especially liked my "Happy Birthday, Love" written on his bathroom mirror with my red lipstick. I knew Sam would feel awkward if I gave him too much attention around his mother.

We were suddenly interrupted by the delivery of Sam's cake from Notto's Bakery. The very large cake was put temporarily on the dining room table where we admired its creative message: Happy Birthday to the King of the Castle on the Hill. The beautifully decorated cake had a fancy iced crown placed in the center. It was a personal joke between Sam and his friends. They teased him relentlessly about being king of the castle on the hill of Colebridge. Sam took it well, trying to make light of it all.

"Now all we need is a birthday present and we have a party!" I teased. I took his hand and brought him to the back porch off the kitchen. I had a new, large stuffed reclining wing-backed chair covered in newspapers. It had a large bow on the top. Sam looked shocked.

"Go ahead and tear it off!" I instructed. "Happy Birthday! Didn't you catch sight of this when you were making coffee in the kitchen? You will love this!"

Without a word, he began tearing the paper from the large chair, trying to figure out its purpose. "A chair, right?" he asked, trying to be cute.

"Yes, a chair for you to have in our upstairs bedroom," I started to explain. "You need a place to relax up there without having to come down here to the den. I have just the spot for it by the bay window and the cream color will be perfect in that room."

"Wow, Annie, this is a pretty well-thought-out gift, I would say," he finally offered. "I guess I'd better try it out!" He sat down and pretended to sleep with a big smile. "I could spend the day here, it's so comfortable! Thank you, Annie!"

"When Kevin and Kip show up today, I'll have them take it upstairs for us," I told him. Sam got up from the chair and hugged me tightly.

"You're always thinking of my comfort!" Sam said, giving me another squeeze. "I'll bet I'll find you in that chair more than anyone!" I nodded with a big smile.

"Well, what's going on out here?" Helen said, coming out to the porch.

Thankfully, Sam took the conversation from there, telling her what a great gift I had given him. He bragged about how I kept it a secret and always came up with such clever ideas. He even asked her to try it out, but, of course, she declined. I'm sure the whole conversation was making her uncomfortable. We went into the kitchen to offer her some breakfast. Sam went outdoors to do some watering, leaving me alone with Helen. I kept busy preparing food and cleaning up so she wouldn't feel she'd have to engage in conversation.

"I see you have added some furniture since I was here last!" Helen remarked.

"Yes, we likely have!" I noted as I poured myself another cup of coffee to join her. "We have more to go, of course, with all these rooms, but I want to take my time with each one. By the way, do you like how well the red and white quilt goes in your room? I really love it, Helen. I'm not quite finished decorating in there, however. I'd like to put some family photos on one of the walls to make it more personal. If you have any to pass on from your family, I'd appreciate it. Sam had a few, which we display in the study." I could tell she liked the idea.

"I'll check into that," she nodded in agreement. "I'm glad you like the quilt. "You know Pat pieced the top and had a friend of hers quilt it! She knew you liked red and white."

"Yes, which makes it much more special. I must write her a thank-you note. She is quite a good quilter, isn't she?"

"Yes, she has a quilt in a competition at some major show in Florida, I believe," she added as she drank her coffee. "I suspect she'll win some award again."

I thought it ironic I, too, would have some part of a quilt entered in that show, and began to explain all the details to Helen about the Jane Austen quilt. She knew of Jane Austen, the writer, but seemed to be amused and somewhat confused as to why we made a quilt about her. I began to realize Helen herself never quilted, but the family grew up with many quilts. Pat was the only one to pursue the craft, and did it extremely well. At least Helen sounded proud of Pat's accomplishments.

By early afternoon, the barbecue was smoking, giving off an enticing aroma inside and outside the house. The tables were arranged with last year's red-and-white checked tablecloths, adorned with small pots of red geraniums in the center. The drinks were iced, ready to serve. No one noticed the heat of the day, except Helen. She remained inside until most of the folks had arrived. I ignored her, giving that responsibility to Mother and Harry, who arrived happily together. I was going to enjoy every minute with Sam and all our dear friends.

Harry Stone was no stranger to many folks. Mother was dressed casually in clothes I had never seen before. Mother and Harry did look quite cute together, I had to admit.

It was great to see Uncle Jim again. It appeared that Aunt Julia and Uncle Jim were civil to one another since their divorce, which helped us all. I was pleased he did not choose to bring a date. Sarah was entertaining Mia, as Paige, Sally, and Abbey were in a private conversation with Kip. It was no surprise that he was the latest and greatest to get their attention!

Amanda and William finally arrived with a plate full of brownies and a gift for Sam. Amanda immediately went over to Mother. The two had bonded together nicely. Nancy and Richard also dressed casually, which was refreshing to see from their day-to-day formal wear seen at the funeral home. Paul and Roy from Martingale came with dates, but Harry, Aunt Julia's former beau, did not show up, which was not surprising.

Sue mostly clung to Aunt Julia as if the two single ladies had something in common. It was so cool to see everyone mix and Sam was enjoying every minute. The weather was not giving anyone a reason to not have a good time.

At the start of dusk, the white Christmas lights strung around the gazebo and bunting were coming alive and Kevin lit some candles that were treated to keep the bugs away. The temperature was starting to cool down, making for a comfortable evening.

"May I have everyone's attention?" yelled Uncle Jim as he hit something against metal to make a noise. "I say it's time to sing and embarrass my buddy, Sam, here on his birthday and thank him for a great party!" Everyone applauded. "We have a special treat this evening. To lead us in song is the famous Kip Blackstone who brought his guitar."

Kip? A singer, as well? Everyone expectantly cheered as Kip put on a cowboy hat and led us to sing *Happy Birthday*. There wasn't a normal version of the melody in the group, which was hilarious. This was a fun surprise for Sam and me—and such a sight to behold. I looked at Abbey sitting next to him as he sang. She was going to be his biggest fan here tonight, along with everyone else.

"Hope this little surprise was okay, Anne," Kevin whispered to me from behind. "He typically sings country western music and is pretty good, don't you think? I thought it might add something to the party."

"It was wonderful, Kevin," I said, giving him a hug. "He is really quite good! You did a great job thinking of everything, as always. Everyone's having a great time and the food is so delicious! Thanks so, so much!" He grinned as he eagerly accepted my compliments.

Sam came up to us and bragged about his great party. He then pulled me aside and looked into my eyes. "You know I really love my chair, but I'll never forget my first present from you. Remember?" he teased. I did remember, as I blushed to recall a very seductive dinner, shared privately together, with me wearing an outfit I knew would please—just for him.

Out of the corner of my eye, I saw Helen watching us as we embraced. Does it make her happy to see her son happy... or not? I think it will remain a mystery. Hmmm...

CHAPTER 46

❧❧

On Sunday morning, we were recovering from a successful birthday party once again. With little clean up, the outdoors appeared as if no one had been there. After breakfast, Helen surprised me by offering some assistance.

"I noticed walking down the hall upstairs that you've added a desk in that cute little room off your bedroom," she observed. "Are you doing some writing, Anne? I know you love to write."

"Yes, you're right," I happily responded. "I brought the desk from home and I've finally started to write some things about the Taylor house."

"Yeah, Mother, Anne calls that room the waiting room," Sam said, jumping into the conversation. Helen looked puzzled. "In other words, it's waiting for whatever!"

"You mean like a nursery?" Helen said with anticipation. I wanted to run out of the room. I didn't look up as I continued to load the dishwasher.

"Whatever awaits us," Sam tactfully responded. Helen shrugged her shoulders and dropped the subject.

We continued the day eating leftover goodies from the party and watched a slow rain appear in the afternoon. Helen went upstairs to rest and I took the opportunity to present my idea to Sam about hiring Kip as a gardener. He listened intently without interruption or reaction. I ended by telling him the Taylors had a gardener and reminded him that it was quite a showplace at that time.

"You say he's done some repair work and painting at the country club?" he asked, displaying a bit more interest. "I do a have a lot of things around here that need attention—like the back screen door. I'm just too busy now to get to some of that, so perhaps we could give him a try. I take it we can trust this guy, unlike the Steve that Kevin recommended."

I didn't respond. I wanted to forget all of that. I calmly told him we could just give him a try to see how he worked out. I didn't want to show my real excitement regarding it all.

The next morning, Sam took Helen to the airport. She seemed to have enjoyed her visit, despite the hot weather and not having Sam all to herself. It was nice, however, to send her on her way. Perhaps I was the one that was not eager to share Sam. It was all part of the learning process of being a daughter-in-law, I supposed.

I headed to the shop without an early walk so I could catch up on things left undone. This was beginning to be a habit I did not like. Before I knew it, my walks could disappear completely. As soon as Jean and Sally arrived, the chatter began about the great birthday party.

"Did you and Paige have a good time?" I asked as I

glanced through my e-mails. "You know, you both could have brought dates."

"I know, but I don't get to do much with just her, so this was fun!" she answered, smiling. "Paige thinks you and Sam are just perfect for each other. How about that rock star, Kip? That was a nice surprise, wasn't it?"

"Absolutely delightful, Miss Anne," Jean chimed in. "Abbey especially thought it quite jolly, it seemed!" We laughed. "On another page, Miss Anne, have you heard from Nancy or Isabella regarding our quilt entry? When do you suppose we'll be enlightened on its award?"

"I don't think she gave us a timeline on that!" commented Sally. "I hope we'll know either way, don't you?"

"I'm sure she'll let us know right away," I said, barely listening as I continued reading e-mails. "I learned from Helen that Sam's sister Pat has a quilt in the same competition. She must have entered something quite good to be in that show. She was the one that made the top to my red and white quilt, you know. I need to send her a thank-you card today, before I forget completely."

"By the way, Anne," Sally began, "did you go to the wake for Mrs. Collins?"

"No," I answered sadly. "I sent Ted a nice note with my card and my donation to the heart association. I wonder how they are all doing. I'm really surprised I haven't heard directly from Ted."

"The Miss Helen went home today, I take it?" Jean asked.

"Yes, and she was in much better spirits this time," I shared. "I'm afraid Sam gave her somewhat of an impression that we were waiting to get pregnant. He probably had to tell her something, knowing how she feels about it."

"Going to give it a go, Miss Anne?" Jean asked in a serious tone.

"No, no, no," I emphatically answered. "That's for another time in my life, you all know that!" They broke into giggles at me taking the question so seriously.

"The literary club is tomorrow night, girls!" Jean reminded us as she went outdoors to empty the garbage. How could it be that time again, I thought to myself.

When she came back inside, we asked her about the topic for the evening. She said no book had been assigned because everyone was too busy working on their quilt blocks.

"I think we are losing a bit of interest from the gang, if you get my meaning," Jean confessed. "I think I'll begin the meeting with one of Jane's quotes from *Northanger Abbey*. She cleared her throat and said, "'The person, be it gentleman or lady, who has not pleasure in a good novel, must be intolerably stupid.'"

"Oh," Sally said, surprised. "That will get them reading, for sure!" We laughed.

"Are you serious?"

"I think you should, Jean!" I responded with interest. "You need to shake things up a bit. In fact, I think it would make a great program to recite Jane's quotes and then have some discussion on how we all might interpret them. I wrote one down last week from *Mansfield Park*, because I write and wanted to remember it. Jane wrote, 'Let other pens dwell on guilt and misery.' It was her way of saying she was all about writing good things and feelings." I told myself to remember that quote.

"You're right, Anne," said Sally. "Even though there were disappointments she would describe, she was never mean spirited with her words. I like the program idea, don't you, Jean?"

"Jolly good thinking, Miss Anne," Jean joyfully responded. "We will give that a go for sure! This will be a mighty good challenge for the Janeites!"

CHAPTER 47

I left early that day to run into Gabardine Printing down the street to make some changes on my brochure and get a few office supplies. Like Miss Michelle's and Notto's Bakery, they continued their ownership through many generations on Main Street in Colebridge. Embracing the influx of modern technology was likely a challenge for them through the years, but it was also a blessing and the secret to their continued success.

When I walked in, I was surprised to see Bill Gabardine and Ted talking in the next room, with what appeared to be a business-like discussion as they held papers in their hands. I ignored them and continued with my requests to Linda, who was always glad to see me. She worked the front desk for many years and probably knew more about their business than anyone.

"Hey, Anne," Bill said, coming toward me, "long time, no see!"

I quickly glanced at them both, but Ted totally ignored me and walked out the door, taking me quite by surprise. "Good to see you, too!" I said smiling. "I turned in my requests to Linda who has always taken care of me just fine."

"That's great," he said, patting me on the shoulder. "We just want to be helpful and we appreciate the business, as always." He paused for a minute as if he wasn't sure how to say what he had to say. "Anne, it's none of my business, but what's up with Ted not speaking to you just now? I thought the two of you were cool with each other after you broke up."

"Well, yeah, I thought so, too!" I quietly responded. "He probably had a lot of things on his mind. I sure was sorry to hear about his mother. I thought the world of his family."

"A shock, for sure!" Bill said, shaking his head. "I guess you heard she died from an overdose. Some say it was on purpose, others say it was an accident. What a shame!"

"What?" I asked in disbelief. "Mrs. Collins?"

"Oh well, you know how gossip can be in this town," he said, now with a tinge in his voice that sounded like regret. "Ted didn't say anything to me, of course, and you can't blame him. Forget I said anything. If you didn't hear anything about it, there's probably nothing to it."

"I sure hope not, Bill," I said, feeling a bit in shock. "It is hard enough to lose your mother under normal circumstances."

We said good-bye and I went out the door feeling ill. How could I forget such a horrible statement even if it was likely gossip or rumor? Sometimes Bill reminded me of the stereotypes of some old ladies, the way he gossiped. He shouldn't have even repeated what he heard. I remembered Mrs. Collins as a God-fearing sweet person, doing all the right things in life. Is that why Ted left without saying hello? Did he not get my card? Was he embarrassed at what may or may not have happened? Was he mad at me for not attending the funeral? Oh dear, it was all not good. I walked down the sidewalk in sheer dismay. Why had I not heard this from Mother or anyone else who knew the Collins family? I wanted to forget I had heard any of this.

Having dinner at home that night was welcomed as I shared Chinese cuisine with Sam. He seemed to be pleased with another take-out dinner, enjoying every bite. I sure was lucky on that account. He showed me his fortune cookie that read: The best is yet to come. Mine read: Another hurdle may be around the corner.

We laughed and knew we could easily apply their meanings to our current life. I certainly knew I had many hurdles coming my way. It would be so cool to know what the future would hold for the two of us...or would it?

"What's wrong, Anne?" Sam asked, sipping his drink and looking directly into my eyes. "You haven't been yourself all night."

"You're probably right," I answered, shifting in my seat. "I heard something today that probably was a rumor, and until I know the truth, I would rather not discuss it. It was unpleasant and it's been on my mind."

He looked puzzled. "I understand. It happens to me at work more than you can imagine," he shared as he took our plates to the counter.

"I'm just hoping the best for all concerned," I said with a sigh. "I'm going to turn in early with a book, honey, if you don't mind. Thanks for cleaning this up. I'm really tired."

"Not at all, Annie," he said, kissing me on the forehead. "This will be a cinch, and I may do some reading in the study."

Tucked in bed, I couldn't think of anything else except the words Bill had said about the Collins funeral. It was hard to think of her as having any kind of serious problems. I had to convince myself that if there were any truth to the rumors, my friends or family would have called me about it. For the first time ever, I really felt sorry for Ted. He was her favorite son and she let everyone know it. There was not a bright side to any of this, true or not.

The next morning, I watched from my bedside as Sam prepared his clothes for two days of travel. He really had the packing routine down to a science. He, too, was using the waiting room for his travel luggage and supplies to make his preparations quicker and easier. You could wait for a trip, a book, or even a baby in that waiting room! As he packed, he gave me the go ahead to talk to Kip about doing some yard work for me and he would arrange for any other jobs when he returned. I listened with much satisfaction.

"I hope he'll be a better recommendation than Steve!" Sam said with regret in his voice. "Make sure you have as much information about him as you can." I nodded, knowing full well I had learned my lesson in that we had to be more careful about who we let work on this secluded estate.

After I saw Sam off, I stopped by Notto's to compliment them on Sam's birthday cake, as well as pick up treats for the girls. Nick was already complaining about the coming street festival that would interfere with his customers picking up their orders. I nodded and listened to the same rhetoric from him every year as he hauled his fortune to the bank.

"Why do they always have to have everything on our street and in our park?" he complained over and over. "Isn't there anywhere else in this whole town?"

"Nick! Be glad they are coming here!" I interrupted. "I personally want the exposure and the traffic; and, by the way, it's not our Main Street, nor our park, remember!"

He looked at me, shaking his head. "Well, they don't steal your flowers or write all over your building like they do mine," he went on. "These events go way too late at night and it's nothing but trouble for us the next day. Half these folks only come to festivals. Those are not my customers."

"You really don't know that for sure, Nick," I stated firmly. "How do you know if someone saw a wedding cake you had on display and came here later to order one? How do you know if they told someone else about this neat bakery they saw on Main Street? However, they will remember if someone was grumpy to them here on the street, that's for sure. Lighten up and try to enjoy it!" He halfway grinned, knowing he had asked for the lecture.

I left thinking maybe Nick had a message there. Why did they seem to pick on Nick's building? It surely couldn't be because he was the friendliest guy in town. He reminded me of my grouchy Uncle Fred that died. The glass was always half empty instead of half full.

The day went quickly and I arranged to have a quick bite with Nancy before we went to the literary club. We agreed to meet at Charley's and sat at our usual place. Brad was always happy to see us and responded to our usual order. After we got settled, I got up enough nerve to bring up what was on my mind.

"Nancy, I know you will have ethical reasons not to answer the question I am about to ask you, but I'm going to ask you anyway," I began slowly. "I've been troubled about the death of Mrs. Collins. Can you just tell me whether she died of natural causes like a heart attack or something?"

Nancy looked away, then down. "You're right. I'm not at liberty to discuss any of this with you, but because you were close to her, I am going to respond with the answer no," she sadly confirmed. "Please, however, do not extend this conversation, Anne. You'll have to find out from someone else."

I couldn't believe it. So there was something to this after all. I did drop it, but went ahead and told her how Ted had ignored me at the printing shop.

"Well, Anne, if I recall, you haven't been exactly friendly or very polite to the guy lately." She teased me with a smile. "His reaction to you may or may not have had anything to do with his mother. After all, you were also in a public place, where any conversation about that would have been awkward."

Okay—she had me there, as an eye witness to my behavior with him too many times. "Well, I'll change the subject by asking you if you heard anything about our Austen quilt," I asked with some interest since the girls brought it up at the shop.

"As a matter of fact, I called Isabella's just yesterday and Roxanne answered," she reported. "She said they hadn't heard anything from the show organizers. It's probably too soon to know much. I think we'll do really well in the competition!" Nancy looked at her watch. "We need to get going, I suppose." There was never enough time for us to chat, but we said our good-byes to Brad and went on our way.

I picked up Mother and off we went to find Jean's house full of chatty family and friends. As usual, we quickly headed toward the dining room to get our English tea, which was just what I needed after dinner. I think it always tasted better because it was served in Jean's English china. Sue had made chocolate cake pops that were adorable and quite tasty.

As planned, Jean did indeed start her club with Jane's touchy quote from *Mansfield Park* that was sure to get a reaction. It went over quite well, and then she explained why she chose it. They loved her evening's plan for discussing Jane's quotes. She continued with the next quote. "Jane once sarcastically wrote to her niece, Fanny, that, 'Single women have a dreadful propensity for being poor, which is one very strong argument in favor of matrimony.'" Everyone applauded, laughing.

"No discussion here!" Sue said loudly. "I'll drink to that!" More laughter exploded.

"I think it rather a revealing admission on Jane's part that she was disgusted about having to get married in order to have any wealth at all!" Roxanne said with some rage in her tone.

"In *Pride and Prejudice*, the Mr. Darcy character stated, 'A lady's imagination is very rapid; it jumps from admiration to love, from love to matrimony in a moment,'" Sue said with a romantic whisper in her voice. "I think there is something to that!" The others murmured in agreement. "Jane also mentioned disappointment with love in *Northanger Abbey* when she wrote, 'Friendship is certainly the finest balm for disappointed love.'"

"That's so true," Aunt Julia stated. "Love affairs can come and go, but it's your friends that remain there for you when things go downhill!"

"Hear ye!" said someone from behind me. I then thought of Nancy and how valuable our friendship was through the years, in good and bad times.

"Good discussion so far, Janeites!" Jean continued. "Here's another interesting quote. Jane wrote to her sister Cassandra about being a chaperone to her nieces. She said, 'As I must leave off being young, I find many douceurs in being a sort of chaperon, for I am put on the sofa near a fire and can drink as much wine as I like.'" This brought applause and more laughter.

"Can't you just picture that?" commented Aunt Julia. "I've had to be a chaperone for Sarah a time or two, and I would have loved sitting by the fire drinking wine!" More comments erupted. It was obvious that everyone had interpreted this differently.

"Another very good sign Miss Jane was a positive thinker," said Nancy. "She could have complained about feeling old and not in the mix of the party, but instead, she saw the bright side of the occasion." All responded with the chatter of approval.

"I'd like to bring this discussion to a close by quoting Jane's words from *Pride and Prejudice*, which are so appropriate for our jolly little literary club," Jean announced. "She wrote, 'I declare after all there is no enjoyment like reading! How much sooner one tires of anything than of a book!'"

A round of applause filled up the room as more discussion continued between each other. It was one of our better meetings, I thought. Thinking of times long ago and how they managed their rights in such a restricted time for women was very thought provoking in our current world.

As Mother and I prepared to leave, Jean came up to thank me once again for the discussion idea.

CHAPTER 48

The next morning's paper had a wonderful colored picture and article about the Jane Austen quilters. It listed all our names and gave great recognition to Isabella's Quilt Shop for hosting the group. She was a great promoter, no doubt. Maybe I should start a flower club. The very thought of scheduling more women to meet with in my life, and likely the same women, was too much to think about.

The next morning, I got to Main Street very early to take my walk. For the upcoming festival next week, they were already marking booth spaces with numbers. The temperatures were already high, so I stopped by my shop to get a cold bottle of water. When I barely unlocked the door, the phone was ringing and ringing. Who would be ordering so early? I picked up the phone to hear a very serious and familiar voice.

"Sorry to bother you so early, Anne," Isabella urgently

said. "I'm trying to catch everyone in quilt club to tell them we must meet at the shop tonight at five thirty. It's very important. Can you make it?"

How strange, I thought at first. "With Sam being out of town, I was supposed to have dinner with Mother and Aunt Julia, so I don't know," I responded.

"You all need to come here first," she was quick to offer firm direction without allowing me to get in another word. "I was about to call your mother next. It won't take long, but it's very important. I'll see you tonight, then?" Then, she hung up, just like that.

There's nothing like someone demanding where you need to be and when. It must have to do with hearing the results with the quilt. Could the news not have waited—good or bad—until we met again?

Before I left to go home to shower, I noticed the amount of work we had to accomplish today was going to be time consuming. I would never get used to the pressure of huge orders and their time frame on delivery. It was a big responsibility to make it all happen, or the disappointment would be inexcusable and probably unforgiving. I checked the large storage cooler to see if we had enough supply of some of the flowers that were being requested. One entire casket order was to be all yellow roses. Sally may have to call some local suppliers if we didn't have enough and have Kevin pick them up. Everything had to be delivered today, so I didn't waste more time to get home for a challenging day.

I was about to leave the house when Mother called and asked me what Isabella's urgent phone call was all about. I didn't have time to analyze the situation because of our full workday, so I told her to call Aunt Julia. I told her we all may not be able to make it, but we would try. If I made it, we could decide after the meeting whether to go to dinner from there. She wasn't happy with my uncertainty, but the shop certainly came before a quilt meeting, that's for sure.

When I arrived back at the shop, Sally was already right on top of what had to go out when and to whom. She had done preliminary work on the garden club luncheon centerpieces, which would be Kevin's first delivery. Three funerals and an evening banquet also needed our attention. Luckily, Sally seemed to think we had enough of the yellow roses for the casket spray.

"I sure enjoyed the program last night, Jean," said Sally as she set up more containers to be filled. "I kept thinking of some of Jane's quotes through the night. I specifically remember the dialogue from *Emma* where she wrote, 'One half of the world cannot understand the pleasures of the other.' I can so identify with that. I almost commented about it last night, but then everyone would want to know why. I never enjoyed what most kids enjoyed growing up. I guess I was always worried about more important things in my house, like whether my parents would have a fight each day when I came home from school." We all were silent, feeling we should not respond any further to her comment.

"Probably best you did not, my dear," said Jean. "I cannot devise what might have been said. I do love that quote so, and you should value its contents." Sally grinned. Sally never shared anything dark from her past.

"There were many good quotes last night, especially the last one about reading a book," I offered, changing the conversation.

"Did you get that crack of dawn ring from Isabella this

morning, Miss Anne?" Jean asked. "Al sure got his dander up about her ringing us up at that hour! She had a good deal of eagerness about her call. Perhaps she's got a bit of news on the quilt and can't wait to party. Right, Miss Anne?" I shrugged my shoulders. It sure didn't sound like a party call to me!

"She woke me from a really, really good dream, if ya know what I mean," said Abbey. "Darn her!" She giggled.

"I would venture that included our new Mr. Kip?" Jean said, teasing her. We all had a laugh. "Quite so?"

"Perhaps," Abbey said, blushing. "The same color eyes, for sure!"

Jean laughed. "I was going to get my hair a bit of a trim after work; but I'm not going to miss a party, so I'll pop in."

"None of us are going to show up if we don't get these orders out," I said, on a serious note. "Are you about finished with that piece, Jean?"

"Well, I am ever so worried that in the course of the day, these hyacinths are going to fizzle before tomorrow's end," she noted. "I fancy it should be done right soon! I will carry on as best I can."

Kevin and Kip were in and out. They continued to tease me about needing a second van as they carried out deliveries. I told them to use my car if they had to, which took the wind out of their sails. All the day's activity was an eye opener for Kip, I'm sure. I still hadn't made the hire for his garden work at 333 Lincoln.

"How's everyone doing?" I heard Mother's voice coming in the front door. "I'm here to work and I brought sandwiches for everyone's lunch. I just happened to make some chocolate cookies yesterday, so brought a platter of those, too." We just stopped and looked at her. Abbey and Jean gave out a cheer of welcome.

"You didn't have to do this, Mother!" I said, giving her a hug. "The lunch will happily sustain us and I know you can help us here by answering the phone and assisting walk-ins, so you are most welcome!"

She didn't waste any time putting her purse under the counter as she began showing a customer some choices in our display of live plants. She was so good with people and so many would know her when she was here.

Meanwhile, Mother answered a call from Sue saying she was bringing Mia with her to the meeting. She also took a call from Sam when I didn't answer my cell phone. He told her to tell me to slow down and we would catch up on the phone when I got home this evening. From the way I was enjoying Mother's services, I decided a secretary like her would be divine. Let's see, I also needed a cook, house cleaner, window washer, gardener, repairman, and maybe even a personal shopper! Oh boy. I was very needy—or just over my head.

I took a break and went outdoors to our small patio that had a lawn table and chairs in order to eat Mother's delicious tuna sandwich. I forgot how yummy it was with fresh grapes and nuts mixed in. Kip and Kevin were eating out there as well, and I told Kip that Sam and I would definitely take advantage of his services if he still needed extra work. I told him to come to our house when Sam got home in a couple of days to check things out. He seemed thrilled.

Sally was becoming uptight as four o'clock came and we still had more banquet pieces to do. I didn't remember seeing her like this before, but was pleased she was taking the responsibility so seriously. She lightened up when Mother came to the design room and started placing the bows and candles. Mother was a godsend today. I decided we were close enough to a finale, so I got out drinks and told them we were about to celebrate our accomplishments. They all cheered aloud, except Sally.

"Not so fast," Sally said. "I think the count is wrong here, Kevin. There are supposed to be fifteen of these. I only see thirteen, so I'm going to have to make two more."

"No, you're not. They're already in the van, so just relax," Kevin teased, patting her on the shoulder. "I checked the order and counted them myself." She relaxed with a smile and took the glass I held in front of her.

I was so proud of each of them as I watched my team pull together. It made me all the more certain we could and would need the expansion. I should see the early plans any day now, I reminded myself. Mother took her glass and gave me a wink of approval. I knew she was also proud, watching my little shop blossom into a successful business.

We all gave a cheer when we heard the van door close. It was four forty-five. We locked the front door and agreed to meet up at Isabella's for the surprise party, as Abbey playfully called it.

CHAPTER 49

When Mother and I walked into Isabella's, everyone was seated as if a program was ready to begin. We sat down and looked about the room to see if refreshments were set up as she did for our other meetings. The tables were empty and not where they usually were placed for our club meetings. Sue and Mia joined us in our section of chairs as Mia fussed at trying to get her way about something. Sue was frustrated and Mia wasn't her usual happy self, especially when she'd see people like us that she knew. She wanted to sit on Sue's lap and ignore everyone else's attention given to her. Her lack of energy to run around the shop at this time was probably a good thing.

Isabella then knocked on the table to get everyone's attention. The room fell totally silent. What could this all be about? "Thanks again, everyone, for all of you coming tonight on such short notice," she began with a somber face.

"I've asked you here tonight in this expeditious fashion to tell you that our quilt did not arrive at the quilt show as it should have." Yup, this was not going to be good news.

The room broke into a united gasp. "The worst of it is that we believe it must have been stolen, best we can tell."

Now the chatter became louder with various responses. She was losing control.

Isabella wouldn't look directly at us as, for everyone wanted to ask questions. Nancy and Roxanne were the only ones standing as they nervously paced the floor in front of us. I'm sure they felt extra responsibility, along with Isabella.

Isabella had to bang on the table once again to quiet us down. "If you'll just bear with me, I will recall the chain of events with you that led to this discovery," she said with fright in her eyes. We were all ears, even Mia.

"I sent the package the day after our celebration as I told you I would," she began. "I packaged it properly, as I have done many times. When I brought it to the shipper, I insured it for the appraised value, thank goodness." She took a deep breath, looking like she may hyperventilate right before us. "The package did arrive at its destination, but when opened, it was not there." We gasped again like we were children being told a horror story.

"The show staff panicked, thinking they had made an error of sorts in their process, so they neglected to get in touch with us right away, thinking they may have the explanation. I knew the package arrived there, because someone signed for it and a copy was sent back to us." This was good news, I thought. The silence deafened the room as we waited eagerly for more details.

"When a few days passed and I wasn't hearing anything

about the judging, I thought I'd better call. Many of you were asking me if I had heard anything about the quilt. When I finally talked to the right person in charge, that's when they told me what happened. As you can imagine, they were terrified. They said that in the many years they have been doing this, that only one quilt was stolen, which they recovered. She said, despite the many precautions that they take, quilts can be stolen in many different ways. They had a photo of the quilt, which I had to send when we registered the quilt for the contest, so they knew what it looked like."

"Now what?" an elderly lady yelled from the back of the room. She and others wanted immediate answers.

"Did you call the police?" asked Paige. She was sitting near Isabella.

"Do you think a guy from the delivery truck could have taken it?" asked Abbey, who was now standing. "You know they mishandle packages all the time. They may have seen it was from a quilt shop and decided to help themselves to a nice quilt." Everyone was talking at the same time.

"Yes, they do it at the airlines all the time," complained Aunt Julia.

Isabella banged once again on the table to restore some order. "Yes, all these ideas and thoughts need to be investigated, but for now, I just felt you all had a right to know," she explained as she now perspired. "I'm sorry if you felt I mislead you into thinking this would be some celebratory announcement. I just didn't know what to do. You had every right to know this right away." I felt so sorry for her as she faced an angry, confused crowd.

"Isabella," Mother said, standing up from her chair. "You did all the right things here, and no one is blaming you for any misstep. These things happen everywhere and I'm sure it will eventually turn up."

"It was a terrible risk, as I warned Isabella about," complained Roxanne with her arms folded in front of her. "How can we really trust what the show folks are telling us? What if one of the women helping decided to take it home?" She quickly had others agreeing with her.

I finally had to speak in Isabella's defense before a verbal attack on her got out of hand. I stood. "I can assure you, as a business person, these kinds of things happen all the time," I said in a calm voice. "Given time, these kinds of mishaps are usually explained and corrected. Let's be civil adults about this, ladies. We don't have to make Isabella feel any worse than she already does. This is not her fault!" As I looked at their faces, they were searching for blame, which was normal.

Almost everyone voiced in agreement and nearly clapped. The order of the evening was lost. The quilters were delivered the news and were in shock. I, too, had no idea of any way to be helpful. Who would take a quilt that was so personal and meant so much to someone? Everyone was now swarming around Isabella like she was the victim of the crime. Some were giving her hugs of comfort as she began tearing up.

"Well, whoever diddled us out of our prize ought to be banged up or sent to the nick, as we say at home," Jean said with anger to Mother and me.

"I'm sure it'll be found," I said, not trying to overreact like nearly everyone else in the room. "It sounds to me it disappeared in transit, don't you think, Mother?"

"Yes," she said, shaking her head in disbelief. "There's no point in laboring over this any longer. Let's get something to eat. I'm quite hungry, how about you girls?"

"Great idea!" said Aunt Julia as she got out her cell phone. "I need to call home and check on Sarah to make sure she got home from play practice."

"I need to get Mia to bed, you all," Sue said, getting up to leave with Mia hanging on her. "Thanks anyway for the invitation, but I'm worn out, and this news is not making my evening any better." I couldn't agree more, I thought.

"I have beef stew at home if you want to come back to the house!" Mother offered, feeling bad for Sue.

"No, Mother, you worked hard today like the rest of us," I reminded her. "How about I treat us to pizza?" Their eyes lit up in agreement.

When we got to Mother's house, I kicked off my shoes from an old habit and we gathered around the kitchen table, waiting for the pizza from Pete's Pizza to arrive. Mother and Aunt Julia always loved the thin crust vegetarian and I had to have my usual pepperoni and onion. Our spirits were broken as we started sharing the night's events.

"Wait until Sam hears about this tonight when he calls," I said sadly. "Ironically, his sister Pat has a quilt entered in the same quilt show. Just think how she would feel if her quilt were missing."

"Well, maybe our quilt wasn't the only one stolen, Anne," Aunt Julia suggested. "For all we know, there may have been more. That would be something they wouldn't be willing to share with us, I'm sure."

"You're right, Aunt Julia," I said, in wonder of it all. "We'll know in time, if that's the case. That will not be an easy story to hide from quiltmakers."

The long-awaited pizza arrived and we dove into its delicious texture and taste before we continued with the topic at hand.

"The interesting thing about this quilt is that there is a whole number of people who feel violated instead of just one maker," Mother noted, after she took her first bite. "We all put so much thought into each block. It may as well have been an entire quilt for all of us."

"Good point, Sylvia," Aunt Julia said in agreement. "I heard Jean tell Isabella that there is a website called stolenquilts. com where you can show a photo of your stolen quilt, in case someone tries to sell it. I suppose, like missing children, the sooner you report it, the better your chances are about finding it. Isabella already seemed to know about it."

"Oh, good," said Mother.

"I think it has to be someone that would know the value of a quilt, and believe me, that's not everyone. Am I right?" I asked, trying to think it through. "I certainly would not know the quilt market right now."

"Heck if I know," said Aunt Julia. "Remember when we would be quilting with Marie in the basement and she would talk about the 'quilt police' coming after us if we didn't do something right? Do you think they could handle this?" We busted out laughing, fondly recalling Aunt Marie's cheerful sense of humor.

"Speaking of the quilt police, they are going to come after us if we don't finish Jean's quilt pretty soon!" Mother reminded us.

"Oh, I kind of forgot!" I admitted. "Yes, we do! I'm surprised Jean hasn't said something to us."

"She's too kind and mannerly to speak up about that," said Aunt Julia. "I'm free this Sunday afternoon, if you two are!"

"Sure," said Mother. "I'll call Jean and Sue, Anne, if you

can make it!"

"What else could I possibly do on a Sunday afternoon with my boring life?" I teased. They all laughed, having fun at my expense.

We had a plan, just as we did many times while sharing our pizza and enjoying one another's company. We may have to call on the quilt police plus Aunt Marie and Grandmother to help find our Jane Austen quilt.

CHAPTER 50

T he next morning, we all could breathe a little easier as far as orders were concerned. Abbey was off and Jean wasn't coming in until noon. Jason Cunningham was due to meet with Sally and me in the afternoon when Jean was available to watch the front room.

"So, did you tell Sam about the latest crime in Colebridge last night?" Sally asked, seeking my reaction.

"Oh yeah," I said. "He didn't call me until midnight, however, so I was pretty groggy. I'm not sure what I even told him. It was short, I know. He'll be home sometime this evening."

"I'll bet Roxanne is giving Isabella fits about that missing quilt," Sally said, revisiting the quilt meeting. "Remember how upset she was that it was being submitted for competition?"

"Yeah, and it showed last night as she paced the floor and unnecessarily embarrassed Isabella for entering it," I said,

265

with sympathy in my voice. "I feel sorry for Isabella having to face all of us. We have to remember the shipper is going to have some responsibility here, so it will likely be traced down."

"Do you think Isabella really told us everything?" Sally asked, suspicion entering her tone of voice.

"Why wouldn't she?" I questioned. Just then, Kevin came in the back door to load the first delivery, and perhaps what may be the only delivery of the slow day.

"Good morning, ladies!" Kevin said, evidencing a good mood. "I heard at the donut shop this morning that the infamous Jane Austen quilt got stolen." Sally and I looked shocked at the thought of the story getting out so soon.

"When I heard one of the guys with an English accent tell about it, I figured it must be Jean's husband, Al. However, I've never met him."

"Oh boy, I'll bet he got his 'knickers in a twist,' as Jean would say!" Sally said in jest. We all laughed.

After lunch, Jean arrived just as Jason Cunningham came in the door. Jean quickly asked if we had heard any latest news about the quilt. I felt like telling her to ask her husband. I'm sure his donut shop cronies would have more news than us!

We used the large table in the design room for Jason to spread out all the blueprints. Sally started with a mental list of questions before Jason could tell us much of anything. I immediately took notice of the little square drawing that was labeled Anne's office. That was pleasing enough for me at the moment. I was amazed how he was able to squeeze in a sizable consultation room, which could also be used for employee meetings. Sally was elated with everything she saw. As I watched and listened, it was surreal to me, almost too good to be true.

Our parking lot was nearly gone, with the exception of two parking places. I did like the way a carport area took care of protecting our van, as well as leaving us a patio area for our lawn table and chairs. His added landscaping touches were excellent and I would definitely use the suggestions.

The biggest changes were adding more design space and expanding the cooling room. The front room of the shop would basically be the same except for a larger refrigerated case for walk-in customers. The current case would be put in the new design room, if needed. The expense for all of this would have to be digested in time, I suppose. As Jason said earlier, now would be the time to plan for the future, while we were going to this much expense and trouble. For a second, I wondered if Sam would think the same way.

He said they would start in the rear of the property where the biggest construction would occur and it would be less disruptive as we kept the business running. He told us he typically uses Collins Construction because of their quality of work and experience in Colebridge. Collins Construction was Ted's uncle. It had been in the family for some time and I knew also that their reputation was great.

"Our biggest challenge here is to get a variance on fewer parking spaces, more than the outside appearance of the rear addition." Jason explained. "By the city ordinance, we need more spaces. That means going before the Board of Adjustment. I also think you need to visit with each of your neighbors on each side of you so they know how disruptive this may be. The Landmarks Board and the Board of Adjustment will be asking them about you. The last thing you need is for your neighbors to protest what you are doing here."

Well, I knew Gayle's landlord would absolutely have no problem. However, on the other side was Mr. Crab, as we called him, who would be the first to complain even though he was never at his shop. I would have to handle him with kid gloves.

When Jason left, Sally and I looked at each other in amazement. This was really going to happen! We both couldn't have been happier. With her support and drive, I really didn't feel I was going through this alone. I also realized I was leaving Sam out of the entire process. Was this a good or a bad thing? I guess it remained to be seen!

Jean was thrilled when Mother called her in the morning to tell her about the Sunday quilting. "Sylvia asked me to supply more of my quilting thread," Jean mentioned.

"I need to go to Isabella's to get more quilt soap for Mother, so I'll just get some, Jean. It's the least we can do to make up for our procrastination here," I offered.

"Mighty fine, Miss Anne," she said, clearly pleased. "I fancy the last roll will occur, do you not think so, Miss Anne?"

"It depends on how much we eat and talk," I teased. "I have a feeling you may be right. It is a beautiful quilt, Jean. You should be proud."

"Quite so, Miss Anne," she concurred.

It was good to see Sam that evening. He suggested we meet up at the Q Seafood and Grill to catch up. When I arrived, he was sitting at a nice corner table with a candle lamp that made him look more romantic than ever! I had so much to tell him, but I didn't want to spoil what I saw as a rare romantic evening. I asked Sam all about his trip, but wasn't absorbing much as my head was already filled with flower shop expansion information. His eyes glistened in the light as he spoke. When he asked about the latest news regarding the stolen quilt, I touched base with reality.

"No good news, I'm afraid," I began my lead in. "It's being investigated, so we just need some time. I do have good news, however, with the first meeting that Sally and I had with Jason Cunningham." I wanted to make sure I was referencing both Sally and me when I spoke about the expansion. I didn't want it to be another Alex King scenario for Sam to visualize.

The once-romantic image on his face soon faded away as I began talking about the meeting. He was looking at me like I was performing instead of explaining. I couldn't tell if he was really absorbing anything. There was no reaction whatsoever when I beamed about personal touches that I liked. I admired him for pretending to listen without any interruption, or maybe he wasn't listening at all. I had to remember that he was listening to my dream, not his. It was just like him to politely handle all of this because he loved me and really did want to see me happy.

When our favorite grilled salmon dinners arrived, I changed the subject to our beautiful house, the new chair in the bedroom, and my latest news of Kip being able to help us. He mostly nodded, as if he were really tired from a long day. He didn't add much to the conversation and just agreed with me for the most part. We were interrupted at one point by one of my good customers and her husband who just wanted to say hello. He graciously stood to be formally introduced. This was the best part of Sam's personality. His business skills and proper upbringing made him quite the gentleman.

He was never curt or catty in his description of others, which I always thought was so commendable.

When our coffee arrived at the close of our meal, I said, "So do you still love that independent and 'knows what she wants in life' girl that you met one Thanksgiving Day?"

"Yes. Yes I do," he admitted, without smiling, "as long as my sweet Annie still knows she wants her Sam."

When he smiled, I breathed a sigh of relief. I took it as a good sign regarding all I had told him that evening. We both took special care to make the rest of the night as romantic as possible. When we arrived at 333 Lincoln, we stopped at the south porch to embrace and kiss. We were surrounded by the sound of the summer crickets playing in the background. We both knew this was really the best part of the day as our bodies embraced and our minds became uncluttered. Having Sam to share my world was not just the icing on the cake, but the cake itself. Hmmm...

CHAPTER 51

The next morning I not only awoke to the smell of coffee, which wasn't unusual, but to a bacon aroma that crept up the stairs. It certainly enticed me to get out of bed and indulge in what Sam was cooking. I put on my light knit robe over my contented body, brushed my teeth, combed my hair, and followed the breakfast aromas down the stairs.

"Pancakes, anyone?" Sam asked with a big grin when he saw me. "Here, taste the perfect crispness of this bacon, would you?"

I opened my mouth to accept the heavenly crunch in my mouth. "So, what brought on the big breakfast today, Mr. Dickson?" I asked, pouring myself some coffee.

"I burned a lot of calories last night!" he teased. "A man has to keep up his strength, don't you think?" He gave me a wink as he flipped another pancake.

"Oh indeed," I added with a grin. "I would like two of

those cakes and maybe three of those bacon strips, if you're taking orders."

"Yes, ma'am," he responded. "I think that can be arranged if you'll sit right here."

As Sam prepared to join me, I thought about how we had untraditional roles in our married life. It was always my mother who prepared breakfast for my father who was coming down the stairs. She always prepared a large breakfast each morning. After Father's death, she still wanted to prepare my coffee and something light for me as I continued to come down those very stairs.

This morning, I was taking full advantage and also skipping my morning walk in order to spend more time with Sam.

On the way to work, I carried all my extra calories to Isabella's Quilt Shop. I learned long ago that if I didn't take care of my errands before my busy day at the shop, I could easily forget or lose track of their importance.

"Good morning, Anne," Isabella greeted from her cutting counter. "I guess you're here to check on any updates like all the others, I'll bet."

"No, no. I'm here on an errand and as a paying customer, I'll have you know!" I said cheerfully in defense of myself.

"Well, that's refreshing!" she responded, coming toward me. "How can I help you?"

"I need a couple of these quilt washes!" I said, grabbing them off the counter in front of me. "Mother brags about this so. She also sent me for two packages of the Craftsman quilting needles. I need size 8, if you have it, and a couple of the spools of thread that she uses. I forgot to ask the brand, so I hope you know. Most of us like these needles very much, but they keep disappearing, for some reason. We're trying to finish quilting Jean's quilt. We got a little sidetracked with some kind of block challenge."

She laughed. "That basement of your mother's has a lot of strange things happen, I hear," she teased. "Here is the thread I know she has purchased before, and if it's for Jean's quilt, please just let me contribute it! We sell a lot of this soap and use it here when we wash quilts for people."

I didn't want to respond to her remark about strange occurrences, so I just laughed, agreeing with her. "Thanks for the thread, Isabella," I said sincerely. "I will tell Jean about your contribution." I paused, choosing the right words to say. "You know, Isabella, in regard to our missing quilt, we all feel your pain on this matter. I apologize for all of those who are not reacting kindly to you in this incident. Your heart was in the right place. It is very natural for some to play the blame game. I have a business and I know how things like this can happen, believe me."

"Thanks Anne. It means a lot that you say this." She paused, putting her hand to her mouth. "There's something I'd like to share with you that I couldn't possibly do with all the others at our meeting." Isabella took a deep breath.

"What's that?" Isabella looked about the shop to make sure it was just the two of us within hearing distance. Did I want to hear this or not?

"When our package arrived at the quilt show's receiving department, the box wasn't empty," she said softly. I waited for more information.

"A white chenille bedspread was folded up inside the box." She shook her head. "The show staffers at first took it to be a joke of some kind. They were not going to contact us until they knew for sure that nothing happened on their end—for liability purposes, of course."

"Oh! My word, Isabella!" I did not know whether to laugh or cry. "What was that doing in there?"

"It beats me, Anne," she continued. "With the weight of the spread, it felt like there was a quilt inside. When someone opened up the box along the way, as they suspect happened, they inserted this bedspread as a replacement for the quilt. No one would become suspicious of anything until it arrived at its final destination!" Her voice was shaking.

"But, Isabella," I rebutted, "what if after, and I mean after the quilt arrives at the destination, someone opened the box, saw the quilt, admired the quilt, and decided to keep it for themselves? They inserted the bedspread, sealed it back up, and pretended it just arrived." She listened intently as if trying to imagine the sight.

"This would also address my theory that the thief would have to be someone that had knowledge about quilts, and also knew they had one of value. They could even justify the crime by saying it would be covered by insurance. A show staffer could be such a person."

"All worthy theories, Anne, but it still doesn't help me get the quilt back," Isabella lamented. "I'm not there to do any inquiry; and, believe you me, they have covered themselves with their precise procedures in shipping and receiving. They even sent me a photo of the bedspread in case I didn't believe them. Can you believe that?"

I tried to picture it all. "Have you talked to the police here?" I finally asked. "We are really just taking their word for it. Something's not adding up."

"Yes, I did talk with them," she said, her disappointment

showing. "There isn't really much they can do, they said. I'm going to have to rely on the shipper to do his due diligence in the matter, I suppose. Let's just hope the insurance company doesn't question all of this and does comes through on the appraisal value. I do want to make sure that everyone who made a block for the quilt gets reimbursed rather quickly, which may not happen right away from the insurance company. I may have to do more from the shop's perspective as well. I have to demonstrate good intent here."

"That's crazy. You don't have to do that," I said with total confidence.

"Oh, believe me, Anne, I do," she stated, just as confident. "My business is already down. They all have taken this quite personally, I'm afraid. Roxanne doesn't let me forget for a minute about what a mistake it was to send it off. I'm ready to tell her to fly a kite, and if my business doesn't pick up, I won't need her here in the shop, anyway!"

"I'm so sorry," I said, feeling badly for what she was experiencing. "Just keep your spirits up and let everyone do their job. I'd better get going, as I still have more errands to run. If you want to be among friends, you can join us on Sunday to quilt on Jean's quilt."

"Thanks, I may just do that," she said smiling. "I love Jean. She always brightens up my day when she comes in. She is quite a good hand quilter, too!"

"Yes, she's not one to like machine quilting; so that's why we offered to help her with this quilt. Plus, she has been such a big help to me in many ways. Thanks again for the thread."

I stopped at the post office and the drug store before I joined my family at Brown's Botanical. When I arrived, Sally said I just missed Nick Notto who was in complaining about the early delivery trucks and congested traffic for the festival tomorrow. Early tourists were no doubt arriving in hopes of any prior sales and activities. I loved the hustle and bustle of anticipated events. Nick did have a point in that many of his customers would be picking up cakes and would have to struggle with the traffic. He should probably consider a reliable delivery service. The weather report was hot and humid, like a typical Missouri festival!

CHAPTER 52

C'an you see now what I'm talking about?" I asked Kip, showing him around our yard and gardens the next morning. "I can't keep up with it all, and fall will be here before we know it."

"To be honest with you, Mrs. Dickson, I think you've done a pretty good job here," Kip said as he looked around. "This place is beautiful and your herb garden is certainly thriving. I can tell you have a good eye because your placements of color and plants throughout the gardens and yard are quite attractive. These gorgeous lilac bushes must have been here for years! I'm sure I can be a great help here if you want. This potting shed is a really old treasure, isn't it? I could see the personal touch you've given it when I peeked inside."

"Sam said I could expand it, but I just can't," I explained. "I need to keep it as authentic as possible. I love it and wish it could talk to me!"

"As I looked around the yard, you could always extend off the back screened-in porch to an attached greenhouse," Kip suggested. "Perhaps something in an octagon shape would add to the charm your estate. You have plenty of room there."

"Are you kidding me, Kip?" I quickly responded. "Do you know how much trouble I'm already in with this flower shop expansion?" He laughed, getting the picture.

I started picking some lilacs for an arrangement in the house. "I'm glad Sam did not hear this conversation. He's in the garage doing something. He said to send you in there when we're done discussing my plans for you."

"I'll just check on the place every couple of days to see what needs to be done," Kip suggested. "I had to monitor grounds similar to this at the country club. You've already done all the hard work when you moved here, I'm sure. I will also spray and fertilize as needed, unless your mower guy does that."

"That would be great, but I'll check with him," I responded with gratitude. I was so pleased to have his help. I really wanted to make this a showplace like it was many years ago. As long as Sam and I could afford it, I wanted the best for the Taylor house.

The next morning, Sam was off to play golf with Uncle Jim, and Mother picked me up to attend church with her. It had been some time since I did this, but I knew I was planning to spend most of the day quilting with her anyway, so I thought it was a nice idea. As I sat in the sparsely populated pew at church, I thought of so many who were in trouble and pain that needed God's help. I was so blessed and grateful for all I had. I asked God to guide us to solve the mystery of our Jane Austen quilt and wanted Him to ease the worry Isabella was feeling. Somehow, I knew all this had a simple explanation. Quilters were good people with good intentions, weren't they? Hmmm...

Before the others arrived at Mother's, we both shared a delicious meat loaf sandwich. The first to arrive were Sue and Mia. They also brought along their other family member who ruled—little Muffin. Muffin, wearing a new pink collar, knew to run immediately to Mother for her expected treat. Sarah came with Aunt Julia. Sarah really took to quilting, unlike most girls her age. Jean was the last to arrive, bringing a lovely platter of fresh cranberry and orange scones. I had experienced them before at one of the literary club meetings, and it was all I could do to keep from grabbing one of them before they traveled to the basement.

When we found our places around the frame, Mia immediately resented our attention being diverted from her. She was used to Sarah entertaining her, but Sarah wanted to quilt with us. After running in, out, and under the frame a few times, Mother found her some new children's books to occupy her.

"Anne, you haven't said anything to us about the strange passing of Ted's mother," Aunt Julia inquired, bringing the subject up unexpectedly.

"Well, I really don't know anything but rumors," I repeated. "Mrs. Carter next door told Mother she was quite depressed, but never bad enough to commit suicide. I think she knew her quite well and used to play cards with her. Frankly, I would like to know exactly what happened, also. I never heard a word from Ted. Neither Mother nor I went to the wake, but I did send Ted a personal note and a donation to the heart association. I really lost touch with them all. She was a dear lady, I'll say that. I really liked her."

"Perhaps that's all we need to know," Mother calmly said. "I think everyone liked her."

Suddenly there was a knock at the door, and Mother went upstairs to answer.

"Hi, Sylvia," Isabella cheerfully greeted. "Anne thought I might be able to give you a hand this afternoon on Jean's quilt."

"Of course!" Mother said, showing her in. "Please come in. It's great to see you. Your timing is perfect. We are down in the basement about ready to share some of Jean's delicious scones." Everyone nearly stood up and cheered at the sight of Isabella coming down the stairs. I hadn't told any of them that I had invited her.

"I hear there is an urgent call out to get this quilt completed!" Isabella joked, as she observed the quilt. "Oh my, Jean, this is a beautiful quilt! I brought my thimble, so where would you like me to quilt?" Jean's approval showed as she got up from the chair to give her a hug.

"You can have my spot," said Sarah. "I'm going upstairs to call a friend of mine."

"I'd be happy to, Sarah!" Isabella gladly offered. "My goodness, your stitches are very small for a beginner!" Sarah blushed and thanked her before she flew up the stairs.

As soon as Isabella sat, Mother offered her tea and the availability of the scones on the counter. Isabella wasted no time and put on her thimble. She knew right where to continue quilting in Sarah's absence.

Aunt Julia was, of course, the first one to ask her about the stolen quilt. I hated that the topic had to come up so soon, with Isabella hardly becoming relaxed in our midst. You could have heard a pin drop waiting for Isabella's response.

"I'm afraid I have nothing new to report, you all," she said, not looking up from her quilting. "Tomorrow's newspaper is going to have an article about it, I hate to say, photo and all. The same reporter that was at our meeting for the debut is doing the follow-up story since he heard about its disappearance. I hate all this attention."

"Maybe it'll be helpful," Mother said. "You never know who might recognize the quilt. There may be a lead or two from it."

"In vain, I have struggled to see how this quilt has taken leave," said Jean, frustration in her tone. "Such ill fortune happening to such jolly quilters—right here in Colebridge!"

"I agree, Jean," Mother said sadly.

"It's such a black eye for the quilt shop," Isabella said, shaking her head. "I really felt the national attention would be such a reward for everyone's hard work and creativity."

"Stop thinking that way," I said, wanting to defend her. "It is not your fault. It was a grand idea."

"I haven't heard of any such roar, Miss Isabella," Jean added in an effort to comfort her. "It takes a special breed to be so cruel."

"I did register it with the stolen quilt website," Isabella noted. "I can't believe how many quilts get stolen every day. As I scrolled down to see them all, I noticed there were so many from all over the world. Most of them are stolen and sold to dealers for cash, so the pictures on the web get pretty much exposure in many ways. They say this is pretty successful, according to the website information."

"So there's a black market for quilts, or an underground racket of sorts on quilts?" asked Sue, innocently.

"I suppose, like everything else, there probably is," agreed Isabella. "This quilt just wasn't an ordinary quilt. That's why I agree with Anne that someone took a liking to its uniqueness and thought they could make some money."

"I've been meaning to call Pat, Sam's sister, to see if she won anything with her quilt at the show," I shared. "I thought she may even have some insight into their registration process, and I wanted to check to see if she had any problems."

"They are not about to let a rumor of any kind get out about a stolen quilt or no one would want to enter a quilt again," Isabella complained. "They have left the ball in our court as the sender to file the insurance claim and that will likely be the end of it." Murmurs were shared around the frame as more takers munched on the delicious scones.

I was waiting to hear whether she was going to share with them about the chenille bedspread, but she didn't say a word. I'm sure she chose not to for the right reasons, so I remained silent. We watched Isabella quilt tiny stitches. She certainly was a pro at this craft, as we all observed.

"Well, I'll bet no one will remove these perfect stitches from the quilt," Aunt Julia remarked. Those who knew the story of Aunt Julia's stitches being removed snickered at her comment.

"Now, Julia, don't go there," Mother said before anyone else could comment. Isabella remained silent and kept quilting. Of course, Aunt Julia was referring to Grandmother Davis removing her stitches as we were quilting Aunt Julia's quilt some time ago. Aunt Julia took it personally, blaming us at first. Many things disappeared and appeared in this basement, so we blamed Grandmother.

It was time to roll the quilt in the frame. There was still

enough for another quilting. Today, it seemed we did more talking and eating than quilting, which happened on certain days.

"Maybe Grandmother Davis can help us find the Jane Austen quilt," suggested Sue, bringing the sore subject up again. Isabella looked at me for some explanation. "Ignore all this, Isabella," I said. "My grandmother and Aunt Julia have issues. They both are sweethearts, except Aunt Julia is still with us and Grandmother has passed on."

She still looked puzzled as we all grinned. "I see," she said. "Well, if she can be helpful anyway, that would be great and most heartedly appreciated!"

"I say we leave poor Grandmother out of this mishap," Jean suggested in a teasing tone. "I would venture that we ask the spirit of Miss Jane Austen. Let's hope she wasn't so horrified at our dashing quilt that she had it vanish upon us! My curiosity is all awake on this one!"

Mine certainly was as well. Hmmm...

We exhausted our topics and Sarah was pestering Aunt Julia to go home. Mia had settled down to the point of almost taking a nap. Jean was thrilled with the new stitches to her quilt and thanked us with all her heart.

Isabella was the last to leave. You could tell she was absorbing any friendship and support she could in light of this unfortunate incident. I assured her I would pass on anything I learned regarding Pat's experience with the show. I knew the risk in Isabella's credibility was at stake here, no matter the outcome.

CHAPTER 53

A hot and crowded festival on Main Street bit the dust for another successful year. The formerly trash-lined street was nearly cleared away of debris and the only ones complaining were the ones who didn't make the money they anticipated. Money had a way of "keeping the peace," as they say. Some residents were never happy because it was a party in their backyard and they didn't receive a dime—only wear and tear on their property. I certainly could see their point. I know how protective I would be of my property at 333 Lincoln.

Knowing I had a meeting with Jason Cunningham this morning had my stomach in a twist. The come-and-go nausea almost felt as if I were coming down with something.

When he arrived right on time, the front of the shop was full and I was helping someone on the phone with a sizable funeral order. I watched him browse each corner and crevice, taking a photo now and then and making a few notes.

"This little shop of yours is going to pop at the seams if you don't do something soon, Anne," he teased as I hung up the phone. I grinned at the very thought of it. "I think it's amazing how you have functioned with a place this size."

We went outside to the shaded table and chairs for privacy as he began bringing me up to date with our schedule and what had to be done next. My stomach churned even more when he told me it was vital that I attend the Board of Adjustment meeting with him to ask for our parking variance. The heat was making it hard to breathe as I tried to listen to his report. I wanted to pass out, but kept listening. He had already visited with some of the board members and he felt we would have a good result. Putting it off no longer, I asked Jason to get me some water. What was wrong with me?

"Let's get you back into the air conditioning," Jason quickly said, taking my arm. We sat down by my desk and Jason asked Sally to get me some water. I felt better in the cool air and accepted a bottle of water from Sally as she looked at me strangely.

"Thanks, Sally. The heat really got to me out there. Thank you," I said, giving her a reassuring smile. "Please continue, Jason. I'm sorry."

He looked at me with concern before he continued. "You will likely have to be closed on the retail side when we take out this back wall, however, you can still do some business on the phone and web," he continued. "We will try to do this as quickly and as quietly as we can, but some things can't be helped with an addition like this."

The disruption I was envisioning was not pleasant, but I also felt Jason had the project under control and I need not worry. As we went over the blueprints, the excitement of the future helped relieve the anxiety I was feeling. Jason was trying to reassure me that all would be well. I had to admit my nausea and light-headedness was not a normal experience for me. Maybe everything was going too quickly and I was losing control of it all.

Sally was now calling for me to come into the shop, for there was someone asking specifically for me. I said good-bye to Jason and took a deep breath to convince Sally that I was just fine.

"Hi, Mrs. Dickson, I'm Ella Christian," she said reaching to shake my hand. "Do you have a minute to discuss your cleaning arrangements on Lincoln Street? Mrs. Brown, I mean your mother, said I should drop by to speak with you."

"Hello, Miss Christian," I said, observing someone who looked nothing like a cleaning lady. "If you can wait back here at my desk, I'll be right with you," I said, wanting to freshen up in the restroom. I didn't want her to leave, but I needed to get myself together. I splashed cold water on my face, put on lipstick, and returned with a smile.

"Please call me Ella," she said politely. "There is much to love and admire here. Flowers and plants are my weakness, I'm afraid."

Hmmm...was she applying for the right job? "Yes, it's a pretty happy place to work," I said in agreement as I sat next to her at my desk. "I'm pleased to meet you, Ella. Forgive me if I have some interruptions. We have a lot going on here today."

"I see that," she said, putting an arrangement of mixed colored mums down on the desk as if she were about to make a purchase. "This is just the perfect gift I need for a dear friend. I thought about making an appointment, but then I needed to take care of getting these flowers. I'm so glad you are in."

I smiled, hoping to convey approval of her visit. "So, Ella, are you the one that cleans Harry Stone's house?" I asked bluntly to get to the point of her visit.

"I am," she said, smiling. "I'm actually a second cousin of Harry's, and when his wife died, I started helping him out with some domestic duties. I have been there ever since. I met your mother at his place and she asked if I would consider taking on any more cleaning. She is a sweetheart, by the way. I'm happy he has found a suitable companion."

My mother...a suitable sweetheart companion, I repeated in my mind. "Yes, we all are pleased," I said, trying to be kind. "Our house is quite large, Ella, I must warn you, or maybe my mother told you." I watched for a reaction but did not see any.

"That doesn't bother me, Mrs. Dickson," she admitted. "I hear it's quite lovely and I'm sure it will be no problem. Frankly, I need to pick up some more income. I have a very small retirement to live off of, so when your mother mentioned this, I thought I'd like to give it a try. Of course, I'd like to see it first and then discuss compensation." She was businesslike, which fit her appearance.

"No problem," I said quickly. "How about meeting at the house tomorrow in the late afternoon? If you are good enough for Harry, you'll be just fine for me!"

She grinned. "Great," she responded with a big smile. "Harry will be happy to give you a reference. I'm afraid I haven't cleaned anywhere else, as I have always worked as a secretary."

As she went out the door, I saw the professionalism she likely had through the years as a secretary and wondered why she retired to clean houses. Her love of flowers might be a bonus to 333 Lincoln as well. Was this another situation too good to be true?

The day could not pass quickly enough, as I still felt somewhat weak. I was glad to be home. Sam had called to say that he was going to be late and for me not to wait for dinner. Dinner. The very thought was certainly not appealing right now. I just remembered I hadn't had lunch, so no wonder I was feeling light-headed. I just wanted to have a drink and relax.

I changed into my jean shorts and T-shirt before going back downstairs to make myself a very cold glass of lemonade. I grabbed a few pretzels and headed for the south porch. I sat on the chair and put my feet up to reflect on the day. This expansion truly got the best of me today. Why had it affected me like that? I should feel excited and energized at the thought. I had to be sure to keep these feelings from Sam.

The heat was still strong with a little breeze, but the drink was cooling me down. I needed to check on the plants. Watering every day was becoming very time consuming, and I was enjoying that part less and less. I decided to walk toward the potting shed and noticed some perfectly manicured shrubs and moist grass and soil. It was no doubt the presence of Kip showing off his handiwork. I was relieved as I admired it all. Was this the kind of result I was going to get from my new gardener? I liked it!

Finally, Sam pulled up to the garage. As he walked toward me, he looked whipped as well. When he observed my drink, his forced smile asked me if I had one waiting for him. I kissed him on the cheek and led him into the house as I bragged about Kip's gardening.

Sam seemed to be distracted and gave me a tired response as I filled him in on the day. He immediately fell into the den chair he loved so much. I went to get his drink and noticed that when he removed his tie, the look on his face looked like he was in pain.

"Are you okay, Sam?" I asked, realizing this husband of mine had a stressful job and heart condition.

"It was a long day and I could have used my pills, but I forgot them today," he said, aggravation growing in his voice.

"Oh, Sam, do you want to take one now?" I asked, trying not to panic.

"No, I'm fine," he said, putting his head back. "I just need to rest a bit." I looked at him as he closed his eyes. I wasn't about to tell him I could have used a few pills today myself.

"Isn't this quilt club night?" he asked with closed eyes.

"Well, normally it is, but we haven't met since Isabella told us about our missing quilt," I explained.

"Your mischievous grandmother didn't have something to do with that too, did she?" He smiled with his eyes still resting.

"I'm hoping she can help us find it," I teased. "Speaking of Grandmother, I hope she will approve of me hiring Harry Stone's cleaning lady tomorrow. She is meeting me here to see the house."

I looked for a response, but Sam left me with silence. He was asleep. I covered him with the afghan and went upstairs to relax on Sam's recliner. The phone rang as soon as I sat down. I jumped to get it before the second ring so as not to wake Sam.

CHAPTER 54

A m I calling at a bad time, Anne?" Mother asked cheerfully on the other end of the phone line. Not waiting for my answer, she asked, "Did Ella Christian stop by the shop today?"

"Yes, thanks for telling her about us!" I said with renewed interest. "She's coming by tomorrow afternoon to look at the house."

"Oh, what time?" she asked with concern. "I was hoping you'd come with me to take Isabella to lunch tomorrow. I owe her so much for helping me with my quilting and I need to pick up some things there. I haven't used my twenty-five dollar gift certificate yet, have you? Besides, I think she needs cheering up and a few cash sales don't you?"

"You're right about that," I sighed. "I should let you use my certificate as well, Mother. I don't know what I'd use it for. I'll check my schedule at the shop in the morning, but I can likely be there at the quilt shop to meet you about noon. That will be early enough before Ella comes. After you make your purchases, maybe we can go to Donna's. I'll bet Isabella would like that."

"That would be so nice," she said with approval. "Is Sam home?"

"Yes. He's totally exhausted in the den. I worry about his long days, Mother. Today, he said he should have taken a pill, but did not have it with him."

"You need to watch him, Anne," Mother warned. "Men are so proud and macho when it comes to their health, but then the minute they become ill, they turn into big babies!"

We both laughed, remembering how my father was just that way. My role as a wife confused me as to how much to intervene with a husband's well-being. He was an intelligent man who made decisions every day. I don't think I would like him second-guessing what I felt was the right thing for my body. I guess I just need to let him know how much I care and let it go at that.

I undressed for bed and decided to leave Sam exactly where he was without disturbing him. I adjusted the thermostat to make the room temperature cooler and crawled between the sheets. As tired as I was, I began tossing and turning with the thought of Sam's heart condition. I could not get the scariness of his heart problems off my mind. Had I been wise to not ask him more about how he felt? I didn't want to baby him. I had to start thinking of something else. My mind went to Ella Christian, which was a good thing happening for me—a cleaning lady for 333 Lincoln. Do I dare tell her about Grandmother, or wait until Grandmother introduces herself? Suddenly, I had a vision of someone tearing down my walls at Brown's Botanical! What if I couldn't fill the orders for my customers and they went to my competitors? This could be a real nightmare! Would Sam be the first to say, "I told you so?" No, it would be Mother, and I can just see her look.

My wandering negative thoughts went to poor Isabella. Sleepless nights always seemed to make my normal concerns worse. I'll bet Isabella tosses and turns every night, wondering about the location of our quilt. How was she ever going to resolve this? I was so glad I wasn't her right now. I personally thought she was making a mistake by discontinuing the club. It made her look guilty or as if she had something to hide. Could Grandmother help solve this theft? I had asked myself that before. Do I ask her out loud like I have in the past? I really think she helped us out with the funeral quilt that went missing. Or, was it that she borrowed it for a while and then decided to return it? Please stop thinking, I told myself! It all made my stomach churn as if I had a flu bug or something. It was unlike me to not feel well. I pulled up the cover from the foot of the bed.

I'll bet Jane Austen could never live my kind of life. In *Mansfield Park*, I remember reading her quote, "Life seems but a quick succession of busy nothings." Did she mean not to sweat the small stuff or was she bored with life's little nothings? The infiltration of Jane in my life was now showing up in my worrisome thoughts. Did I have to worry about her, too? My stomach churned again as I tossed and turned. I felt like throwing up. Did my stomach need food or a simpler, more uncomplicated life? Hmmm...

When I awoke the next morning, I took notice that Sam had not come to bed at all the night before. I got up immediately, not attending to my needs or beauty concerns. I quickly went downstairs to the study to find Sam still curled up, asleep on the couch, instead of in the chair he had previously occupied. He heard me creep into the room. "Come here, woman," he said in his caveman voice. He took my hand and pulled me onto him. I giggled at his energy and vigor so early in the morning.

"My hubby didn't come home last night," I teased, kissing him with his morning breath. He grinned with his incredible, sexy eyes.

"He's home now and wants his little woman right here," he said, squeezing me tightly. We embraced, teased, and flirted until we both fell off the couch. Our silly laughter was fun but we were both mindful that we needed to pick ourselves up and begin our day. All work and no play seemed to be how we lived! Sam claimed he felt better, but I wasn't sure of my condition. A good shower should do the trick!

CHAPTER 55

I left the house that morning later than usual, but was pleased my Sam was back to his old self. I stopped to get my usual Starbucks and treated myself to a scone. My stomach was not very accepting, and the strong early heat of the day was not helping. I really wanted to go back to bed. I was angry at wasting the night away with worry and not taking my daily walk. I wanted the old Anne Brown back.

When Sally and Abbey arrived, I told them my plans for the day. Seeing the unpacked boxes crowding the floor was not justifying my absence, but Sally and Abbey told me not to worry.

"Should I call Jean in today?" I asked Sally.

"Heavens no, Anne! We'll be fine," Sally responded. "I'll soon have Kevin's last delivery finished, so we're in pretty good shape."

I helped with the last piece of the Jackson funeral order,

then left to meet Mother at Isabella's. The quilt shop was unusually empty and quiet. Mother was the only customer and Isabella appeared to be working alone.

"Okay, what are you two up to?" I asked, walking in the door with anticipation.

"Oh Anne, take a look at this gorgeous blue toile," Mother said as she held the bolt in her hand. "I want to change my bedroom a bit and this is as pretty as any decorator fabric I've seen. Isabella said they could quilt a spread out of this for me and I could have someone cover the valances to match. What do you think?" Interesting, I thought. What else was Mother up to?

"I'm not going to recognize our house pretty soon, with all the changes you're making," I teased. "You've had peach and green in that bedroom as long as I can remember, so I think it's time for a change! It's very beautiful! I would love it in that red, Mother. Have you redone my room yet?" She knew I was teasing.

We all happily approved of Mother's choice as Isabella starting measuring what was on the bolt. "I have Roxanne coming in shortly, so we can go to lunch," Isabella said. "You are both so sweet to try to cheer me up. I am really looking forward to this today."

As Isabella and Mother continued to be quite absorbed regarding figuring out the yardage required, I continued browsing in the shop in case there was something I could buy. When I visited any shop, I was never concentrating on the merchandise as much as I was estimating their square footage and how they were using their display area. I was always curious about shops that had space to spare and never made good use of it. My favorite area at Isabella's was her book department. I would love to carry all sorts of floral books in my shop! She had a special table and chairs for customers to relax and browse through the books. I'm sure the inspiration paid off in sales. It was fun to just read and look at quilts, knowing I would never make them. I did the same with cookbooks and cooking shows. Go figure. I guess the "wanna-be" cook had its way of appearing.

When Mother finally began paying for her purchase, I had several books in my hand, deciding which one to purchase. They were written about quilt care. I was scared to wash what quilts I had, and Mother had always taken that responsibility on when I lived at home. When I placed them on the counter, two of them slipped onto the floor. Along with it went a yardage chart, two pencils, and a pincushion from the counter.

"Oh no!" I said, lamenting my clumsiness. "I'm so sorry! I hope I didn't damage any of them."

Mother, standing next to me, started to laugh as she bent down to help me salvage the mess. We picked up all we could, including a few straight pins, paper clips, a used receipt, and a few cotton balls, which were barely attached to a scrap of fringe.

"Well, how embarrassing is that—to have my customers clean up the place," Isabella jested. "Here, let me take that. Good heavens! Where did the cottonballs come from? I guess a customer dropped them." She looked at the crunched receipt and it went in the trash with the other litter.

Roxanne now arrived with a somber half hello to us. She immediately began straightening bolts of fabric. Just months ago, I seemed to be her best friend at quilt club meetings. What happened? Was she upset with all of us for letting the quilt leave Colebridge? I tried to engage her in conversation, but she barely responded. So after I made my purchase, we left for Donna's Tea Room.

After Dan, the waiter, told us it was Donna's day off, I learned that the turkey melt sandwich was Isabella's favorite item on the menu. It was mine as well. If you looked around the room, you would always see someone you knew, so a few acknowledgments were made before we noticed Donna had new menus to admire.

As if we couldn't avoid it any longer, it didn't take long for the subject of the stolen quilt to come into our conversation. Isabella put her head in her hands as if she were about to cry. I began to wonder if this lunch was really a good idea.

"I really don't know what to do next," she said softly, shaking her head. "I'm getting more and more negative feedback from customers, like it's entirely my fault! I was afraid as time went on that this would be something some could not forgive. Some people won't even speak to me outside of the shop." I listened, not knowing for sure what to say. Mother had a concerned look and was also speechless. Mother looked to me for a response.

"Well, I think you may have to be more forthcoming with the information that you do have, Isabella," I suggested. "Why don't you call a meeting on our regular quilt club night and tell them everything?" I took a deep breath before going further. "You haven't told them about the replacement of the chenille bedspread, which would verify to them that someone had pulled a fast one in the shipping process. You haven't let them know the nasty side of this theft that has put you in a terrible position and loss of business. You mustn't let them run over you, Isabella. I'd even show the picture they sent you of the bedspread, so they'll believe you."

Mother looked up with fear on her face. "What picture of what bedspread?" Mother asked, not knowing that part of the story.

Isabella sighed as she shook her head. Isabella went into her purse and pulled out the photo of the bedspread that showed a member of the staff holding it up, as if it were just taken from the box. Mother shook her head in disbelief as Isabella explained the switch that had taken place.

"Are you saying this was in the box you sent instead of the Austen quilt?" Mother asked in disbelief.

"I am, Sylvia," she said, her embarrassment clearly evident. "I don't know what to believe or who to believe. Frankly, I regret the whole thing. I wish I had never started this whole club. I should never have planned to send away what was not totally mine. As much as I hate to say it, I now think Roxanne was right about this."

I had to almost agree with her. It sure carried a lot of responsibility since it involved so many people.

"Oh no, Isabella," Mother said, consoling her. "No one else feels this way. This was some bad luck that will have a good outcome, I'm sure."

I kept looking at the picture Isabella had dug from her purse before I spoke. "Well, this is interesting," I noted. "Look at the ball fringe on the end of this spread." Isabella took the photo from me to look closer.

"What about it?" she asked calmly. "Looks pretty typical for a chenille spread, if you ask me. Most of them have some kind of fringe like that."

"Remember the balls I picked up off your floor today?" I asked.

Isabella shrugged and wrinkled her face. "I think it's exactly the same kind of fringe," I claimed.

Mother now took a closer look, holding the picture in her hand. "I think you're right, Anne," said Mother, agreeing but not really seeing the point.

"So what?" Isabella asked, unconcerned. "I certainly didn't examine it before I threw it in the trash." Isabella paused, now silent.

"I hate to say this, but could that bedspread have been in your shop at some point, Isabella?" I asked suspiciously.

"What are you saying, Anne?" she asked defensively. "Are you accusing me of something here?" The look on her face was now frightful.

What had I done? I continued in spite of her tone. "No, but don't you think that's a little weird?" I couldn't contain the snicker in my voice. "When you get back to the shop, I think I'd get it out of the trash and compare it."

"Anne, what are you saying?" Isabella retorted, the volume of her voice elevated. "I put that quilt in the box myself. Where are you going with this?"

"Maybe nowhere, but since you don't sell fringe, how could it have fallen on your floor?" I pried. "Was anyone else with you when you got this ready to ship?"

"Yes. Roxanne was with me, as a matter of fact," she shared. "I have a witness. However, I recall that we were constantly interrupted with customers."

"So, Roxanne was helping you?" I tried to construct a picture in my mind. "Roxanne, more than anyone, was quite upset about you sending that quilt away for competition, remember?"

"Yes, I know," Isabella confessed. "Once she knew my

mind was made up, however, she finally shut up about it all."

"So, you were the one to finally send it off?" Mother asked.

"Yes. I've said that over and over," she shot back, becoming agitated. "I boxed it and Roxanne was taping while I did the label. I guess you could say we did it together. She's just as upset as I that this happened and resents those who are pointing to the shop as the guilty party."

It was difficult to keep eating with this interrogation going on. Mother kept giving me dirty looks like I had overstepped my boundaries and subsequently made Isabella feel even worse. Finally, between bites, I couldn't help but present the visual picture my mind had created.

"Forgive me, Isabella, but could Roxanne have slipped the bedspread in the quilt's place, leaving the quilt behind, and even worse—keeping it for herself? It certainly would explain those little pieces of ball fringe that fell on the floor. I'm sure you didn't watch her every second. By the weight of the box, you would have never known it was removed."

"Anne! What are you really saying here?" she responded. Her voice was elevated in both pitch and volume. "Roxanne wouldn't possibly pull anything like that! She is not a thief—nor am I."

Oh dear, I guess this came out all wrong. However, I wanted to force her to think about the possibilities.

"Anne, this is crazy," Mother chimed in, ready to fiercely defend her friend.

"Maybe not," I continued calmly. I was determined to make my point. "From my conversations with Roxanne, she would have liked to have had the quilt to herself. She is a bit over the top with Jane Austen, if you ask me. She even came into the shop to complain about the quilt leaving." Isabella just sat there shaking her head in disbelief as her face whitened.

"Look. There has to be some kind of shadiness going on here, Isabella. That is why folks are finding it so mysterious. Think about who would want this quilt badly enough to pull something like this. The quilt had to be switched in the transportation process or before. The likelihood of it happening in front of the quilt show staff when it arrived is nil. I doubt if they could ever get by with anything like that." I finally paused, waiting for some response, but there wasn't one. Mother was in shock at my behavior and Isabella's mind was churning just like my stomach.

"I've got to go," Isabella quickly announced, getting up to leave. "I've got to digest this! Thank you for the lunch." She put her napkin on the table and headed toward the door without a formal good-bye.

CHAPTER 56

M other and I looked at one another, shocked. Mother's gaze at me was one of disapproval. I hadn't seen that look in a long, long time. I somehow felt I had been helpful, in a cruel sort of way. It was time Isabella started thinking outside the box on this matter or the mystery would go on forever.

"I've got to hand it to you, Anne, your imagination took this to the next level," Mother said in disgust. "I hate that you had to be the one to suggest this type of scenario. We may have lost a good friend just now. Frankly, Anne, if this is really what took place, she would have figured it out for herself, don't you think?"

"Sometimes we can't see what's really right in front of us, Mother," I stated. "She had made up her mind that Roxanne couldn't have done this, so she wouldn't think about it. I have a feeling our quilt never left the quilt shop. Roxanne would not have been able to send an empty box, so with the weight of the bedspread in there, Isabella thought nothing if it!"

"That is a pretty harsh judgment you're making against Roxanne, Anne," Mother scolded. "Quilters would never do anything like what you're suggesting! I think there were many of us in the group who would have liked to own that quilt, don't you think?"

"Maybe so, but I think the dishonest one here is Roxanne, not Isabella," I said, giving the waitress my credit card for the lunch. "I hope I said something that jogged her memory, since she left here so fast."

"I think she didn't want to hear any more and I really feel bad about that, Anne," said Mother, concerned. "I'll give her a call when I get home and apologize."

"Whatever, but I guess we'll know in time what happened, Mother," I said, leaving the table. "I'm not sorry I suggested my theory."

Thankfully, I got to the house in time to meet Ella. Hopefully, she would be my new house cleaner. I had the house fairly straightened in hopes that she wouldn't think we were untidy. I couldn't help but wonder if Grandmother was going to let this go smoothly and without any interference. Ella arrived, professionally dressed as if she were being interviewed for a secretarial position. I met her on the porch and briefly showed her the grounds of 333 Lincoln. She seemed envious of all the flowers and was also moved when she saw my potting shed. She commented that she had a sizable rose garden and spent her extra time there when she could. From her body language, I could tell when we walked in the entry hall that she approved and admired the grandness our home.

"You are a very lucky lady, Mrs. Dickson," Ella said as we went up the stairs to the second floor. "Hopefully these stairs won't be a problem. Occasionally my knees act up. They sure are good for exercise, however."

When I showed her our master bedroom, she especially was complimentary about my choice of cream and white colors. She noted the bay window and commented about how many windows the house contained. I assured her the window cleaning was being addressed.

"How do you feel about cleaning an attic?" I said bravely as I pointed to the door. "I have been just too busy to attempt it myself." I was hoping my lie was not evident. "I know it's more stairs, but once it's done, you shouldn't have to go up there again."

"Sure, that's not a problem," she immediately answered. "It may have to be done on a separate day, of course."

After the tour, we came downstairs and settled on a satisfactory fee. She seemed pleased and I walked her to the car. I felt very relieved. Ella would make the house shine, Kip would keep the blooms and garden going, and Jason would expand my shop. My dreams somehow were too good to be true.

I went inside to change clothes before Sam was due home. I looked in on my neglected waiting room that was still waiting for my writing. I smiled, knowing that I would always be waiting and writing. Jean told us once at the literary club that Jane had times when she was too busy or depressed to write. In that day and time, they had so much everyday correspondence to keep them busy. It's a wonder she still wanted to work on her books. What a shame so many of Jane's letters to her sister Cassandra were destroyed.

It would have told us so much more about her. As for myself, I hated to see the written word disappear, especially when it came to letters people had written to one another. Were people saving tweets and e-mails? Not so much. Perhaps when Jane would look at her little writing desk, it was her waiting desk, like mine!

I checked my messages when I got downstairs and there was one from Isabella and Mother. Isabella's message announced an emergency meeting of the Jane Austen Quilt Club tomorrow night. Hmmm...I was glad she decided to take my advice and bring the group together again. She obviously decided to stand up for herself. Mother's message was asking me if I had gotten the message from Isabella. Sam was ringing my cell phone and said he was bringing home pizza and salads from Pete's. It sounded great, as I barely nibbled on our stressful lunch. I decided to prepare lemonade for the warm summer supper on the south porch, just like the Taylors did years ago. I smiled at the thought of how Mrs. Taylor likely had a delicious dinner prepared for Mr. Taylor. Maybe they had a cook and a maid. That was a question I never pondered before. If they had a gardener, why not a cook? Hmmm...

"Hey, Miss Annie, any special news to report from your day?" Sam asked as we took our drinks to the porch. "How about the nausea you had this morning?"

"I'm fine now—just not enough sleep with so much on my mind." I reported. "I had a very productive day, I think, despite a very interesting lunch with Mother and Isabella." He didn't respond to my lunch comment, which was good.

"I've been too busy to keep track, Anne, but you don't think you could be pregnant, do you?"

I looked at him in shock and then burst into laughter as I looked at Sam's serious face. "Excuse me, Mr. Dickson, but your wife happens to be on birth control pills!" I said, overreacting. "I think it's just been all the stress with all the changes, not much sleep, the heat, meeting with the cleaning lady, and you name it!" I laughed, but Sam looked at me, not saying a word to further the conversation. I changed the subject by filling him in on the interview with Ella and telling him that she agreed to clean the attic. I told him how pleased I was that things around 333 Lincoln were falling into place.

"So it makes Mrs. Dickson very happy," I bragged. "Does it make Mr. Dickson happy, as well?"

He broke into a grin, knowing I had dodged the discussion of starting a family...once again.

CHAPTER 57

The next day was terribly busy with challenging orders and many disruptions. The chatter of the anticipated quilt meeting in the evening added to the mix. I kept quiet as I heard each one's interpretation on what the meeting might be about. I knew most were guessing the quilt had been found, but I wasn't so sure. If Isabella had not found the quilt, the group would be terribly disappointed after she called them together so urgently.

I was still worried about how much I had upset Isabella at lunch. I hoped she understood my point that brainstorming with her was to make her think about all the different scenarios that could have happened. I suppose I'd find out tonight if there were any fragments left to our friendship. Since we were all heading to the meeting after work, we decided to enjoy appetizers at Charley's before I picked up Mother. Brad was thrilled to see all the Botanical girls in

ANN HAZELWOOD

one visit and we munched on artichoke dip, potato skins, and chicken strips. It was fun to enjoy their company outside the shop. I did consider them like family and friends, but also reminded myself that as an employer, I needed to draw the fine line so problems would not arise in the shop over relationships. We all concurred that it would be a much nicer evening if we could continue our party, but Jean reminded us that we wouldn't want to miss any important announcements from Isabella.

"Cheerio, Mr. Brad," Jean said as we all left the restaurant.

"Have fun, you all," Brad responded, laughing.

The quilt shop was packed, and everyone was visiting among themselves as they always did before our meetings. Some were even making purchases, which had to please Isabella very much. I looked about the shop and there certainly wasn't a Jane Austen quilt hanging on the wall. Perhaps this was just an update for the group, as I had encouraged her to do.

Isabella finally got our attention with her usual banging on the table. You could hear a pin drop in the room, it was so still. She looked very nervous as she began to speak. "Thanks so much for coming out tonight," she began. "I want to also thank you for your patience and understanding in regard to our beloved quilt. If I may quote Jane as she wrote in *Emma*, 'How often is happiness destroyed by preparation, foolish preparation!' I made such a big deal to prepare for this competition that I destroyed the joy of what this quilt was to be about. I saw the pride in each of your faces when we had the finished quilt hanging on the wall. That truly was my reward. Most of you challenged yourselves to try something new, knowing it would not be the best or as good as someone else's. Each of you brought out your own personality in your block. I think Jane would have been amused and flattered." The crowd continued to be silent as they mentally reminisced about their own individual block. Where was she going with this?

"Just so you know, we did receive a check from my insurance company," she continued. "I was very pleased that they compensated us promptly and without question."

So this was the reason to get the group together? Mixed underlying comments were now being shared among the crowd. She was going to have to get control of this group before someone said something derogatory. Isabella banged on her counter to get everyone's attention once again. "The even better news, my friends, is that we won't need it!"

What? Did I hear her correctly? Huge sighs and cheerful voices filled the room in anticipation. Isabella had to pound on the counter once more to gain their undivided attention. My heart was pounding as well. What in the world happened in the last twenty-four hours?

As she looked at our faces, she reached under the counter and pulled out our beautiful Jane Austen quilt. Everyone started to applaud and yell aloud. When they settled down a bit, Isabella began her explanation. She briefly told us the quilt had gotten into the wrong hands, giving me the impression she was not going to go into the details with everyone, which was probably smart. She shared she was very relieved, as it had been a nightmare for her.

"I am not here to put blame on any one person or any organization, as we are all human, but there truly was an error in the shipping process that was unintentional," she explained. "I was just glad to see it again with my own eyes.

I couldn't help but think of Jane Austen's quote in *Love and Friendship* when she wrote, 'Run mad as often as you choose, but do not faint.'" We broke into laughter.

"When I received the quilt back in my hands, I wanted to run like heck, hoping I wasn't dreaming, and that I wouldn't faint!" She joined the others in laughter. "When someone suggested weeks ago that perhaps Jane's spirit would help us find the quilt, I had my doubts. I was worried we had insulted this loving author and she would have no part of our nonsense, but I now know I was wrong."

I watched as Isabella won back the hearts of her customers, with few questions asked. She said she'd like to display the quilt in the shop until we decided what to do with it at our next quilt club meeting. More approving applause erupted.

Mother put her arm around me, pleased about what had just taken place. It was a wonderful sight to behold.

"Now, my friends, as part of our celebration, I had Norma prepare refreshments and cake to celebrate the joyous return of our Jane Austen quilt!" she announced. Hmmm... Roxanne would have typically taken care of this and I noticed she was not in attendance.

"Where is Roxanne, do you suppose?" asked Mother in a suspicious tone.

"I think the two of us can assume she had a role in this, don't you?" I asked softly, so no one could hear.

"I have to give you credit here, Anne," Mother said in disbelief. "You opened a can of worms for Isabella to explore. It obviously didn't hurt!" She squeezed my arm affectionately.

Before everyone went to the refreshment table, the ladies all came closer to the quilt to reacquaint themselves with their quilt blocks. I was just as curious to see if the My

Pemberley quilt block made it back in good condition. For some reason, it looked even better than before as I stared at its bold columns. It took many hours, but as I stitched away, Jane's writings had occupied my thoughts. Her courage and independence in *Pride and Prejudice* with Mr. Darcy brought her to Pemberley, just as mine did to 333 Lincoln. It was a surprise Cinderella story for each of us.

"You were right about Roxanne," Isabella said quietly to Mother and me. "The ball fringe I pulled out of the trash matched the photo exactly. When the shop closed, I got directly in Roxanne's face and told her I wanted the quilt back immediately. I said I had proof of the switch she had made, and if she returned it promptly, I would not tell anyone or press charges. It took a leap of faith and it worked! She was shocked, that is certain, and did not attempt to deny it. Having told her I had proof scared her, I think."

"Oh my," I said, imagining the horror of such a scene. "How scary this must have been for you, Isabella." I gave her a hug of support. "I take it she is no longer employed here?"

"You've got that right," she said putting her hands on her hips. "I can't thank the two of you enough for helping me through this. Why are we sometimes blind to what is right before us? Please keep this quiet for me. I just want my shop and customers back again. Thanks so much for hanging in there with me through this whole process. You never gave up on me like so many of the others. You both are dear friends. I will never forget this."

Jean now approached us with drinks. She handed one to Isabella and congratulated her on a good outcome. "You made it through this, Miss Quilt Shop Lady. I would venture that someone had an openness of heart. We are trying to take in the meaning of it all, as Jane herself so often did. Now, would you be so kind as to get on and cut me a piece of this lovely chintz? I shall be grateful."

Taking the bolt in hand, Isabella laughed and said, "I shall be delighted, Miss Jean!"

Mother, Aunt Julia, Sue, Mia, and Sarah all joined me as we looked at each other in disbelief and pleasant satisfaction. It was not the time to ask for details, but instead to just enjoy the Kodak moment we shared so frequently.

Holding the refreshments in our hands, I decided a toast was in order. My stomach was again unsteady with all of the excitement, but I raised by glass and announced, "Here's to the Jane Austen Quilt Club bringing success and happiness back to the Colebridge community once again." We clinked our glasses. "Hear, hear! Life is good!" I announced to my loving family.

"I think a better way to say this, my dear, is what I recite each morning: 'This is the day the Lord hath made; let us rejoice and be glad in it!'"

"Amen!" we all heartily agreed.

The disappointments and unexpected joys would always be embraced, as the Colebridge community continues!

What you can look forward to:

Will the Jane Austen Quilt Club be able to continue?

Will Ella be accepted by Grandmother Davis
as the new cleaning lady?

Will parenthood continue to be a sensitive
subject between Anne and Sam?

What will the next drama be on
Main Street in Colebridge?

More Books from AQS

#1415 $24.95

#8853 $14.00

#1256 $14.95

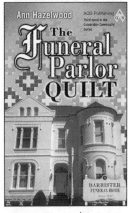

#1257 $14.95

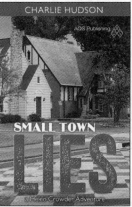

#1258 $14.95

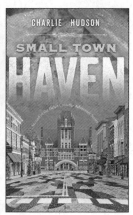

#1424 $14.95

Look for these books nationally.

1-800-626-5420

Call or Visit our website at
www.AmericanQuilter.com